I0628980

BOOK FOUR OF THE MACHINISTS

CAPTURE

CRAIG ANDREWS

Capture

Copyright © 2017 by Craig Andrews. All rights reserved.

First Print Edition: 2017

ISBN: 978-0-9991784-0-9 (print edition)
ISBN: 978-0-9991784-1-6 (ebook)

Interior formatting: Streetlight Graphics

No part of this book may be reproduced, scanned, or distributed in any printed or electronic form without permission. Please do not participate in or encourage piracy of copyrighted materials in violation of the author's rights. Thank you for respecting the hard work of this author.

This is a work of fiction. Names, characters, places, and incidents either are the product of the author's imagination or are used fictitiously, and any resemblance to locales, events, business establishments, or actual persons—living or dead—is entirely coincidental.

ALSO BY CRAIG ANDREWS

FRACTURE

SPLINTER

MARTYR

CAPTURE

EXPOSURE
(forthcoming)

To receive *Heritage*, an exclusive prequel novelette
set in the world of The Machinists, sign up
for the Craig Andrew's mailing list at:

http://eepurl.com/IEjIr

For additional bonus content, and to be the
first to hear about giveaways and
promotions, follow Craig Andrews on Facebook at:

https://www.facebook.com/craigandrewsauthor

For Gala and Gary, who welcomed an opinionated, foul-mouthed boy into their family and loved him as their daughter did.

CHAPTER 1

Sᴇᴅʀɪᴄ Lᴀɴɢ, Kɴɪɢʜᴛ Cᴏᴍᴍᴀɴᴅᴇʀ ᴏꜰ the Knights of Rakkar, rode the elevator to the fifty-second floor of the Patron's high-rise. Located in the heart of Frankfurt, the sixty-three-story structure was one of the tallest buildings not only in Germany, but in the entire European Union. Built in a postmodern design, the building was pencil shaped with a square base that rose fifty stories before taking on a cylindrical shape, which was then topped with a pyramid. By all appearances the home to the financier of Sedric's operation was a contradiction of forms—not unlike the Patron himself.

Sedric stood with his hands clasped behind his back, hoping his stoic expression hid his mounting unease. The elevator floor vibrated as the digital display cycled through the floors it sped past. *Forty-one. Forty-three. Forty-five.* By *forty-seven*, the elevator shuddered, its brakes kicking in and slowing the car to a stop.

Upon arriving at the fifty-second floor, the elevator dinged. Its doors opened, and Sedric strode purposefully into the austere interior. The walls on one half of the floor were made almost entirely of glass, offering an unobstructed view of the whole floor. Inside glass rooms, workers dressed in white lab coats consulted files, typed furiously on keyboards, and studied three-dimensional projections of what Sedric assumed was a digital representation of the Blood Wand.

Part of him bristled at the sight of the artifact being a subject for study. The mere existence of the magi race was a demonic plague infecting the good people of Earth. To have the relic in the open, to have it studied—*touched*—was akin to studying the devil himself and was, in many ways, contrary to Sedric's primary mission of eradicating the magi altogether. But such were the ways of the modern world. The Knights of Rakkar needed funding, and the Patron required the Blood Wand.

"A sacrifice for the greater good," the Rakkaran leadership had called it. And Sedric wasn't about to argue—not when the other parts of his mission were coming together so well.

Dressed in black military-style fatigues, Sedric stuck out among the lab workers like a fur trader at a technology summit. Those who looked at him quickly looked away, returning to their work. His presence wasn't entirely out of the ordinary—especially since their work was centered around the ancient magi artifact that he had given to the Patron weeks before.

Ignoring the growing tension that made his steps feel light and off balance, Sedric turned away from the glass rooms to the private section of the floor. The digital terminal beeped and flashed a green light as he scanned his access card across its plastic casing.

The door clicked open, and Sedric stepped inside a corridor of white unadorned walls that felt like a cross between a clean room and a hospital. He wound his way through the halls, passing various doors and rooms, but never another soul, until he came to a pair of double doors that could have been stolen from one of the magi manors he had become so familiar with. Stationed outside them was a pair of thickly-built guards dressed in black suits with black ties.

"Is he inside?" Sedric asked, stopping outside the door.

"One moment," the guard to his right said in a thick German accent. He held one hand to his ear, alerting the Patron of Sedric's arrival. His other arm was held out before him, barring Sedric's entry. The gesture wasn't necessary. Sedric knew not to try to push himself inside uninvited, and besides that, should he need to, he could easily make short order of the two guards and anyone else inside.

Since branding himself with the Blood Wand, he had manifested magi abilities, which of course, was the entire reason he was here. Not because of *his* abilities—those remained a secret between Sedric and his Knights—but because of the abilities the wand could grant to someone else.

"You can go in." The guard opened the door.

"Thank you."

Sedric stepped into a room that must have been one of the most advanced hospital rooms ever constructed. Light spilled in through a wall of glass at the far end of the room, glistening off tiled floors and white walls, filling the room with a warm yellow light. Beyond was the picturesque cityscape of Frankfurt's downtown business sector. Sedric's eyes, however, fell on a young girl of no more than eight years old sleeping on a gurney at the center of the room. Tubes and wires stretched from her disease-riddled body to various machines and pieces of medical equipment. A quiet beep accompanied the display of her heartbeat.

Sitting beside the girl and holding her hand was the Patron. Not quite into his middle years, he was of average height and build, though softer than Sedric for having spent his life working behind a desk. His brown hair was short and disheveled, beginning to show signs of gray, and while dressed in a pair of charcoal slacks and a white button-down shirt that likely cost more than Sedric made in a year, he had the appearance of a man who hadn't left his daughter's side in days.

Sedric's footsteps echoed through the room as he moved to stand beside the seated man. Sedric remained silent, unwilling to taint the man's private moment with his daughter with uninvited words.

"Do you have children, Sedric?" the Patron asked, keeping his voice quiet, as if afraid of waking the girl.

"No," Sedric said. "My lifestyle never lent itself to having a family."

"That's too bad. Just by their very presence, children have a way of showing us what's important in life. I mean, look at me." The Patron gestured at his unkempt clothing. "I run a company that's worth more than many countries, and yet I haven't spoken with anyone outside this room since we..."

"Since you...?" Sedric looked at the girl with renewed interested. Her chestnut-colored hair, draped across a green medical smock, framed an innocent face. White gauze poked out from under her left sleeve. "You branded her?" He couldn't keep the surprise out of his voice.

"We don't have much time left, Sedric. She's getting worse."

Sedric opened his mouth, but his words died in his throat. The Patron had branded her ahead of schedule, *well ahead* of schedule. There was no way his team had spent enough time properly studying the artifact and extracting its secrets. Sedric knew all too well the abilities the Blood Wand could imbue, but those abilities would be useless to the girl. She needed the powers only the magi clerics had—the power to heal. Only then would she have a chance. To move forward without a concrete idea of the wand's capabilities meant the Patron was getting desperate.

"When?" Sedric managed to choke out.

"Yesterday."

"And...?"

"And I'm still waiting for her to wake up." A single tear streaked down his left cheek.

"It must be a pretty traumatic experience for one so young," Sedric said slowly. He of course knew the pain associated with the branding but wasn't about to let the Patron know that. If the Patron even suspected Sedric had branded himself before handing over the Blood Wand... well, it wouldn't have a positive outcome. Fortunately, Sedric's well-known stance on the magi worked in his favor. The idea of Sedric branding himself would be unthinkable, though if the Patron ever chose to inspect him, Sedric would have no way to hide it.

That would be an interesting day.

"Her doctors said she was strong enough," the Patron said. "And she was asleep of course."

"Of course."

The Patron let out a deep sigh and gave his daughter's hand a squeeze before standing and making his way across the room to the sink. Looking at himself in the mirror, he wet his hands and ran his fingers through his hair in a failed attempt to make himself more presentable. "Tell me again what you know of the wand."

"It's old," Sedric said without preamble. "At least two thousand years, though probably older than that, and it gave the magi race second life after their number nearly died out."

"It's supposed to give magi abilities." The Patron watched Sedric from the mirror.

"Yes, though I guess *what* abilities is the real question." *Which is why I'm surprised you didn't wait to study it before staining your daughter with it.*

The Patron pulled a couple paper towels from the dispenser and dried his hands. "But you think it's something that can save my daughter."

"I wouldn't have brought it to you if I didn't."

The Patron turned and leaned against the counter, watching Sedric with an expression the Knight Commander couldn't place. "I hope you understand the trust I'm placing in you, Sedric. There are experimental treatments, and then there is this. If something goes awry, I don't need to remind you who's responsible."

Sedric had to bite his tongue to keep from snapping back. He hadn't reached out to the Patron, and neither had the Rakkaran leadership. The Patron had come to them seeking information, and after confirming the existence of the magi, he'd been the one to make the proposal. He'd even insisted that the Knights refer to him as "the Patron" in a ridiculous ploy to keep his true identity a secret. Not that it had been overly difficult to figure out, but that was another piece of information Sedric kept from the man. In any case, the Patron had agreed to bankroll the Knights' efforts in eliminating the magi, but in return, he wanted their help in finding a way to use their abilities to treat his ailing daughter.

How he had discovered the magi or the existence of the Knights themselves remained a mystery. Sedric hadn't pressed, either. The agreement had seemed like such a simple proposal, and after learning about the Blood Wand, Sedric had realized there might be a way to tackle both objectives at the same time. But with the Patron already laying the idea of failure at his feet, he needed to tread lightly.

"There is no need for reminders," Sedric said evenly. "We all know what is at stake."

"Good." The Patron glanced at his daughter's motionless body. "Then you won't object to a new idea."

"A new idea?"

"In case the wand doesn't do what we hope it'll do."

"A contingency plan."

"Sure."

"What did you have in mind?"

Sedric found himself smiling as the Patron laid out his scheme. It wasn't terribly clever—Sedric would have recommended it himself if the Patron hadn't—but it would inflict more pain on the magi than simple death ever would have. And that, of course, was Sedric's true objective.

"I'll see it done," Sedric said.

"That's great, Sedric. Thank you. When can I tell our team to expect the first returns?"

"Soon," Sedric said. "Soon."

He had no intention of letting the magi sit idle for any longer than he had to.

CHAPTER 2

P ANIC FLARED THROUGH THE ECHO. Startled by the sudden
wave of foreign emotion, Jaxon froze the Mahari in
midpose. He sent his own feeling of curiosity back
through the forbidden connection that allowed him to feel
Leira's emotions as if they were his own. Wherever she was,
she would feel his voiceless question instantly—not in the
form of words, the echo wasn't a telepathic link, but as a
wave of external feelings similar to what he had felt.

Beyond what he had experienced firsthand, Jaxon knew
little about the echo—it was forbidden, after all, and rarely
spoken about—but he had come to appreciate how close the
magi link had brought him and Leira, though he supposed
that hadn't prevented him from being terrified when he had
discovered they'd formed the bond. If the magi leadership
ever discovered it, Jaxon and Leira would experience their
unimaginable wrath. More than that, it meant Jaxon would
never experience another moment of privacy.

Every flash of annoyance, moment of irritation, pang of
guilt, or spike of amusement would be instantly shared with
the one person whose opinion he valued most. The one person
he loved more than any other. The one person he never wanted

to hurt. But where all magi abilities had consequences, they also had benefits, and in times like this, when the magi were fighting a vicious enemy hell-bent on their destruction, those benefits far outweighed any disadvantages.

Sweat chilling his exerted body, Jaxon waited for Leira's response. Before long, a wave of urgency flooded through him as she pleaded with him to find her.

I'm coming, Jaxon responded, trusting the words would translate into a feeling she would understand. He grabbed his compression armor top from a nearby tree limb and pulled it over his head, frustrated that the Mahari had been cut short again. He couldn't remember the last time he'd been able to complete the magi kata without being interrupted. War was inconvenient in that way. Keeping that war invisible from the outside world and ensuring that the existence of the magi race remained a secret from the rest of humanity was even more problematic.

Concern reverberated through the connection. Leira had felt his frustration and was worried.

I'm fine, Jaxon thought, stepping back onto the path that led to the Klausner Manor. It was little more than a narrow trail, nearly hidden among emerald green grass, colorful wild flowers, and thick trees. Having spent years in the mountains and forests of the Pacific Northwest, Jaxon had instantly taken to the familiar setting of the Swiss Alps and worked to find time every day to spend at least a few minutes in its beauty.

He found Leira waiting with a full squad of magi—twelve in all, including Allyn, Nolan, and Nyla—in the driveway of the manor. Their compression armor and grim expressions told him everything he needed to know.

"Report," Jaxon said.

"There's been another attack," Leira said, confirming Jaxon's fears. "We're needed."

Jaxon cursed. The attacks were growing more frequent. The Knights of Rakkar had them on the ropes and were pressing the advantage.

"Who?"

"The Friedl Family."

"That's..." Jaxon did the distance calculations in his head.

"An hour away," Leira said.

An hour was an eternity in battle—especially when the Knights of Rakkar raided magi Families in the same way Vikings had once terrorized the coastlines of Europe. Unlike the Vikings, who'd raped and pillaged, fueling their economy, the Knights cared only about death and destruction. They pressed hard, acted fast, and retreated when the magi mounted a strong counterattack. It was death by a million paper cuts, but the magi were hemorrhaging.

"Who else has been called?" Jaxon asked.

"The Blackburn Family will be the first to arrive."

"Good," Jaxon said. "That will give us some time."

"There's something else." Leira grimaced as if she didn't know how to put it into words. "The reports are... *strange*. The Knights' strategy is different. We can't be sure, but they might be taking prisoners."

"Prisoners? Why now? They haven't done that before."

"We have no idea."

"Does the arch mage know?"

"We've sent word," Leira said.

"Good," Jaxon said. "Then we'll meet him there. When do we move?"

"Now. But, Jaxon... *we?*"

"I'm coming too."

A ripple of surprise washed through the echo. Jaxon

hadn't been directly involved in a mission since the McCollum Family had retaken the contents of the McCollum library back when they were running from the FBI. But the situation was too big.

After today, the war with the Knights of Rakkar would take on a different tenor, escalating to new levels, and the members of the Forum and Arch Mage Westarra himself would converge on the site of the battle to see its aftermath for themselves. That presented opportunities. At the very least, being present would ensure the McCollum Family was up to date with plans and strategies, and if the war really was changing, Jaxon would make every effort to ensure his Family knew how.

"Load up," he said. "I want to be there before the arch mage arrives."

CHAPTER 3

FORTY-NINE MINUTES AFTER JAXON ORDERED the McCollum magi to load up, they arrived at the Friedl Family's estate. Split evenly among three SUVs, which had recently been retrofitted with reinforced doors and bulletproof glass, they rumbled past a destroyed gate, racing down a private driveway. Signs of battle lined both sides of the paved path: vehicle wreckage, low-burning fires, and fallen bodies marred what had once been a well-cultivated property.

Allyn watched through the tinted windows, wielding in short bursts. His red coils of electricity appeared and disappeared with a steady, anxious rhythm. Beside him, on the middle bench seat of the SUV, Nolan watched through the other window, his hand clenching and unclenching in a similar cadence. Even as veterans of war, the magi struggled with nerves.

It wasn't without good reason. Through the reinforced doors and windows, Allyn heard muffled bursts of gunfire and intermittent explosions. *The battle isn't over then.*

Allyn shared a look with Nolan. The former FBI special agent was clearly as surprised as he was. Since the Battle of Zurich, the Knights hadn't engaged the magi in an extended battle. At the first sign of reinforcements, they retreated, preventing their forces from being boxed in and taking heavy casualties. It kept the magi forever on the defensive—a losing strategy, in Allyn's opinion.

The SUVs crested a gentle hill, and the Friedl Mansion came into view. Made of gray stone and whitewashed timber, the mansion was closer to a castle than a traditional home. The paved driveway forked in front of the mansion, the pavement turning to cobblestones that circled a large fountain. The front of the mansion reminded Allyn of how the McCollum Manor had looked before it burned, though that had lacked the natural-colored timber that accented the Friedl Mansion's whitewashed walls. It had also lacked the enemy's tactical vehicles that were currently parked in its driveway.

A large tank-like vehicle with a twenty-foot steel rod had crashed into the front of the mansion, punching a hole the size of a car through the front entrance. The windows were shattered, the walls burned and stained with soot. Bullet holes and blood streaks further marred the once-majestic property.

The SUVs rumbled to a stop where the pavement met cobblestone, and with practiced efficiency, the magi streamed out. Wielding fire, energy, and electricity, they jumped out of the vehicles, using the doors as cover. Gunfire and shouted orders suddenly became louder, but Allyn couldn't see any individual Knights. Dressed in black tactical gear, complete with helmets, and often carrying man-sized shields, they wouldn't be difficult to spot.

"They're inside," Jaxon said. "Form up into your squads. Today, we smash the Knights against the strength of our Order." Once the twelve magi formed their previously determined squads, Jaxon gave them their orders. "Leira, take your squad around back and enter from the rear. Nolan, hang back and watch our six. Give me a signal if anything goes amiss. Ren, we go first and enter through the front."

We.

The change in command was as subtle as possible. In previous operations, Ren had led the assault, but because Jaxon had come, the chain of command had clearly changed. If Ren was surprised or irritated by the last-minute adjustment, she didn't show it.

"Let's go," Jaxon ordered.

"Wait," Canary said. The young machinist in Nolan's squad cocked her head to the side, listening to something only she could hear. Her lips moved, inaudibly repeating the radio broadcasts and communications she heard as part of her ability. Unlike the rest of the machinists the McCollum Family had found, Canary couldn't turn her abilities on and off. She was constantly bombarded with radio waves, cell phone communications, and other electronic signals.

It wasn't until after fleeing the McCollum Manor, where Canary had been sheltered from the onslaught by Liam's jammer, that her abilities had first appeared. Unable to relax or sleep, and constantly repeating what only she could hear, she'd been rendered inept. Jaxon had thought Canary mentally broken and had ordered her separated from the rest of the Family. Once they were safe within the walls of the Hyland Estate, they had discovered Canary was, in fact, another machinist with abilities about as unique as they came.

"What is it?" Jaxon asked.

"I don't know." Canary closed her eyes, a pained expression pinching her face. "There's a lot of chatter."

"What kind?"

Canary didn't answer. She didn't even so much as show she had heard Jaxon.

"Canary," Jaxon said again. "What kind of chatter?"

Canary began to speak, but the words that came out of her mouth were not her own. She spoke in a monotone voice, almost like a child repeating the words of an adult, oblivious to their true meaning.

Confused, Jaxon watched the young girl. "Okay," he said, turning to Nolan. "Stay on it. Tell me if it changes or begins to make sense. The rest of you, move out."

The two squads moved at his command, leaving Nolan's group behind to watch their asses. Allyn followed Jaxon and Ren, Nyla and Rory at his side. Each of the squads were mixed with a balance of magi, clerics, and something only the McCollum Family could provide—the machinists. That unique ability had quickly proven their Family's worth and earned them a spot as one of the arch mage's go-to squads—a far cry from the ostracized position they had held only months before.

Entering the Friedl Mansion was like stepping through the mouth of hell. The dead, dying, and wounded were scattered across the marble floors of the main entrance. Fallen magi and Knights lay in pools of blood, water, and the remains of what had once been a grand chandelier. Their moans and cries of pain echoed through the chamber, dampening the sounds of battle deeper within the mansion.

The entrance opened into a wide chamber with vaulted ceilings and a single grand staircase looming directly ahead. As they advanced, the other four magi branched out, peering into nearby hallways and ensuring an unexpected force wouldn't flank them from behind. Knowing their rear was covered, Jaxon made for the staircase and the high ground it would provide. Before he got there, though, a squad of Knights emerged from behind the staircase. Engaged with another magi force, they were retreating and didn't see Jaxon's squad approaching.

The air in front of Jaxon warped as he unleashed a massive concussion of air. The shockwave struck the Knights in the back, hurling them forward, and back toward the other advancing magi force, who made quick order of them.

"Jaxon," the squad leader said in a heavily-accented voice. He was a middle-aged man with a strong face, prominent nose, and salt-and-pepper hair. Allyn had met Konrad Blackburn when the Knights had attacked the Blackburn Family. "Thank the First Families. You're here."

"What's going on?" Jaxon asked. "The reports were strange."

"It's a full-scale attack," Konrad said. "Larger than anything I've seen."

"How many Knights?"

"Two platoons, at least. Maybe more."

Two platoons... almost eighty Knights. Except for the Battle of Zurich, that was a larger force than anything the magi had encountered.

Why now? And why the Friedl Family?

Having been misled by the magi leadership before, Allyn wondered what they were hiding now. What other secrets or ancient artifacts could the Friedl Family be privy to? And how had the Knights known about them?

"But the Friedl Family gave them a hell of a fight," Konrad continued. "Even taken by surprise, they made the Knights earn every inch with blood. The mansion was overrun by the time we arrived, but the Knights had lost nearly half their force. With you here, I have no doubt we can repel them."

"Where's the main battle?" Jaxon asked as a new barrage of gunfire echoed through the mansion.

"It's hard to say," Konrad said. "Best we can tell, the Knights took down the front door and streamed inside.

Others entered from the back, but they're not fighting in a coordinated fashion. It's almost as if every squad is on their own."

"Are they looking for anything?" Allyn asked.

"I don't believe so. Why?"

"Nothing," Allyn said, catching a sharp look from Jaxon.

"Stick to the main level," Jaxon said. "We'll take the second and third. But keep your head. Something feels different about this."

Konrad nodded and ordered his squad forward, disappearing deeper into the mansion.

"Let's go." Without waiting for a response, Jaxon took to the stairs.

Allyn followed, the carpeted steps squishing underfoot as he ascended. The staircase opened on a landing that branched off into two hallways, leading to the northern and southern wings of the manor.

After a glance in each direction, Jaxon moved left, toward the sound of battle. But before he had taken more than a few steps, an explosion rocked the mansion, stopping him midstride. His eyes instantly found Allyn's. The explosion hadn't come from a powder or chemical—it had a more natural quality about it. Allyn and Jaxon recognized it immediately.

"Nolan!" Allyn said.

Jaxon bounded past him, racing down the stairs. Allyn was on his heels, followed closely by Nyla, Ren, and Rory, who reassembled their formation. As Allyn exited the mansion to where Nolan and his squad remained, his eyes immediately fell on five heavily-armored tactical vehicles racing down the driveway.

"Inside the mansion!" Jaxon bellowed. "Now!"

The entire magi force obeyed, hurrying through the wrecked entrance. Allyn found cover against the wall and watched through a shattered window as the five vehicles formed a V. The lead vehicle drove straight toward their SUVs, showing no signs of slowing down, and a crash of metal on metal wailed as the lead vehicle drove *through* the SUV, flipping it up and tossing it aside.

"What the fuck is going on?" Allyn said.

"It's a trap," Nolan said. "And we just fell into it."

"Silence," Jaxon said. "We have the fortified position. We still have the advantage."

"A fortified position that's crawling with more of those assholes," Nolan said.

"I said cut it out," Jaxon said, more sharply this time. "How many Knights do you think are in those vehicles?"

"That's a Lenco BearCat," Nolan said. "They're used by SWAT and police forces around the world. Each one will be able to hold up to ten Knights."

"Fifty Knights," Jaxon said.

"Fifty *more* Knights," Nolan corrected. "When do we order the retreat?"

"We're not leaving the other Families behind."

"Jaxon," Nolan said. "Those are damn near tanks on wheels. They have us outgunned and outnumbered. This is not a battle we can win."

"I said we're not leaving the other Families behind."

"Jaxon—"

"Enough!" Jaxon bellowed, tearing his eyes from the threat outside to the one splintering his squad. "I am in command here, and my word is law. Does anyone have a problem with that?"

Nolan clamped his mouth shut, and nobody else spoke up.

"Good," Jaxon continued. "Nolan is right, though. We can't compete with that kind of firepower."

"Whatever you're thinking, think faster," Allyn said. "They're almost here."

"They're going to be invincible inside those vehicles," Jaxon said. "We need them out."

"You want to poke the hive?" Nolan asked.

"Yes. Can you hit one of them with an energy blast?"

"You're damn right."

"Do it, then."

"My pleasure."

Nolan stepped into the open mouth of the mansion and wielded. The ball of light in his palm quickly grew to the size of his head, but Nolan wasn't finished. He continued to project his energy into the blast, increasing its size and intensity. By the time it was nearly four feet in diameter, the ball of energy was white-hot and distorting the air around it.

With a bellow of rage, Nolan hurled the blast forward. A separate concussion sounded half a heartbeat later, propelling the blast forward with even greater intensity.

The BearCat swerved to avoid the blast, but its lumbering mass was too great to turn in time. The blast struck the right-front corner of the vehicle, and a shockwave of white light hurled the front of the vehicle into the air. Metal shrieked across stone in a wave of sparks as the BearCat slid to a halt on its side, the right-front tire billowing blue smoke.

The other four BearCats skidded to a stop, their sides angled toward the mansion.

"Down!" Jaxon shouted as the sides of the BearCats opened up and gun barrels emerged.

Allyn hit the deck just before bullets punched through the face of the mansion, shattering windows and destroying wood and stone. The assault continued for five seconds, ten, maybe longer, before Allyn lost count. By the time it stopped, his ears were ringing, and he could barely hear Jaxon issuing more orders.

Nolan didn't appear to have the same issue, though, and

was wielding again. He wasn't alone this time—Jaxon and Ren readied fireballs, while the air warped around Rory as he prepared a concussion of air.

"Now!"

Nolan shot up from his position of cover, launching a second energy blast toward the nearest BearCat. Rory immediately propelled it forward, and Jaxon and Ren unleashed their attacks a moment later. The energy blast struck the side of the BearCat, tipping it onto its driver's side wheels, exposing its underside for the briefest of moments. But that's all it took. The two fireballs struck the underbelly of the BearCat, exploding against the fuel tank. A ball of fire threw the tactical vehicle high into the air and then sent it crashing into a third one on its descent.

More gunfire erupted from the remaining two vehicles, but with three of the five destroyed, the counterattack lacked the intensity it had before.

"Again!" Jaxon ordered, and the team of magi readied their next attack.

The second attack wasn't as successful, however—the fireballs failed to ignite the fuel lines—but it was enough to prove to the Knights that they weren't safe inside the BearCats. The rear hatch fell open, and a full squad of ten Knights streamed out, guns blazing.

Bullets peppered the walls around Allyn, and someone in his squad cried out in pain. He wielded, ready to repel the Knights, but when he rose and prepared to unleash his first volley of attacks, he realized they weren't making for the mansion. The single squad had split into two sub squads, each one moving to a separate crash site.

They're rescuing the wounded.

"At will! At will!" Jaxon bellowed, and the two full squads of magi unleashed their full strength.

The Knights arrived at the first crash site before the first wave of magi attacks hit. Taking cover behind the reinforced steel of the BearCat, a pair of Knights took aim and provided cover fire while the other three were out of sight, presumably helping the injured. Fireballs and ice blasts struck the side of the tactical vehicle but were nearly completely ineffective.

Allyn's trio of static charges struck next, crashing against the broadside of the BearCat. Red coils of electricity unwound, expanding in a wave that enveloped the vehicle like the tendrils of a great kraken ripping a ship apart. Conducted electricity hit the Knights who were in contact with the BearCat's steel exterior, frying them where they stood.

The Knights from the other crash site saw their comrades fall and moved so they weren't in contact with the vehicle's exterior. Behind them, the remaining BearCat rumbled into position, its rear hatch open, allowing the first wave of survivors to rush inside. Allyn readied another attack, aiming to pick off the fleeing Knights before they could get inside the vehicle, but before he could launch the attack, gunfire erupted behind the magi.

Allyn cursed, ducked, and dove into a nearby hallway. The gunfire continued, striking magi who hadn't been as lucky, while others found new cover in the adjoining hallways. Allyn watched in horror as the fallen magi were riddled with bullets. In a single instant, a third of their number was cut down.

"Fuck! Fuck! Fuck!" Nolan shouted.

Allyn reassessed the situation. Nolan, Nyla, and Rory were on his side of the entrance. Across the corridor, Jaxon, Leira, and Ren had found refuge with a small number of other magi. Jaxon's eyes found Allyn's, and the elder magi pointed at him then motioned back down the corridor to where the gunfire had originated.

"He wants us to flank them," Allyn said. "Come on."

Allyn took the lead, moving down the hall away from the central corridor, then cut into a separate hallway that emptied into the mansion's main-floor living space—a great room with a full kitchen, living room, and informal dining rooms.

Staying low, the foursome moved into the space, using the kitchen counters as cover. The central corridor split the back wing of the house in half, and using the wall for cover, Allyn risked a peek around its corner. The central staircase obstructed his view, but he heard movement above.

"They're on the stairs," Allyn whispered then waved Nolan and Nyla toward the other wall. Once in position, he motioned the entire squad down the central corridor, moving in pairs down either side toward the front entrance. They kept their eyes trained above, searching for the enemy force.

Jaxon emerged from his hall, peering in Allyn's direction, and a split second later, a barrage of gunfire hammered his location. The older magi ducked back behind the wall, narrowly avoiding the salvo.

Allyn froze, holding up a fist, silently ordering his squad to stop. The carpeted stair creaked. Someone shuffled. A magazine was removed and replaced, a fresh round chambered as a Knight reloaded.

They're advancing, Allyn mouthed to his squad.

The stairs creaked again as a boot appeared on the stairs inches above his head. The single boot was quickly replaced by more as a squad of eight Knights advanced.

Allyn kept his fist up as his squad remained in position behind the stairwell, obscured from the Knights' view. He held his breath, fearing his heart, thundering in his chest, would be loud enough to alert the Knights to their presence.

But still they advanced, guns trained on where the other squad of magi hid.

Allyn continued to wait. He had to be sure there weren't more above, but by the time the Knights were halfway down the corridor and closing in on Jaxon's position, Allyn couldn't wait anymore. He ordered the attack.

A fireball and an energy blast streaked down the corridor, taking two unsuspecting Knights in the back. The remaining Knights, thrown by the explosion and the following shockwave, crashed into walls and hallway furniture at unnatural angles.

Nolan sent two more blasts into the corridor, ensuring the fallen Knights wouldn't rise again, while Allyn and Rory spun on the stairs, their attention focused on the landing above. Two guns blazed as Allyn spotted the two remaining Knights positioned atop the stairs. Allyn and Rory's attacks crisscrossed, striking opposite attackers, and the corridor went silent.

"Clear!" Allyn shouted.

"Clear!" Rory repeated.

At the far end of the corridor, Jaxon emerged tentatively then, when he wasn't fired upon, stepped fully into the corridor. The rest of his squad followed his lead.

Allyn and Rory bounded up the stairs and surveyed the landing above. After a quick search didn't uncover any remaining Knights, they hurried back downstairs, rejoining the magi force, which had repositioned itself at the front of the mansion, where they could see the work being finalized outside.

By the time Allyn and Rory joined the squad, the two remaining functional BearCats rumbled out of view, moving around the corners of the mansion.

"Where are they going?" Nolan asked.

"Retreating?" Allyn suggested.

"Then why not go back out the way they came in?"

"Because they're not retreating." Jaxon spun and raced down the central corridor to the back wing of the house where Allyn and his squad had been only moments before.

They arrived in time to see the BearCats round the corner of the house, moving parallel with the back of the mansion, tearing through hedges and colorful gardens. As they came to a rest, a squad of Knights, led by the helmetless Knight Commander Sedric Lang himself, sprinted from a separate entrance to the house, rushing across the grounds. He jumped onto the side of the BearCat, taking hold of one of the various handholds, keeping his other hand on his assault rifle.

Sedric laid down a barrage of cover fire as a mass of new bodies followed in his path. Most had guns and were firing at an unseen magi force, but others didn't and seemed to be putting up some sort of resistance.

"Are those...?" Nolan's voice trailed off.

"Oh my God," Allyn said. "They're prisoners. They're taking prisoners! Come on!"

Allyn was sprinting from the back of the house before he knew it. Someone shouted after him, but he ignored them, pushing for the pair of BearCats. Their rear hatches were open now, the magi being herded inside. Wielding, he thought about sending a series of static charges in their direction but couldn't risk hitting one of their own.

The BearCats started forward when Allyn was still at least twenty feet away, and quickly, the distance grew between them. Sedric remained on the side of the vehicle, his rifle under his right arm, pumping more rounds into the mansion. He rode without fear, barely even flinching as ice blasts and fireballs shattered and exploded against the vehicle's armor. Allyn's movement must have caught his eye, because he turned and, seeing Allyn sprinting after them, *smiled*.

He waved as the BearCat disappeared from view.

CHAPTER 4

SUNSET ARRIVED AT THE FRIEDL Mansion before the arch mage. By then, the remaining Friedl Family members, aided by the Blackburn and McCollum forces, had thoroughly searched the grounds for remaining Knights and carefully laid the fallen magi in the gardens, where their loved ones could mourn.

Seventeen magi were dead. It was an unthinkable number that included one fifth of the Friedl Family and a good number of the Blackburn and McCollum advanced forces. The twenty-three dead Knights gave the survivors a tiny semblance of satisfaction, but for most, it wasn't enough. The battle had been the bloodiest to date—for both sides—and if the overwhelming sense of dread in Allyn's gut was any indication, it was only the beginning.

He sat on the edge of the fountain, watching as magi worked into the night on their first attempts to rebuild. He should have been helping. He should have swept, mopped, mended, or consoled, but he just couldn't bring himself to move. He wasn't exhausted; he was exhausted of being exhausted, of feeling the same damn emptiness again and again. So he stayed out of the way and watched.

Sometime later, Nyla sat beside him on the edge of the fountain. She laid a hand on his bare arm, white light illuminating at their contact as she began to probe his condition.

He pulled away, breaking her touch. "Don't."

"I want to make sure you're not injured."

"I'm fine."

Nyla sighed but didn't press the issue. She sat there, listening to the soft trickle of water and the cries of the mourning mothers, fathers, brothers, and sisters.

"What the hell happened today, Nyla? Since when do the Knights take prisoners?"

"I don't know," she said. "I don't know any more than you do."

"And then we just stood there. We didn't even go after them."

"We'll get them back, Allyn."

"Are you sure?" he asked sharply. "I don't know how. We don't even know where to look."

"I..." She sighed, pursing her lips, apparently rethinking what she was going to say. "I choose to believe we'll find them, because it beats the alternative."

Allyn shook his head. It wasn't that he disagreed with her; he didn't know *how* he felt. His feelings were a jumble of contradictions.

"What happened to me, Nyla?"

"What do you mean?"

"I just witnessed... no, I just took part in the death of forty people, and all I can think about are the few that were taken alive. Everything else is just..." He held up his empty hands.

"I don't have to be an empath like your sister to know that's not true, Allyn."

"It is," he said defiantly. "There's this... *emptiness* inside me. A void where I should feel something. Anything." He looked at his feet and rolled a rock under the sole of his shoe. "What's wrong me with? You should feel *something* when forty people die. When five children were just murdered."

"You do," Nyla said. "You're angry."

"You're damn right I'm angry! I'm angry I don't feel *more.*"

"Our bodies have a way of protecting us, Allyn. Of shielding us when the horrors are too great. What you're feeling now, what you're *not* feeling, says more about what just happened than it does who you are."

"It's getting worse." He rubbed his hands together as if trying to wash away the blood. "The war. The battles. All of it."

"Yeah."

"I don't know if I can do this."

"I don't know if I can do it, either."

Allyn looked up, really seeing Nyla for the first time. Her silver hair glowed softly in the moonlight, and blood streaked her soft heart-shaped face. It was an odd contradiction—someone so beautiful stained by violence.

Nyla avoided his gaze, taking her turn to be timid. "We've seen more than anyone ought to see. And it takes a toll. It definitely takes a toll."

"Nyla, I..." He didn't know what to say. He'd felt so alone for so long that he had never given any thought to how the violence was affecting the others—especially Nyla and the other clerics. She'd been stalwart, a figure of unshakeable certainty, and the magi had asked more of her than any of the others. When the battles were over and Allyn had the luxury of watching the aftermath from a distance, Nyla had been on the front lines, healing the injured, taking on the burden of their wounds and pain.

She met his eye, giving him a fragile smile that said more

than words ever could. She knew. And she knew that he knew as well.

"We'll be okay," she said.

"And if we aren't?"

"Then we'll be there to pick each other up."

───────── ••• ─────────

Darkness had completely fallen by the time the arch mage arrived, and by then, most of the magi had turned in. Unable to sleep, Allyn was on watch, using the quiet as a time of reflection. The emptiness he'd felt before had evolved into something else. Not anger, exactly, but a form of it. It was like anger, confusion, and the sense of being overwhelmed all rolled into a tight ball that was constantly at the forefront his mind. He picked at it as if it were a scab, irritated by it but, at the same time, taking comfort in its existence. In the fact that he felt something. That his body was trying to mend itself.

Shortly after graduating from high school, his best friend, Grant, had joined the army. They'd said their goodbyes but stayed in contact, and Allyn had even visited him on base, but with every visit he'd noticed small, nearly imperceptible changes within his friend. First, it was small things: liking different music and watching different movies. Then, after a while, his taste in girls and the things he did for fun began to change too. Worse, Grant's mood began to change, and he became much quicker to anger.

By the time Grant had been granted a medical discharge, he was a completely different person. He and Allyn were still friends, of course. They still had their shared childhood experiences and could laugh about those times, but little by little, they drifted away. Grant wasn't the same person, and Allyn had changed too, but in a different way. Finally, the differences became too great to overcome. Hanging out weekly turned into monthly then bi-annually on each other's birthdays, and at some point, even those excuses weren't good enough.

Am I changing like that too? Who am I drifting away from?

He hated to think about it, hated to admit it, but knew deep down that no one could experience the horrors he had without changing in some way. Thoughts like those and memories of distant friends still plagued Allyn when the lights of a motorcade appeared like two glowing white orbs weaving through the trees that circled the mansion grounds.

Thinking the Knights were returning to finish the job, Allyn felt his heart skip a beat. Just as he was about to sound the alarm, he noticed the rumble of the engine lacked the throaty sound of the BearCats, and the lights were too low to the ground to have been from one of the tactical vehicles.

It's the arch mage, Allyn realized bitterly. *He finally showed up.*

Allyn alerted the others on patrol, and by the time the arch mage's car and two more filled with prominent members of his Elemental Guard had parked, the Friedl Mansion was once again bustling with activity.

There was no pomp or formal greeting. Arch Mage Westarra didn't wait for it, and it wasn't the right occasion. Instead, he nodded to Allyn and the rest of the guard while entering the mansion in a rush.

Allyn was called to the meeting twenty minutes later. Inside a large formal sitting room, he found Jaxon and Leira with Arch Mage Westarra, six members of his Elemental Guard, Grand Mage Curtis Friedl, and Konrad Blackburn of the Blackburn Family.

"Allyn," Arch Mage Westarra said, "thank you for coming."

"My apologies for being late," Allyn said tightly, wondering what he had missed in the minutes it had taken the others to assemble.

Westarra waved away the apology. "Sit, please, all of you."

Allyn found a seat next to Jaxon and Leira in an oversized armchair near the fire. It was helpful to have a unified front when addressing the arch mage, and Allyn suspected they would need it.

"Jaxon and Konrad have already debriefed me, so we don't need to dwell on the details of the battle," Westarra said. "But clearly this was a... *setback*."

"A setback, Your Grace?" The words were out of Allyn's mouth before he knew it. After everything he'd been through—the emptiness, the anger, the confusion—Arch Mage Westarra's feeble words were too much. They finally gave him something to latch on to, something to channel his ball of conflicting emotions into. "Seventeen magi are dead, Your Grace. That's more than a *setback*."

Jaxon opened his mouth, but Arch Mage Westarra held up a hand, cutting him off. "It's fine, Jaxon. I was only trying to be polite. You're right, Allyn. I apologize. This was a massive defeat—the worst massacre we have suffered since the beginning of the war. And clearly, our strategy needs to reflect this new reality."

Westarra's gaze lingered on Allyn for several moments. Allyn couldn't tell if the arch mage was looking for his approval to proceed or asserting his own authority, but he nodded anyway. He was relieved the arch mage was willing to revisit his strategy. Their current one wasn't working. It was too defensive. If they were to stand a chance, they had to take the fight to the Knights.

"How long after the attack began did it take us to respond?" Arch Mage Westarra asked.

Us? Allyn wanted to ask. There had only been two Families

who had come to the Friedls' aid, and no support at all from the arch mage or his Elemental Guard.

"We arrived thirty-two minutes after we received the call, Your Grace," Konrad said.

"And we were just over an hour, Your Grace," Jaxon said.

"And by your own admission," Westarra said, looking at Konrad, "the enemy was already within the mansion walls."

"Yes, Your Grace."

"Then, clearly, your response time was too slow."

"Our *response* time, Your Grace?" Jaxon asked slowly, his voice tight. Either Jaxon wasn't as good at hiding his emotions as he had once been, or Allyn had grown to know the man well enough to see when he was fighting to control himself.

"Yes," Westarra said simply. "Had either of your two Families arrived sooner and prevented the Knights from entering the mansion, the number of casualties would have been greatly lowered. Do you disagree?"

Jaxon locked his jaw, and Konrad shifted uncomfortably in his seat.

"My apologies, *Your Grace*," Allyn said, laying the formalities on thick, "but it sounds to me like you're blaming this on us. The McCollum Family is *three thousand* miles away, and there are two Families closer to the Friedls than the Blackburns. Maybe a more appropriate conversation would be why the fuck nobody else showed up."

Westarra blinked, looking as though he'd been slapped, and Allyn immediately regretted cursing at the arch mage. Kendyl had once asked him why someone who had practiced law and was trained to keep cool under intense pressure struggled to hold his tongue in front of the magi leader. The only answer he'd been able to come up with was that he'd never had to confront a judge after being shot at.

"You may not have grown up within this Order, Allyn," Arch Mage Westarra said coolly. "But you are still a respected member and a representative of the McCollum Family. I expect you to act like it."

"Of course, Your Grace," Allyn said. "I apologize. It's no excuse, but it's been a long night. It won't happen again."

"See that it doesn't." Westarra turned to the others. "You are here because of your unique set of abilities. Had Canary not been here, we wouldn't have had the lead time we had, and the Knights' ambush would have been more successful. She was the difference—*you* were the difference between a narrow victory and complete and utter defeat. I recognize that. I really do. Why no other Family offered aid is another problem, which I'll see to personally."

"Thank you, Your Grace," Jaxon said.

Irritated, Allyn shifted, his gaze going from Jaxon to Konrad to Westarra. They were still dancing around the real issue.

"What is it, Allyn?" Westarra asked. "You're squirming in your seat like you're sitting on a hot coal."

"Uh..." Allyn's face grew hot under the weight of everyone's gaze. "It's just that—"

"If you have something to say, say it," Westarra said. "By the First Families, you haven't held anything else back."

"It's not the other Families I question, Your Grace. It's our strategy as a whole."

"Explain."

"We're fighting a war of attrition, Your Grace. The Knights are bleeding us dry, harrowing our Families like a raiding party attacking supply lines. That's not a war we can win—we don't have the numbers. Every day, every battle, the odds get stacked further against us. And now they've started taking prisoners. If we weren't prepared before, we certainly aren't now. Something needs to change."

"What would you have me do?"

"I'd have us attack."

Westarra gave him a dismissive expression and rose from his seat to pace behind his chair. "We've been over this. After the battle in Zurich, when Jaxon and I first visited you at the Klausner Manor, we discussed this."

"We did, Your Grace."

"And I disagreed with you then."

"I remember."

"Why would now be any different?" Westarra asked. "The magi have many enemies, Allyn, but our biggest enemy is exposure. The pain and the fear you feel today, the concern you have for our future, would be nothing compared to what you would feel if that enemy reared its ugly head and our existence was known. We cannot fight a war we can't control. We cannot fight a war off our land. We must keep the secret. Against all else, we *must* keep the secret."

"War, by its very definition, is out of control, Your Grace. And unless we fight back, there might not be a secret to keep."

Westarra opened his mouth to speak, but Allyn cut him off. He refused to be dismissed. The magi leadership needed to hear this. They'd been trying to fight a war from the outskirts for too long. "Excuse me, Your Grace, but this war has changed. And if we don't change with it, it's going to come to an end very quickly."

Westarra took a deep breath, looking from Allyn to Jaxon. "And how do you feel about this, Jaxon?"

"I think it's always wise to review one's stance, Your Grace."

"You sound like you're on the Forum, Jaxon. Speak clearly—I won't have you politicking in a private meeting."

"I agree with him, Your Grace. You fear an offensive

strategy will result in unexpected consequences, but I disagree. It's the only way we can choose the battlefield."

"I see." Arch Mage Westarra turned to the representative from the Blackburn Family. "Should I assume you are in agreement with this as well, Konrad?"

"I..." Konrad shot an uneasy look in Allyn's direction. It appeared he wasn't ready to be lumped in with an insubordinate outsider just yet. "The battle had a different feel to it, Your Grace. I'll say that. But I wasn't privy to your previous discussions, and I am not as familiar with these Knights as Allyn and Jaxon are. Still, nobody has as much experience going against this enemy as they do, so who am I to disagree with them?"

"A tempered endorsement if I ever heard one," Westarra said sarcastically. "What about you, Leira? You are the true, senior-most member of the McCollum Family here. What do you have to add?"

"I agree with Allyn, Your Grace," she said without preamble. "I watched as my father battled Lukas for many months. Like you, he tried to contain it. Tried to keep word from spreading. And that prevented him from doing what he needed to do. I don't want to see my people burn up the same way my home did."

Westarra nodded. "Thank you for your honesty, Leira. And thank you all for your... *candidness*." He shot Allyn an amused look with that last part. "I'll take this into consideration. In the meantime, I want you two to draw up how you would proceed. I want to see what your strategy would be."

"Yes, Your Grace," Jaxon said.

"Thank you, Your Grace," Allyn said.

"Don't thank me yet," Westarra said. "I expect to have an answer in two days. And you'll be presenting it to the entire Forum."

CHAPTER 5

IAM RESTED HIS CHIN ON his fist, gently tapping his finger against his lips. It was, in his opinion, a pretty respectable impression of the statue of Socrates at the Academy of Athens. Not that he'd been there to see it in person, of course. Until very recently, he'd never even traveled on an airplane, let alone left his secluded home in the Pacific Northwest. Now, he had been to two countries, a real man of the world.

It was almost ironic, then, that he sat in the Klausner library, staring at the wall of books and wishing more than anything to be back home.

How can they all be so useless? He had been through all of the books, maybe not thoroughly—he didn't have time for that—but slowly enough to decide if they warranted a closer inspection.

They're for show, nothing more.

The wall was little more than decorative art. Trophies. A status symbol among the magi. He should have known; the clues had been there all along. The first should have been how the rest of the *real* art—the sculptures, ancient bowls and cups, and handmade vases—were mixed in with the books, filling holes and making the wall more attractive.

That's not entirely fair, a contradictory voice inside him said. *Your library wasn't any different.*

And it was true. The McCollum library had proudly displayed its own decorative pieces—though Liam liked to think of them as something more than that. The difference was that the McCollum library had been climate-controlled, the air kept a crisp sixty-five degrees Fahrenheit and free of moisture that would have ruined the texts. The artifacts had benefited from the regulated environment, but beyond that, the artifacts weren't truly on display. The library had been underground, away from prying eyes and curious fingers. The Klausner library *was* different. Centrally located within the main floor of the manor, the wall of books was the magi equivalent of a huge television.

Sighing, Liam stood and stepped up to the bookshelf. He ran his fingers across spines as he passed. He might have missed something, overlooked a small, nondescript tome that held the answers to the questions that had kept him up for countless nights since his imprisonment. Since the first time he'd seen Knight Commander of the Knights of Rakkar wield.

How deep is the connection between the magi and humans? And why does the Blood Wand work on both?

He absently touched the brand on his upper arm, tracing its pattern through his compression armor, knowing even as he gazed at the books that the search for answers was pointless. The information, if it existed at all, was a closely guarded secret. It wasn't something he would find in a random library. There was only one place he would find something like that: the arch mage's personal collection.

The real question was, how could Liam convince the most

powerful magi in the Order to allow him, a young magi of no real regard, into his personal archive?

Magi of no regard? his internal voice of derision chided. *Stop discounting yourself. You're the first magi since the Reaping to have been touched by the Blood Wand, and the only magi in the Order with both machinist and magi abilities. If there's anyone the arch mage will make an exception for, it's you.*

The thought brought a smile to his lips. Even months after manifesting the magi abilities, Liam still could hardly believe the change. He'd wished for the abilities for so long, had worked so hard, and then when it seemed as if they would never develop, he'd resigned himself to the harsh reality. Allyn had helped with that process, of course, and Liam's life had taken an unexpected twist when the two of them had discovered the new abilities being developed among the magi. But it hadn't stopped him from still feeling like an outsider. A disappointment.

After all, the fundamental difference between humans and magi was the ability to wield. And if a magi didn't have that ability, then who were they? *What* were they? Liam had never felt comfortable with the question, even after the Blood Wand had given him everything he had longed for. Even if, for the first time, Liam was starting to feel as if he belonged.

Liam stopped, his finger sliding from the spine of a book to rest on the shelf. *It's all related.* The new questions were just an extension of the old. *He* and his perspective were the only things that had changed. As it were, the central question had evolved from "where do I belong?" to "*why* do I belong?"

Liam returned to his chair, again taking the pose of the ancient philosopher. He'd have to think on the realization, see if it would help him come at the question from a different angle, maybe open his search to new possibilities.

"Am I interrupting something?" Allyn asked.

Liam blinked, snapping out of his thoughts, and found Allyn standing in the doorway. "Hmmm?"

"What are you doing?" Allyn stepped into the room, stopping beside the chair opposite Liam. Nearly a full day had passed since Allyn and Jaxon had gone to assist the Friedl Family, and he looked as though he hadn't slept at all. Dark rings circled swollen eyes, and his pale skin had a red tint as if it were forever stained with blood.

"Just thinking," Liam said. "What happened to you? You look terrible."

"Thanks," Allyn said with a sarcastic laugh. "It's a long story. And if I look half as bad as I feel, then I'm sure I'm quite a sight."

"The rumors are true then? The battle didn't go well?"

Allyn shook his head, his body deflating, and Liam thought for half a second that he would have to catch Allyn before he fell to the floor. Allyn steadied himself, though, and sat on the arm of the chair.

"You should get some sleep," Liam said.

"There's no time," Allyn said. "The arch mage has agreed to review our strategy. Do you still have the Knight Commander's logbook?"

"Of course."

"Good. It's time we dust that off and use it to our advantage."

"All right," Liam said. "When do you want to start?"

"Now," Allyn said. "We have a date with the Forum."

CHAPTER 6

JAXON STOOD AT ATTENTION WITH Grand Mage Klausner, Arch Mage Westarra, and a mix of McCollum and Klausner magi as the motorcade carrying the members of the Forum rolled onto the Klausner grounds. There hadn't been enough time to assemble the entire Forum, but those who were local had made the trip, and the rest would participate via videoconference.

Five magi SUVs came to a stop and shut off their engines. Their drivers hopped out to open the doors for the grand mages. Men and women Jaxon recognized by sight, but had never met in person, climbed out and stretched stiff bodies. They greeted the arch mage first.

Westarra thanked them for coming and directed them down the line, where Jaxon and other magi welcomed them. The assembly wouldn't start for another few hours, but the members headed straight inside, likely to meet privately with the arch mage and other members of the Forum.

Jaxon hadn't gotten the invitation, and part of him wondered if he would. He was acting Grand Mage of the McCollum Family, a position recognized by Arch Mage Westarra and the Forum. Purposely excluding him from a meeting where every other member of the Forum was present would be a show of disrespect he hadn't seen or felt since the Forum had dissolved the McCollum Family.

He wrestled down a pang of irritation. There was no sense in agonizing over something that hadn't happened yet. If he didn't get the invitation, he would take it up with the arch mage later.

"Welcome, Grand Mage Friedl," Jaxon said as the next grand mage moved down the line. "We are with you." The last bit was a deviation from tradition, but the man nodded his appreciation and moved on, giving Jaxon a clear view of the last two members to arrive. The first was another he recognized by sight but had never met. But the second...

"Father?" Jaxon said, completely breaking decorum.

The magi around him, forever shielded by tradition, acted as though they hadn't heard the outburst. Grand Mage Wesley Green strode forward confidently, saluting the arch mage in the magi fashion before making his way down the line toward Jaxon.

Watching with nervous anticipation as his father clasped arms and accepted the Family's welcome, Jaxon wondered what he would say to the man who had nearly disowned him. In the end, he decided to hide behind the veil of convention.

"Welcome, Grand Mage Green," he choked out when his father stopped in front of him.

"Thank you," the elder Green said. His father was broad of shoulder, his skin darker even than Jaxon's, with gray peppering his closely cropped hair. He'd aged since Jaxon had seen him last. The hard lines of his face grew deeper as he studied Jaxon, weighing him. It was everything Jaxon could do not to flinch, blink, or show any sign of being intimidated.

"Return home," his mother, Talisa Green, had said when

they'd last spoken. "Return home, or we will be forced to remove you."

She and his father hadn't agreed with his decision to remain with the McCollum Family after Graeme's death, and were vehemently against him assuming the interim grand mage mantle. If his father's current grim expression was any indication, it seemed he had come to make good on that promise.

"This is a surprise," Jaxon said quietly. "What are you doing here?"

Wesley cast a sidelong glance at the remaining magi, who were beginning to disperse, the formality over. "It's been too long, Jaxon. It's time you and I had a talk. There's much to discuss."

A cold feeling of dread washed over him. His father wasn't the talking kind of man. If he said they needed to talk, then something was seriously wrong.

"Come." Wesley took Jaxon by the shoulder with a firm hand and directed him inside. "Let us find a quiet corner and speak as father and son."

Jaxon led his father into a private study on the first floor of the manor and closed the door behind them. The room was lightly furnished with a pair of leather armchairs resting in front of a small fireplace. Jaxon motioned for his father to sit, then did so himself.

"We're both busy, so I'm just going to get straight to the point," Wesley Green said.

If Jaxon hadn't been so tense, he might have laughed. His father was making excuses for being direct and straight to the point—as if he had any other means of communication.

"You disobeyed me," Wesley said, leveling his gaze on Jaxon.

With a stare that could force a mountain into relenting, Jaxon's father was one of the most intimidating men he had ever known. Worse, the man knew it and often used his reputation to his advantage. But Jaxon had grown up since the last time his father had leveled that gaze at him. He'd faced down men who wanted to kill him, defeated other men who wished to imprison him. And he wasn't in any mood to be manipulated by a man who too often acted like a petty bully.

"You'll have to be more specific than that, Father."

"You didn't return home when your mother and I commanded you to."

"I had other responsibilities."

"None greater than your Family."

"Which is why I remained," Jaxon said. "The McCollum Family is as much my own as the Green. Besides, wasn't it you who taught me to honor my commitments? I promised I would see this Family to safety, and I remained so I could."

"You're more important than the remnants of a splintered Family, Jaxon."

"We're not splintered anymore," Jaxon said. "You know that. You voted against the McCollum Family's readmittance to the Forum and lost, remember?"

"All the more reason for you to return home. You promised the Family safety? Fine. You've done that. They're more stable now than they have been in years. It's time you returned home."

"I still have more to learn."

"And it's time you learned it from me." His father took a deep breath, his mask of strength cracking. The mask reappeared quickly, returning to the same dour appearance Jaxon knew and expected.

The brief glimpse of humanity unnerved Jaxon, and he was suddenly less angry. His father was many things—a respected leader, accomplished magi, and dedicated husband—but devoted father wasn't one of them. He was hard, ever the leader, even to his children, and never let down the façade of the strong grand mage. Seeing his father's frailty was akin to watching a hero turn human before his eyes.

"I didn't order you home solely for your safety, Jaxon. It is time you reclaimed what is rightfully yours. It's time you became grand mage in more than name alone."

It took several seconds for the words to register, and when they finally did, Jaxon didn't know how to respond.

"You're abdicating?"

He doesn't expect me to believe such nonsense, does he? My father will be grand mage until the day he... Jaxon's blood ran cold. He looked at his father, *truly* looked at him, and what he saw shook him to his very core. Wesley Green looked tired. His eyes were duller, the wrinkles of his face deeper, his skin oddly colored. What Jaxon had originally chalked up to travel fatigue suddenly took on a different meaning.

"I'm dying, Jaxon." Wesley leaned forward in his seat with a wince. He rubbed his hands together and dropped his tone. It wasn't what Jaxon would call compassionate, though it had lost a bit of its edge. "I only have a few months left, maybe a few weeks, before my body begins its steep decline."

Jaxon sat back in his chair, shifting awkwardly, unsure what to do. His first thought was to comfort the man, but he wasn't sure he even knew how.

"Say something, Jaxon. Tell me you'll fulfill your duty."

"Duty." Jaxon almost spat the word. "It's always duty with

you, Father. Always responsibility. You just told me you're dying, and all you're concerned about is—"

"Your Family needs you."

Jaxon shook his head. He couldn't tell what he was angrier about, his father's condition or his lack of empathy. "How?" he finally asked, afraid of the answer.

"How am I dying? It's cancer. My own body is fighting me."

"And there's nothing they can do?"

"I've already been undergoing treatment, but it's only slowing the inevitable."

Jaxon watched his father, looking for a crack in his story. But he knew it was useless. His father was telling the truth, and sooner than Jaxon probably realized, his life would be devoid of one of the most influential people in his life.

He looked away, his vision going blurry through unexpected tears. He and his father had never been close, but there had always been respect. And despite how hard the elder man could be, he was still Jaxon's father, still the man who had carved him into the person he was today. Jaxon had never truly imagined a life without that constant presence. Thinking about it now... He could barely complete the thought.

"I'm not gone yet." His father let out a long breath, as if what he was about to say next took more effort than everything he'd said previously. "I'm done ordering you about, Jaxon. I'm asking you instead. Return with me to the Green Family, and let me spend my last days teaching you the things I should have taught you years ago."

Jaxon left the Klausner Manor behind, seeking a place of

solitude. He moved south, scaling the steep mountainside that shielded the Klausner Manor from the rear.

Thick, tangled knots of beech roots rose from the ground, providing Jaxon with footing and handholds as he began his ascent. The forest vegetation wasn't as diverse as it was at home, but in many ways, it was more beautiful. Where the Pacific Northwest was largely varying shades of green, the Schwyzer Alps shone with an array of crimsons, golds, violets, and blues. The very air felt alive with color.

And the smell... The vibrant sensations tickled the inside of his nose. He filled his lungs with the sweet smell and held it in, letting it purify him from the inside out.

Having left his phone behind, Jaxon didn't know how long the hike took, but he eventually found what he was looking for—a secluded, rocky plateau sheltered by trees that overlooked the town and manor below. He shed his shirt and hung it on a nearby branch before dropping into the opening pose of the Mahari. For weeks, he'd sought refuge in the magi kata, and for weeks, he'd been interrupted. He wouldn't let that happen again, not after what he'd been through.

He started slow, easing into the familiar cadence, steadying his breathing and dropping his heightened heart rate to a more sufficient level. He felt the burn in his muscles and pushed them, stretching them, gradually building up the Mahari's intensity.

Most young magi new to the magi kata didn't know it directly mirrored its magi's emotions. They assumed the kata was some kind of cleansing ritual designed to bring the magi's emotional state back to center. However, the Mahari was not an outside force acting upon the practitioner like a massage of the spirit. In reality, the Mahari helped a magi realize their feelings by putting their inner thoughts and emotions to action.

Hidden anger resulted in sharp, jagged movements that escalated as the kata progressed and the anger boiled to the surface. Uncertainty manifested in a slow, tentative dance where the Mahari became mechanical, whereas grief and sorrow brought about inconsistent, often distracted movements. No, the Mahari was not an outside force. Instead, it allowed practicing magi to understand their current emotional states, and from that understanding, they could take the appropriate action.

Jaxon, of course, didn't need the Mahari to uncover his emotional state. He knew the tangled mix of emotions that writhed inside of him. Even at that moment, as far from the conversation as he could get, he still relived the key moments of their discussion. And mirroring the memory of the conversation, his movements increased in intensity, picking up speed, sharpened by aggression.

"And it's time you learned it from me."

Jaxon stumbled, his knee slamming into the rocky earth. The words had been the turning point in their conversation, the first step on the path that had led to Jaxon putting the pieces together. He waited there on one knee, breathing heavily, the image of his father's expression burned into his vision like an afterimage. He stood, banishing the thought from his mind and falling back into step. The movements came habitually, his body going through the motions, his mind entirely disengaged.

You're thinking too much. Clear your mind.

He closed his eyes, filling his mind's eye with complete blackness. He focused on the strain of his muscles, the weight anchored above the balls of his feet, the last vestiges of warmth from the setting sun.

The void inside him swelled with energy as he channeled his body heat and drew it to his core. The temperature outside suddenly felt much colder, and if he hadn't been in control, his body would have shivered, sending goose bumps across his flesh. The void full, Jaxon projected the energy into his hands, and it surged through his body like blood through his veins. Then he was wielding.

His eyes snapped open, but he didn't see the world as he had before. Where he'd seen the setting sun casting the landscape in a golden hue, he saw fire. It enveloped his hands, flickering across his vision as if the world itself were aflame. He threw his hands skyward, and a pair of fireballs flew high into the sky, leaving behind trails of black smoke. A moment later, two more fireballs soared after the first, and brilliant explosions flashed as the second attack met the first.

He repeated the process twice more, launching fireball after fireball, hitting the first volley with the second as if he were skeet shooting. Then, with a primal roar, he stretched his hands toward the heavens. The end of the Mahari was near. Anger swelled inside him. Anger at his father for dying, for not fighting harder, for being so damn cold when telling his own son he would soon be alone.

Jaxon's composure broke. He lost control, and his anger fueled the fire burning inside him. He continued to wield. He had to get it out. Had to get rid of it before it consumed him.

The fire manifested itself around Jaxon's arms, similar to the way the coils of electricity wrapped around Allyn's. It wasn't normal fire, though. This was alive, unharnessed, burning hotter than normal. And already, he could feel his core body temperature drop. This was why he always instructed young magi not to feed their abilities with emotion—one could lose control quickly and pay the price. Magic, of course, had consequences.

Arms still raised to the sky, Jaxon *released*, and the fire streaked upward, burning the leaves of the surrounding beech trees. Though reckless, the fire pouring from him was cathartic, and Jaxon continued until his body was spent. Then, weak and suffering from the first stages of hypothermia, Jaxon cut off the fire and dropped to his knees.

Tears, the final remnant of his emotions, streamed down his face. On this side of the kata, he felt empty, and in the absence of his own emotions, Leira's were stronger than ever. She was near and drawing closer, concerned. He hadn't told her his father had arrived unexpectedly, and he hadn't had time to tell her of their conversation or that he might have to break the promise he'd made to her outside the Hyland Estate when he'd vowed to protect the McCollum Family.

Thinking about it was nearly enough to tear him apart. He was being pulled in opposite directions by equally strong forces, and if they weren't careful, they would break him.

Leira found him as he was pulling his shirt back over his head. She stopped when she saw him, her eyes looking him up and down like a concerned mother checking her child for bumps and scrapes. Once she saw that he wasn't injured, she stepped out onto the bluff with him.

"It's beautiful," she said, looking at the scene behind him.

Jaxon turned, following her gaze. The first lights of Schwyz glowed below, filling the impending night with yellows, blues, and reds.

"Yes, it is."

"But that's not why you're up here."

"No," Jaxon said. "I needed... I was tired of being interrupted." He regretted the words the moment they left his mouth. "Not that you're interrupting," he added quickly.

Leira smiled, and a wave of amusement accompanied the expression. She stepped past him, nearing the edge of the bluff, and sat down, bringing her knees to her chest.

"You know," she said, "I've never had the same need to

get away as Liam has. Maybe it's because my father didn't keep me as close and let me leave the manor to see parts of the world Liam could only read about. Or maybe I just don't have that desire. But as beautiful as it is, Jaxon, I'm tired of it. I miss home."

Jaxon remained where he stood, watching Leira awkwardly. He'd faced countless enemies and fought in countless battles, but nothing intimidated him as much as baring his soul to the woman he loved. He was terrified about what came next. He couldn't stand the thought of hurting her. Of letting her down.

He shuffled over and sat down next to her. "Me too."

"No. I miss *home*. I miss having a place that was ours, that was mine. I miss hunting in the forests and swimming in the creek. I miss reading in Liam's library and watching him catalogue the books and texts. I miss walking the same halls my father walked, eating in the same dining room that thousands had eaten in before me. I miss cooking in the same kitchen my mother..."

Jaxon draped an arm around her, pulling her close, and she buried her face in his chest. Leira's mother had died shortly after Liam was born, and all Leira had left were vague memories and stories told by those who'd known her. She didn't even have a photograph—the fire at the McCollum Manor had claimed even that.

Though Leira rarely talked about any of it, Jaxon knew the emptiness weighed on her every day. That void in her life defined Leira in ways he could never comprehend. Still, he was a little surprised she was bringing it up.

It's the war. It's weighing on all of us.

"You know what I miss?" he asked. "I miss the smell. The aged wood of your father's study. The crisp, clean air of Liam's library. Even the smell of wood smoke that had

57

soaked into the walls over the centuries." He gently rubbed her upper arm with his fingers. "But most of all, I miss how, no matter how many fires you had going or how hot you got them burning, the manor was always *cold*."

Leira gave him a single quiet sniff of laughter.

"Seriously," he said. "The place was an icebox. Even in the summer."

"Maybe you should have tried wearing sleeves."

"Ha!" Jaxon barked. "No chance."

They sat in silence for a while, taking comfort in the silence of each other's company.

"I'm sorry," Leira said eventually. She pulled away and turned so she was looking at him. "You have a lot going on. Between Allyn and the Forum. You don't need my distractions too."

"It's okay. It actually feels good to be distracted." Jaxon took one of Leira's hands in his.

"When is the session with the Forum?" she asked.

"Tonight."

"Is Allyn ready?"

"I don't know," Jaxon said honestly. "I haven't had a lot of time to spend with him since we returned."

"Really?"

"I had to welcome the members of the Forum."

"Oh," she said. "Well you should talk to him. He's expecting your help, and it's not fair for you to leave him on his own. Not when you spoke against the arch mage too."

"I know," Jaxon said. "I was..." He licked his lips. "Distracted."

A pang of nervousness rang through the echo as Leira's eyes fell to the ground. "Your father was with them, wasn't he?" She phrased the words as if they were a question, but there was little doubt she already knew the answer.

"Yes," Jaxon said, fearing his ability to say more. He'd

known he would have to tell Leira of his father's request, and of his own decision, but he hadn't expected to so soon.

Leira watched him intently, visibly anxious by the unanswered question, and when it became apparent Jaxon wasn't going to say anything further, she pressed. "It's... *unconventional* for a Forum member to travel so far."

Jaxon nodded. He couldn't hide from the truth any longer, not when she was asking him directly. But even though he knew he had to tell her, his words fought like hell to stay inside.

"He isn't here for the assembly," Jaxon began. "That was only the excuse. He's sick, Leira. He's... he's dying."

Leira sucked in a sharp breath, her hand covering her parted lips. "Oh, Jaxon. I'm so sorry. Is there any...?"

"Hope? No."

She took both of his hands in hers, her thumbs rubbing his calloused skin. The echo vibrated with her emotions. Concern and sadness mixed equally with anxiety and regret in a contrary jumble, making it difficult to determine where his emotions began and hers ended.

"It's cancer. It's spread through his body."

"How long?" It was a delicate question, which Jaxon could tell she was uncomfortable asking.

"A few weeks. Months, if he's lucky."

Leira shook her head. She had lost her father too, and if anyone understood the pain he was going through, she did. But the loss of her father had brought her and Jaxon closer together, whereas the loss of Jaxon's would drive them apart.

"It's time for me to go home, Leira. It's my father's dying wish that I return to the Family and take up his position as grand mage. I know I promised to stay, promised to remain until the McCollum Family had returned to full strength, but I can't. I'm sorry, Leira. I have to break that promise."

A single tear slid down her cheek, and it was as if it were a knife plunging directly into Jaxon's heart.

"I understand," she whispered, but her thumbs stopped massaging the backs of his hands. If the echo were any indication, she was too overcome with her own emotion for his to take precedence any longer. "How long do we have?"

"I don't know," Jaxon said. "But I imagine he'll ask that I return with him."

She nodded and took a deep breath, regaining control of her emotions. "You're doing the right thing."

"Then why does it feel like I'm being torn in two?"

She smiled a tear-riddled smile. "Responsibility is a terrible burden, and sometimes the right decisions are the ones that hurt the most. But that's also how you know they're the most important."

"Thank you," Jaxon said.

"For what?"

"For this. For being you. If you weren't so strong, I don't know if I'd be able to get through it."

Leira squeezed his hands. "No matter how much distance is between us, Jaxon Green, we'll still have this. This isn't over, and it isn't our end. That, I commit to you."

Jaxon returned the gesture. "This is not our end. That, I commit to you."

There, on the bluff overlooking the lights of the Klausner Manor and the town of Schwyz, Jaxon kissed her. And for as long as his lips held hers, everything felt right in the world.

CHAPTER 7

ALLYN PACED HIS ROOM, GOING through his various talking points in preparation for his session with the Forum. The movement helped keep the worst of his anxiety at bay and allowed him to focus more on the merits of their petition than on the fact that he knew next to nothing about the Forum proceedings. The plan that he, Jaxon, and Liam had come up with was strong, and if the Forum made their decision based on nothing but the facts, then Allyn felt confident that they would prevail.

It wasn't until a knock came on his door that he realized night had fallen across the manor.

"Come in," Allyn said.

The door opened, and Jaxon stepped in. He was dressed in formal magi attire Allyn had rarely seen worn. Utilitarian in design, the sharp lines and stiff shoulders of the dark clothing were ornamented by brass buttons that had been polished and shined. Allyn, who didn't have formal attire, was dressed in compression armor. It was a newer style than he was accustomed to, reinforced and padded in the chest, shoulders, and back. The new armor was one of the various minor benefits of working alongside the arch mage's personal guard.

"It's time," Jaxon said.

Allyn didn't move. There was something *off* about Jaxon. *More nerves, maybe?*

He doubted it. Jaxon wasn't the type of person to get nervous. He also wasn't the one presenting. *Something to do with the arch mage or the Forum then?*

The thought almost sent him into a panic. If Jaxon was nervous about something, Allyn should be downright terrified.

"Are you all right?" Allyn asked. "You look..."

"Later," Jaxon said. "We don't have time."

But Allyn wasn't going to give in so easily. "Should I be worried?"

"It has nothing to do with you. Now, come on. We don't want to be late." Without further discussion, Jaxon turned and exited the room, leaving the door open in expectation that Allyn would follow. He did, and together, he and Jaxon made their way from the second level of the manor down to the first before stopping in the hall outside the grand entrance.

"Remember," Jaxon said, "as your Champion, I will escort you into the proceeding, introduce you to the Forum, and take my place among them."

"I remember," Allyn said.

"You refer to the arch mage and members of the Forum by their title, and their title only. No first names. No Family names. Titles."

"I know."

"And you do not speak out of turn."

"Jaxon, we've been over all of this. I will be respectful and adhere to your traditions."

"Good," Jaxon said. "Because you represent the McCollum Family *and* me."

"I understand. I won't embarrass you."

"I know, Allyn." Jaxon took a deep breath. "Let's go."

Jaxon strode forward then stopped under the arch that led into the grand entrance, clearly visible to the members of the Forum. Allyn remained at his shoulder, surveying the space before him. A long rug ran from the arch into the center of the foyer, and sitting in a perfect circle around it in elegant, high-backed chairs, were the members of the Forum.

There were over one hundred Families in the Order, most of them operating out of Europe and North America, but fewer than half had a representative in attendance. Liam had erected cameras throughout the space to broadcast the assembly to the rest. Following Allyn's remarks, the Forum would enter a deliberation phase, looping in the remaining members via videoconference.

Like Jaxon, the members of the Forum were dressed in formal magi attire and wore sharp expressions befitting of their rigid clothing. There was no chatter, whispering, or small talk—an odd detail, considering the men and women of the Forum hadn't seen each other in months. There was only formality and tradition as they watched Jaxon and Allyn waiting in the archway.

"Arch Mage Westarra," Jaxon began, saluting the arch mage in the magi fashion, "members of the Forum." He nodded to the left side of the room, then the right. "Jaxon Green, acting Grand Mage of the McCollum Family, and Allyn McCollum of the McCollum Family ask your leave to enter the Forum."

"Granted," Arch Mage Westarra said. He sat on a small dais at the head of the circle, his back to the front entrance.

Jaxon nodded his respect and strode into the foyer. Allyn followed a step behind, giving Jaxon the reverence his station deserved. The members of the Forum remained seated, trailing the two new participants with their gazes. Allyn and Jaxon came to a stop at the end of the rug, their chins up, backs straight.

"What brings Jaxon and Allyn of the McCollum Family before the Forum this day?" Arch Mage Westarra asked stiffly.

"Your Grace, Allyn of McCollum has been tasked with evaluating the Forum's strategy in the Order's war with the Knights of Rakkar. He is here to share his conclusions."

"Very well," Westarra said. "You may be seated."

Jaxon saluted again and stepped from the rug to take his seat in the circle to the right of Allyn. He remained in Allyn's periphery, his short, controlled movements masking the nervousness Allyn knew he felt. The same nervousness pulsed through his own veins, causing his hands to tremble and his legs to feel weak.

"Allyn of McCollum," Arch Mage Westarra said once Jaxon had taken his seat. "Are you ready to share your conclusions?"

"I am, Your Grace."

"Then you may begin."

"Thank you, Your Grace." Allyn relaxed, allowing his body to fall into the same calm demeanor he'd used while at trial. "Arch Mage Westarra, members of the Forum, after careful evaluation of the Order's current strategy against the Knights of Rakkar, it is my conclusion that the magi Order is leveraging a strategy that will lead to its demise."

Half of the number shifted uncomfortably in their seats, the creaks of leather and strained chair legs echoing against the vaulted ceiling of the foyer.

"It is also my conclusion," Allyn continued, "that this should not surprise any member of this body. As you may well know, the Order successfully repelled a recent attack against the Friedl Family, but did so at great cost. Nineteen members of our Order perished in what was the bloodiest battle to date, and five more are thought to have been taken prisoner by the Knights. Still, it would have been worse had the Blackburn forces not arrived as quickly as they had. Arch Mage Westarra, members of the Forum, the war with the Knights of Rakkar is changing, and our strategy must change with it."

Allyn paused, waiting for the Forum's reaction. It came from the man seated next to Jaxon. Thick of build with dark skin and closely cropped hair, the man had a stern expression much like the one Jaxon had worn too much of late. Allyn blinked, his eyes going from the man to Jaxon, then back to the man. Their resemblance was unmistakable. As was the way Jaxon sat next to him—cautious, almost as if he were intimidated—leaning slightly away.

Wesley Green flew halfway across the world to take part in these proceedings. No wonder Jaxon is on edge.

Grand Mage Green stood and waited for the arch mage's permission to speak. After a nod from Arch Mage Westarra, he began. "The Forum thanks you for your work, Allyn of McCollum, but I question your competence on this subject. Can you tell this body what authority you have to speak on?"

Allyn acknowledged the question with a nod. He and Jaxon had expected the question, and the answer rolled smoothly off his tongue. "It's a fair question, Grand Mage. Prior to my time with the McCollum Family, I had no formal training in the art of war. I haven't served my country in the military, nor have I worked in a dangerous field where leadership was required. I am, most certainly, by all respects, unqualified to speak on such topics."

Grand Mage Green smirked triumphantly. Little more than the tiniest rise in his lips, the expression might have gone unnoticed if Allyn hadn't seen Jaxon replicate the same expression a thousand times.

"However," he said before Grand Mage Green could feel too victorious, "my time with the McCollum Family has afforded me experience I was otherwise lacking. Jaxon Green, a highly respected member of this body and Grand Mage of the McCollum Family, has trained me in the art. I have since eliminated the McCollum Family's greatest threat—a dissenter by the name of Lukas McCollum, whom this body was aware of—then led the Family safely through an FBI manhunt. While still preserving the magi secret, I led the elimination of the last vestiges of Lukas's movement and secured our Family refuge with the Hyland Family—the very Family of Lukas's greatest ally.

"But more than anything, Grand Mage," Allyn continued, "I have seen the enemy up close. I have looked Knight Commander Sedric Lang in the eye, spoken with him, fought him, and *won*. I know how he thinks, what he believes, and what he'll do to achieve victory. With all due respect, Grand Mage, no one within this body is more qualified to speak on the Knights of Rakkar than me."

The smirk vanished from the man's face. He remained standing, however, and by Forum standards, still had the right to speak—and he didn't seem ready to give up. "Well said, Allyn of McCollum. I apologize if I was unclear, but no one in this body is questioning your knowledge of the enemy. I merely inquire on your authority to speak on *strategy*."

"One doesn't have to be an expert in strategy to see when the current one isn't working, Grand Mage." Allyn broke eye contact with Jaxon's father, turning to the rest of the body. "Arch Mage Westarra, members of the Forum, we are fighting a war of attrition. I have seen the enemy. I have seen their resources. And I assure you, that is not a war we can win."

"Please tell us what you would have us do." Wesley Green sat, relenting his right to ask a follow-up question.

"I would have us fight back, Grand Mage. I would have us attack and take this war to the Knights' doorstep instead of waiting for the next attack. I would have us use the magi strength to our advantage. And more than anything, I would have us use the resources already at our disposal."

"You speak of the logbook," Arch Mage Westarra said.

"I do, Your Grace." Allyn surveyed the members of the Forum, taking note of their expressions. Most remained unreadable, but some leaned forward in their seats, engaged and nodding slightly. A smaller number were obviously skeptical, drawing their lips into a line and watching him with narrow, distrustful eyes. Surprisingly, Wesley Green seemed to be watching his fellow Forum members with a hopeful expression.

"After our battle with the Knights in Zurich," Allyn continued, "we recovered the Knight Commander's logbook, which outlined supply depots, bases of operation, and more."

"All of which were empty when we first investigated," Arch Mage Westarra said.

"True, Your Grace," Allyn said. "It was clear the Knights suspected we had recovered the book and had taken necessary precautions. But it's not what we found that I speak of. It's what we *didn't* find."

"Explain."

"The logbook is an electronic tablet, Your Grace. With Liam of McCollum's unique abilities, we were able to uncover *deleted* items."

"You're saying you found more?"

"Much more, Your Grace. Much more." More creaks filled the room as magi shifted in their seats, and for the first time since the assembly had begun, Allyn felt a growing sense of confidence. "And with the permission of the Forum, we can question the prisoners you have locked away to corroborate anything we find."

An inaudible stir swept through the Forum. Allyn had them. He could see it in the way those he'd already won over struggled to hide their smiles. In the way those who had been on the fence sat back in their chairs, fingers to lips in contemplative thought. He moved in for the kill.

"My sister, Kendyl of McCollum, is an empath. With her abilities, we can extract every kernel of information out of the prisoners and verify what they say is true. As I said before, it is my preference that this body use the resources already at hand."

Allyn waited triumphantly for the arch mage to speak. Before he could, a frail-looking grand mage who was easily one of the oldest in the room slowly rose to his feet, using a cane and the arm of his chair for support. With thin white hair, a wispy white beard, and a weathered, sun-beaten face, he looked comically similar to a wizard in an old Disney movie.

"Grand Mage Ricci," Arch Mage Westarra said, granting the wizened grand mage permission to speak.

"Thank you, Your Grace," Grand Mage Ricci said in a surprisingly strong, heavily accented voice. "You make a compelling argument, Allyn of McCollum. But you fail to recognize the true threat. The Knights of Rakkar are the enemy of the day, but the true enemy, the one that this body has fought for ages, is the enemy of exposure. We must keep the secret. Your plan would have us operating in the open, taking the fight to the streets. You risk showing the world who we are, and I cannot support that."

The excitement that had been building through the room fizzled, and Allyn looked around helplessly, wondering if someone would speak in his defense. No one did.

"Please help me make sure I understand you correctly, Grand Mage," Allyn said slowly. "Are you suggesting we risk certain death because of the *possibility* of exposure?" It was an old attorney technique—repeat the question back to the witness to gain a couple more moments of thought. It also sometimes extracted other bits of information that could be used to divert the conversation in a new direction.

"No." Grand Mage Ricci shook his head, his beard swaying back and forth. "Your ideas have merit, Allyn of McCollum. They're rash and dangerous, but I do not think you'll get too much resistance from this body in suggesting an alternative strategy. Where you will find debate is finding consensus on what that strategy needs to be."

Grand Mage Ricci returned to his seat, only for another to rise. The man stood tall and proud, pulling his dark hair out of his eyes.

"Grand Mage Guerrero," Arch Mage Westarra said.

"Thank you, Arch Mage," Grand Mage Guerrero said. "I too echo Grand Mage Ricci's concerns. But where he fears exposure, I fear escalation."

"The war is already escalating, Grand Mage," Allyn said defensively.

"Yes, it is," Grand Mage Guerrero said. "And your plan would have us escalate it more quickly. I propose an alternative. When we first fought these Knights, we slowed the war. Let the fires burn themselves out. Why not do the same today?"

"You're suggesting we hide," Allyn said.

"I propose an idea that has already worked against the same enemy."

"But it hasn't, Grand Mage," Allyn said. "If it *had* worked, we wouldn't be fighting them now. We need to end the war, not delay it. We can't let future magi risk their lives for something we have the power to handle now. And what of the captured magi? Are you suggesting we leave them in the hands of the enemy?"

"You speak of magi loss," Grand Mage Guerrero said. "Isn't the best way to prevent loss to avoid battle in the first place?"

"With all due respect, Grand Mage, the enemy already has their teeth in us, and they've tasted our blood. They know we're weak, and they know where to find us. Just because we roll onto our backs and expose our bellies does not mean the Knights will grant us mercy."

"I'm not proposing we surrender."

"Then what are you proposing, Grand Mage?"

"That we hide."

"I already told you," Allyn said. "They know where to find us. They know where we live."

"Houses can't move. But people can."

"You'd have us abandon our homes?" Allyn asked, incredulous. "That's the magi wealth. The magi history. Losing that..."

"Material possessions." Grand Mage Guerrero waved a dismissive hand. "*We* are the magi history, and besides, Ukiah preserves more of our past than any private collection."

Allyn shook his head, resisting an urge to pinch his forehead. He couldn't believe what he was hearing. The magi were showing a complete and utter lack of will to fight. Worse, the assembly was quickly spiraling out of his control, and he had no idea how to get it back on track. Already, three more grand mages were standing, waiting for their opportunity to speak.

Arch Mage Westarra stood, and the attention of the room shifted immediately. Order was about to be restored. "Thank you for your words, Allyn of McCollum. You have given this

Forum much to think about. Do you have anything else to add?"

"I do, Your Grace."

"Then please continue so we may deliberate."

"Thank you, Your Grace," Allyn said. "And thank you, Grand Mages, for the opportunity to speak before you. A difficult choice has been laid before you, and it's not without great risk. But I have seen this enemy. I have looked them in the eye and seen what they're capable of. I have bled in the defense of this Order while fighting that enemy. And I implore you to listen to what I have to say.

"If we stay the course, if we fight the same fight, pivot to a *safer* strategy, or repeat the mistakes we made in the past, we *will* fail. This, I can guarantee you. And it won't happen fast. It will be a prolonged, tortuous affair, full of death and pain and terrible sorrow. But you have the means to prevent that. You have the power to stop it. Use the logbook. Use the prisoners. Use my sister and the other magi and machinists to rescue our people and ensure the safety of your Families and the future of our Order."

Allyn stood straight and proud, surveying the room. Only silence and expressionless faces greeted him. The time for questions was over. The Forum had once again returned to a state of modest decorum.

"Thank you, Allyn of McCollum." Arch Mage Westarra stood, marking the end of the proceeding. "The Forum will now enter deliberation. You will be notified of our decision. You may go."

"Thank you, Arch Mage." Allyn nodded then turned and left. He exited the room, leaving the Forum behind, terrified that what he had said wouldn't be enough.

CHAPTER 8

ALLYN WOKE TO A KNOCK at his door. It was a tentative sound, as if the person behind it hadn't wanted to wake the others in the residential hall, and exhausted, Allyn wasn't entirely sure he hadn't just dreamt it. He remained in bed, eyes cast questioningly at the door, trying to blink away the morning fog as he wrestled with the idea of climbing out of his warm bed to investigate.

His floor-to-ceiling curtains were drawn, casting the room into darkness, but through a tiny sliver, he could see that the sky outside was beginning to purple with the first vestiges of dawn. The knock came again, a tiny bit louder than before.

Not my imagination then, Allyn thought, throwing his down comforter aside and rolling out of bed. He pulled on a pair of loose-fitting sweatpants that had been thrown over a nearby chair and made for the door. His first thought was that the Forum had completed its deliberation, but he quickly cast the thought aside. It had been barely twelve hours since Allyn had addressed the magi's governing body, and even if they had come to a decision, he doubted they would want to reassemble so early in the morning.

Pulling open the door, Allyn found that the person behind

his early morning wake-up call was Jaxon. The larger man stood in the hall, looking anxious, as if he were arguing with himself whether to stay or go.

"Did I wake you?" Jaxon asked, taking note of Allyn's appearance.

"Yeah," Allyn said. "It's fine, though. What's up? Is the Forum ready?"

"No," Jaxon said. "Not yet. Do you... do you have a minute?"

Something in Jaxon's tone immediately put Allyn on edge. Whatever Jaxon had to say, it was important enough to wake Allyn at an hour usually reserved for young lawyers.

"Of course," Allyn said. "Come in." He stepped aside, allowing the other man to enter, then closed the door behind them. Jaxon made for the pair of armchairs in front of the window and took a seat. Allyn snagged the same shirt he'd worn the night before, pulled it on, and sat in the chair opposite Jaxon. "What time is it, anyway?"

"I don't know... early." Jaxon sat forward in his seat with his elbows resting on his knees, rubbing the palms of his hands together. "You remember last night when you asked if I was all right? If you should be worried?"

"Yeah..."

"Well, I'm... I'm not. I've been given some bad news. My father..." Jaxon shook his head as if he didn't believe what he was about to say. "He's... sick."

"Sick?"

"Cancer," Jaxon said awkwardly. "It's terminal."

"Oh, Jaxon, I'm—"

Jaxon held up a hand, stopping him from saying anything more. "Please don't," he said sharply. "Please don't apologize to me."

"I'm not," Allyn said slowly. "I just... I know what it's like, that's all. I lost my mother to cancer."

Jaxon looked away, his eyes finding the small crack in the curtains. A mountain fog had fallen over the manor grounds, giving the world outside an eerie quality.

"I appreciate your sympathy," Jaxon said. "But this is a personal matter, and I need to keep it that way."

"Of course," Allyn said. "If you don't want me to mention it, I won't. Just know that if there's anything you need..."

Jaxon nodded, his eyes returning to Allyn's. "The thing is, it *does* affect you. My time as Grand Mage of the McCollum Family has come to an end. I'm to return with my father and begin preparing for my succession."

A shiver ran down Allyn's spine, and the room suddenly grew very cold. The timing couldn't have been any worse. The McCollum Family was finally returning to a position of strength, of respect, and more importantly, they were finally healing from the internal wounds caused by Lukas's splinter. With most of their Family half a world away, what kind of instability would Jaxon's departure cause at home?

Visions of another splinter wracked Allyn's brain. He couldn't let that happen. Wouldn't let that happen. Though, if he were truly being honest with himself, he had no idea how to stop it.

Allyn wasn't sure how long he'd been deep in thought, but the moment had drawn on long enough to grow uncomfortable. Jaxon clearly wanted him to say something, but for one of the first times in Allyn's life, he was at a loss for words.

"This isn't the first time my father has summoned me home," Jaxon said, breaking the silence. "Just after we arrived at your family's cabin, my father *requested* that I return. I refused him then, but I realize now that's when he found out. He wasn't ordering me to return home out of spite—or at least, not *only* out of spite. He knew then that he was fighting a battle he couldn't win."

"There's no way you could have known."

"I'm not sure it would have changed anything, anyway. But I didn't tell you then, either, and for that, I'm sorry as well."

"The Family was on the verge of splintering," Allyn said. "We had other things to worry about. I would have made the same decision."

"I just want you to know this isn't something I do lightly."

"I know that, Jaxon," Allyn said. "Who else knows?"

"Only Leira."

"Then I won't say anything."

"I appreciate that."

"You need to tell the Family, though," Allyn said. "They need to hear it from you before word spreads."

"I know." Jaxon sighed. "It's unfortunate we're split as we are."

"What will you tell them? Who will you endorse as the new grand mage? It might lessen the blow if the Family's future wasn't so unclear."

"That's what I wanted to talk to you about," Jaxon said. "There are two paths I see the Family taking. You aren't aware of this yet, but I've spoken with Parke Hyland about merging our two Families. They're disgraced by the Hyland name and looking for a fresh start. And the truth of it is, neither of our Families are strong enough to thrive on their own. So my first thought is the McCollum Family unites behind Parke, naming him grand mage of the newly formed Family."

"Do you think they'll do that, though?" Allyn asked. "Follow someone who isn't their own?"

Jaxon cocked an eyebrow. "They followed me."

"True, but you'd been with the Family for years, and Graeme trusted you. So *they* trusted you too. This is someone completely foreign to them, and someone from a Family that killed many of their own. I can't imagine them uniting behind him."

"I don't disagree," Jaxon said. "The McCollum Family was one of the first North American Families, and before the splinter, it was one of the most respected. They're too proud. No, they'd never go for it. Which is why they'll confirm someone internally."

"You still think that will be Liam?"

"I think he's readier now than he's ever been," Jaxon said. "He's one of the faces of the machinists, and he's the *only* magi in the entire Order who has both sets of abilities. What he lacks in age, he makes up for with pedigree and gifts."

Allyn tapped a finger to his lips, contemplating the idea. Liam would be half the age of the Order's next youngest grand mage, and Allyn had serious doubts the Family would fall behind him. Jaxon had always been more optimistic, often mentioning precedents set by other Families with young grand mages, but what he'd failed to mention was that only one of those young magi leaders had lived within the last thousand years, and none of them had been younger than seventeen.

Still, Liam did have distinct advantages. Were they enough to make the Family's most cynical members forget the awkward, hermit-like teenager he'd been only a year before? It was tough to say.

"What about Leira?" Allyn asked. "She's a well-respected member of the Family. Older too."

"Leira's never shown any interest in leading the Family," Jaxon said. "Fighting for it, yes. Advising, sure. But not leading it. Anyway, we're not making a decision now, and you have work to do. I only wanted to apologize. Thank you for your support and everything else you've done. It's been a pleasure serving with you, Allyn McCollum." He held out his hand.

Allyn nodded and took Jaxon's forearm in his, shaking it in the magi fashion. "Good luck, Jaxon."

"Thank you."

Jaxon stood, readjusted his compression armor, nodded a final time, and strode toward the door. Allyn followed and closed the door behind him. He still didn't know how much longer Jaxon would lead the Family, but one thought crept into the back of his consciousness.

The McCollum Family, as old and prestigious as it had once been, was light on allies. But between Jaxon's time as grand mage and his relationship with Leira, Allyn wondered if Jaxon's new ascension was the beginning of what might become one of the strongest alliances in the Order. And if so, with the McCollum and Green Families working together, there might be no limit to what they could accomplish.

In the darkness of war and the uncertainty of their future, the thought was nearly enough to give him a flicker of hope.

The Forum summoned Allyn back nearly two hours later. An Elemental Guardsman had found him eating breakfast and ushered him into the private study that Arch Mage Westarra had commandeered. As before, the Forum sat in a tight circle with the arch mage the focal point. Within the tighter confines of the room, the tension was palpable.

Standing in the middle of the assembly on an ornate rug, Allyn saluted the arch mage and fell into parade rest, legs shoulder length apart, hands clasped behind his back.

"Allyn of McCollum," Arch Mage Westarra began, "a day's past, this Forum heard your plea that in the wake of escalating tensions and new information, we revisit our existing strategy in fighting our war with the Knights of Rakkar. You are here today because we have come to a judgment."

Allyn watched the arch mage intently, waiting for the blow of failure to land. He hadn't felt terribly confident after leaving the proceedings the day before, and his feeling of disappointment had only grown deeper since.

"It is this body's verdict, a decision made for and on behalf of the entire magi Order, that we agree with your conclusions."

"What?" The word was out of Allyn's mouth before he knew it. He stood there stupidly, gawking at the arch mage and members of the Forum. He couldn't help it—he smiled and found Jaxon sitting beside his father. Seeing both men expressionless, he quickly looked away, his smile faltering. Embarrassed, he returned his attention to the arch mage.

"I said this body agrees with you, Allyn of McCollum," Westarra said. "However..." The words echoed off the coffered ceiling, plunging directly into Allyn's ego. "However, the body disagrees with your proposed alternative strategy. This war is but a single battle amid a much larger war that this body has been fighting for centuries, and winning this battle may cause us to lose that bigger war. This body cannot risk that. We must keep the secret."

"We must keep the secret," the members of the Forum repeated in a single, unified voice.

"Therefore," Westarra continued, "in an effort to remain flexible and agile in this time of war, it's this body's decision to elect a War Council to oversee the Order's war efforts. Comprised of five members in all, the War Council will have unilateral control over the Order's strategy, preparedness, and battle execution. And until such war is ended or shifts landscapes, the council will operate out of this centralized location occupied by the Klausner Manor. This decree has been voted upon and ratified by this body, and the order will subsist until such a vote deems it is no longer necessary and disbands the council. Before we adjourn, does any among this body have questions about this pronouncement?"

"I do, Your Grace," Allyn said.

Arch Mage Westarra smiled knowingly and nodded his permission for Allyn to continue.

"Who is to be on this War Council, Your Grace?"

"A valid question," Westarra said. "I myself will sit on the council. As will Wesley Green, Grand Mage of the Green Family. Due to recent ailments, he will be aided by his son, Jaxon Green. Alivar Guerrero, Grand Mage of the Guerrero Family, and Harold Klausner, Grand Mage of the Klausner Family, will also join us. And, since this was your petition and because this Forum agreed with your initial assessment, you, Allyn of McCollum, Advocate of the Machinists, will also belong to the council."

Advocate. Allyn wondered if it was an official title, and if so, what benefits it might grant. He didn't have long to think on it, though. The arch mage was expecting an answer.

"Thank you, Your Grace," Allyn said with a bow. "It would be an honor to serve on your council."

He surveyed the room, his eyes finding the other members of the Forum who would be joining him on the War Council, and something in their expressions told him that, while he had just won a battle with the Forum, a new battle was already on the horizon.

Arch Mage Westarra inclined his head, acknowledging Allyn's acceptance, then announced the end of the Forum session and asked his newly formed War Council to remain.

"Let me tell you how this is going to go," he said as soon as the rest of the Forum was gone, his tone devoid of all formality. It seemed when the Forum wasn't in active session, its members didn't hold quite so closely to decorum. "This is a council, meaning just like with your positions on the Forum, all decisions will be made by a vote. Those deemed by me, the chair of this council, to be less critical in nature will pass by a simple majority. However, those deemed critical— something like rolling out a specific battle strategy or battle plan—will require a super consensus and can pass with no fewer than four votes. Any questions?"

"Just one, Your Grace," Grand Mage Guerrero said, looking directly at Jaxon. "How many votes will the Green Family have on this council?"

"One," Arch Mage Westarra said. "As I said before, Jaxon is here due to his father's health concerns, and he will only be granted a vote if Wesley becomes too ill and is unable to perform his duties."

"But what about influence, Your Grace?" Grand Mage Guerrero pressed, clearly not ready to give up the fight. "Are we to expect that Jaxon won't have influence over his father?"

"He'll have no more influence over Wesley's vote than those in your private council will have over yours."

"Surely you're not suggesting that what is discussed in these proceedings is to be common Order knowledge."

"Absolutely not," Westarra said. "But don't take me for a fool, Alivar. I'm well aware that Forum proceedings have always been discussed with your own advisors well beyond the walls of the Forum. The only benefit Jaxon of McCollum will have is firsthand knowledge of the proceedings, instead of being forced to make decisions based on relayed information."

"Will other council members be allowed to have advisors in attendance?" Guerrero asked.

"No."

Guerrero stammered, obviously searching for the correct response.

"Are you dying, Alivar?" Westarra asked.

Guerrero blinked, clearly put off balance. "No, Your Grace."

"But you understand Wesley is."

Guerrero shot an uneasy look in Grand Mage Green's direction. "I am aware of his health concerns, Your Grace."

"Good," Westarra said. "Then you'll understand that Jaxon's presence in these proceedings isn't a sign of preferential treatment—it's about necessity."

Guerrero opened his mouth to respond, but Westarra stood, cutting him off.

"Your objections are noted, but this matter is closed. If you wish to speak with me about it further, I will grant you your request, but this is a war council, and we have other business to attend to."

Guerrero bowed, relinquishing his argument.

"Now," Westarra said, "we have told the Forum our current strategy is failing, and it's up to us to replace it with something that gives us the best chance of success while mitigating risk of exposure." He turned to Allyn. "I tasked you with coming up with a number of different proposals, and I understand you've had time to outline a couple of options?"

"I have, Your Grace."

Arch Mage Westarra held his hands before him, gesturing for Allyn to continue. "Then please..."

"Can I grab something first?" Allyn asked. "It'll only take a moment."

"Of course."

"Thank you." Allyn rushed out of the room.

By the time he returned, the group sat haphazardly around the room, all vaguely facing the arch mage's direction. They watched Allyn curiously as he wheeled in a mobile whiteboard that had a map of central Europe taped on it. On the map were a series of small color-coded circles.

"Just let me know when you're ready for me to begin, Your Grace," Allyn said.

"Please," Arch Mage Westarra said, giving him the floor.

Allyn inclined his head to the arch mage and turned so that he was including the others in his presentation. "As Arch Mage Westarra said, he tasked Jaxon and me with putting together a few options. Our idea isn't drastically different from the strategy already in place, and I think that will make the transition from the old to the new easier. It'll also simplify the transition from it to whatever we come up with next, so think of this as the first step in a larger strategy that we still need to solidify, okay?"

He was met with a series of small nods of understanding and a noncommittal expression from the magi leader.

"To understand how *our* strategy needs to shift," Allyn continued unflinchingly, "we first need to understand the enemy's current one. Up until this point, we've thought their attacks were random, but upon closer inspection, there is a geographical trend. The red dots on this map are the Families that have been hit. As you can see, they're split across multiple countries and follow a semi-circular pattern, meaning the Knights are likely operating from a base somewhere centrally located in this area here."

"Are you suggesting you know where the Knights are operating from?" Arch Mage Westarra asked, his voice excited.

"No, Your Grace," Allyn said. "At least, not yet. Liam is working on that now, re-analyzing the data from the logbook. We're hoping he can find something we might have missed before this trend appeared. For now, I want you to focus on the blue and green dots on the map. The blue represents Families that haven't been attacked. And the green represents other Families who haven't been attacked, either, but also fit certain criteria."

"What kind of criteria?" Arch Mage Westarra asked.

"Size of the Family, proximity to populated areas, and—"

"Why would the Knights care about proximity to populated areas?" Grand Mage Guerrero asked. "They don't value secrecy the same way we do."

"I'm not convinced that's entirely the case, Grand Mage Guerrero," Allyn said. "They view this war as a holy war, that they're doing God's work, and I'm not sure they want to expose the demons to the world—after all, this entire war began because they felt we violated the Accords by stepping out of the shadows.

"On a more practical level, where there are people, there are police. By attacking the most secluded Families, they don't have to worry about an armed police force intervening. But we think there's another data point that's even more important than proximity to cities. Look at the red dots and tell me what else you see."

Westarra rose and stepped closer to the whiteboard. He looked at it for several moments, his eyes darting from dot to dot as he attempted to see the pattern Allyn had referred to.

"It also has to do with proximity," Allyn said, giving the magi leader a hint.

"They've attacked Families that are not close to other Families," Arch Mage Westarra said.

"Exactly. Every Family that's been attacked is a minimum of forty-five minutes from the nearest Family."

Westarra looked back at the board. "This is good work, Allyn. This is good work."

"Thank you, Your Grace," Allyn said. "Now if Your Grace would please take note of the green dots. Remember, they represent Families who fit specific criteria but haven't been attacked yet."

"What are they?"

"Potential targets. They're the Families we think the Knights will attack next." Allyn pointed at the three green dots on the map in particular. "These three are small Families, far away from other magi Families and populated areas. This is where we think the Knights will attack next. And we intend to be ready for them."

Westarra stared at Allyn, his eyes twinkling with excitement. "Tell me more."

CHAPTER 9

SEDRIC ALWAYS GOT THE SHAKES before an operation. The trembling hands and quivering knees had plagued him ever since childhood when he would step into the ring to spar or wrestle on behalf of his small Georgian school. They'd always grown worse when he met his bullies and tormentors in the parking lot after class. The tremors had even persisted through boot camp, Ranger school, and three tours in Iraq and Afghanistan.

For the longest time, he'd tried to hide the shakes, fearing they would be seen as cowardice. When his superiors had spotted them, they had tried to train them out of him. For weeks, Sedric had been harassed relentlessly. But nothing worked. The shakes always plagued him right up until the moment the first shot was fired and the battle began. It was then that a cool serenity would wash over him, leaving him at peace.

To some of his former army buddies, battle and war had become a drug. The ultimate rush. An addiction only cured by more fighting. For Sedric, the opposite was true. It was in the heat of battle that he first experienced what it felt like to be *home*, understood what it meant to have purpose. For a time, fighting beside his comrades, fighting for his country had been enough, but as the war had dragged on and the cynicism infected even the army's staunchest supporters, his sense of purpose had begun to waver. It had been at his lowest point, in the weeks following his discharge, that he had found the Knights—or rather, when the Knights had found him—and in their cause, he found true resolution.

So on the eve of battle, Sedric Lang, Knight Commander of the Knights of Rakkar, paid his trembling hands no mind. His soldiers knew that the shakes weren't a byproduct of fear, nervousness, or cowardice, but rather a burning excitement for fighting a righteous war and carrying out the Lord's justice.

He rode in the passenger seat of the heavily armored assault vehicle as it rumbled down an isolated country road. Two other vehicles—both dark-gray BearCats like the one he was in—filled out the formation behind them. It was late into the night, and as close as they were to their target, they drove with their lights off. The vehicles would be nearly impossible to see, though if the magi Family had posted any sentries, they would hear the engines from miles away.

Sedric peeled his eyes off the road, glancing into the back of the BearCat, where twenty Knights were doing a final gear check. They'd been through the ritual half a dozen times since leaving their staging area, but Sedric had instilled the habit into his soldiers, just as his own instructors had drilled it into him.

"Three minutes," he said, and as if it were on his command, the BearCat suddenly veered right, turning from the country road onto a private drive that climbed a small rise, leaving the road behind. The magi homes were all the same, secluded, hidden, and on large plots of land. Though missing some of the grandeur of the other manors and estates, the Schuster Manor was no different.

Shaped like an enormous rectangle, the manor was three stories tall and painted a light yellow with white accents and natural wood shutters. What it lacked in ornate columns and grand entrances, it made up for with its grounds. A four-foot retaining wall circled the main grounds, and a beautiful five-acre lake rested at the manor's rear. Even in the darkness, the land reminded him of home. Replace the paved driveway with an old dirt road and the property could have been mistaken for an old Georgia plantation.

The BearCats sped up as they approached the retaining wall and a steel gate. Ten feet before the gate, the driver punched the gas and rammed the gate with its reinforced steel nose, ripping it from the stone pillars. Stone crumbled under the weight of the ensuing BearCats as their formation split, and they moved into position.

The Schuster Manor had two main entrances, each slightly off-center from the central point of the house, and elevated above the driveway by a pair of staircases. Two BearCats slid to a stop in front of each of the staircases, while Sedric's BearCat glided to a rest in the decorative garden at the center of the circular driveway. Sixty Knights emerged from the vehicles; the men in the front carried battering rams and were protected by shields held by the Knights closest to them.

Sedric waited, anticipating the first signs of resistance, but the manor remained uncharacteristically quiet, its windows dark. For the first time in a while, doubt crept into the back of his mind. He flexed and unflexed his trembling hand, waiting for the first burst of gunfire to erase his nerves.

After a silent countdown, the two lead Knights pummeled the manor doors with their battering rams, shattering the hinges and throwing the doors inward. The rest of the Knights streamed inside, and half their number had crossed into the manor's threshold when the first explosion hit.

A fireball larger than anything Sedric had seen since fighting in the Middle East burst through the entrance, shattering wood, stone, and glass. The Knights nearest the door were incinerated, and the force of the explosion hurled the others away from the manor. Before the other squad could recognize the trap, another explosion ripped a new hole in the manor, tearing through the men outside the second entrance.

In an instant, more than half of their advanced force was down—either dead or severely wounded. Those who remained able rolled onto their feet and raised their guns, providing cover for others who helped pull their fallen comrades to safety. Sedric waited for a tense second, expecting more attacks to come, waiting for the first barrage of gunfire, but save for the crackling fire and the cries of the wounded, the scene returned to silence.

"Second wave!" Sedric shouted.

His own squad mobilized, shoving open the rear hatch of the BearCat. It slammed against the ground with a dull thud and echoed with the sounds of boots as his Knights raced down it and then across the manor grounds, trampling the garden. Sedric's squad was larger than any other—twenty men in all instead of fifteen—and they split into two sub squads, each making for the wounded outside the manor doors. As they did, the magi finally made their presence known.

The second – and third-story windows shattered as fireballs and ice blasts rained down on Sedric's men. The night came alive with battle. Gunfire sang in response as the Knights targeted the hidden magi.

With the battle finally underway, Sedric's shakes vanished, and he sprang into action. He launched himself out of his seat, grabbing Jackie, his M4A1 assault rifle equipped with an M203 under-barrel grenade launcher, and exited the BearCat. Sighting one of the broken windows, he pulled the fully automatic trigger. Ejected casings smoked through the air as they were flung from the rifle. The stock of the M4 kicked against his shoulder with a familiar rhythm. Bullets slammed into the manor, chipping away stone and shattering more glass. He kept his bursts short and controlled, moving from window to window, laying cover fire as the last of the Knights regrouped behind the BearCats.

"Looks like our friends want to play," Sedric said, grinning from ear to ear. "Who wants to have some fun?"

"Let's play, sir!" several of his Knights shouted.

Sedric's smile widened, and he quickly organized the remaining Knights into three squads—two to carry out the assault, and a third to watch their rear. When his men were ready, Sedric emerged from the cover of the BearCats, fired a series of bursts, and switched action to his grenade launcher. The M4 kicked hard as it launched the grenade forward, sending it sailing through a shattered window. The grenade detonated inside, smashing other windows and spraying dust, smoke, and debris outside.

Sedric continued his advance, reloading the M203 with another cartridge, and targeted a second window. *Thunk!* Another grenade blasted from the end of the under-barrel launcher and also landed inside the room. Unlike the first, the second explosion was accompanied by screams and cries from those inside.

Sedric smiled and waved his squads forward. They raced up the steps, guns trained on the interior in front of them, stepping over the bodies of their fallen squad mates.

The inside of the manor was dark, eerily quiet, and more concerning, completely vacant. Not only were there no magi or any resistance to speak of, but the manor was uncharacteristically void of furniture and decoration. That wasn't to say that there was no adornment—it was just that the entrance and nearby rooms lacked the overbearing ostentatiousness that Sedric had seen in every other magi manor.

Is the Family less well-off than the others, or is something else going on?

A sense of unease sweeping through his body, Sedric led the Knights up a nearby staircase. The magi resistance had come from above, so that's where they would go. No more pussyfooting around. It was time to be relentless.

Pausing on the second-floor landing, Sedric searched the dark corners and recesses of the floor, then seeing nothing, crept down a narrow hallway toward where he guessed the original counterattack had originated.

The second floor was much like the first, strangely lacking decoration, including the historical pieces he'd taken great pleasure in destroying in the other manors. To destroy the magi art was to destroy their culture. Destroy their culture and you destroy the people. In Sedric's estimation, he'd inflicted as much damage on the magi by destroying their history as he had by killing its people.

A series of doors lined the hall. Sedric split the Knight force back into two squads, allowing the original squad leader to take lead of the second, then ordered the other squad deeper into the hall. He turned his attention to the first door. The door was closed, the room quiet.

Sedric took up station against the wall, gun barrel up, and commanded the next soldier in his squad to kick down the door. After only one kick, the door flung open, and Sedric dashed inside, gun raised, ready for a fight.

A light haze of smoke still hung in the air, though Sedric

could see through it easily enough. It was a long room with four large windows that overlooked the front entrance. At the other end of the room, beyond the large hole Sedric's grenade had created, was a second entrance, the door also closed. The room was empty. No paintings, vases, sculptures, or books. And more importantly, no fallen magi.

Sedric lowered his gun as his men checked the doors and corners. He knelt beside the blast radius and dragged his gloved fingers across the blackened wood. They came away dark with soot and sticky with something wet. Sedric held the fingers before him, rubbing them against his thumb.

Blood. They were here, and they're injured.

"Freeze," he said sharply, and his men stopped moving. Sedric rose, scanning the floor like a bloodhound searching for a scent.

There!

Two steps forward, Sedric crouched again. It was another droplet of blood. He followed the trail, finding a third. The person had rushed to the second door of the room.

The taste of blood on his tongue, Sedric stormed through the second door and out into the hall, but he hadn't gone more than two steps before he heard the commotion outside. He spun on his heels, colliding with a Knight who'd been trailing behind him, and pushed his way back into the room.

The third squad of Knights, the one Sedric had left outside, was falling into a defensive formation meant to repel a force *away* from the manor. Sedric watched helplessly as the squad split into two sub squads, each taking up position on the manor stairs behind the BearCats. It wasn't a terrible position—the BearCats would repel nearly any attack, the stairs offered a clear vantage of the incoming enemy, and in the event the squads were overwhelmed, the Knights could fall back into the manor itself.

What concerned Sedric was not the appearance of a second force, but the speed with which it had arrived. His Knights couldn't have been at the manor for more than fifteen minutes, and he'd targeted this specific Family because of its distance from the next-closest magi Family. Even if the nearest magi had been notified of the attack the moment it began, reinforcements should have taken at least an hour to arrive.

Sedric backed away from the windows, his eyes narrowing as he replayed the attack in his mind. They'd been met with resistance, but not the same kind of resistance he'd come to expect. Then the inside of the manor had been surprisingly empty. No magi. No desperate people fighting to protect what they held dear. No decoration...

They knew we were coming. But that was impossible. He would bet his life that he had no moles among his men. No leaks. He must have made a mistake somewhere.

Or they got lucky. It was a happier thought, for sure, but Sedric quickly discounted it. Even luck required a level of skill, and that meant he'd left some sort of trail for the enemy to follow. He had to clean up his tracks.

"With me!" Sedric bellowed then stormed into the hall, where he found the other squad leader.

"What are you orders, Commander?"

"Cover our men below," Sedric said. "When I begin the counterattack, return to the BearCats and reinforce C Squad. From there, I leave it to your best judgment."

"How will we know when you've begun your counterattack, Commander?"

"Believe me, son," Sedric said with a wide smile, "you'll know."

CHAPTER 10

ALLYN LEANED AGAINST THE BANK of the pond behind the Schuster Manor, watching the rear of the house with intense anticipation. The long grass circling the pond obstructed his view and, he hoped, the view of anyone inside who might look in his direction. Lined up beside him and stretching out across the bank was the rest of his squad—a mixture of machinists and Order magi, including Nolan, Nyla, and Ren—that numbered twelve in all.

Waiting for Sedric and his Knights to fall into the trap had been more difficult than he had originally imagined. Fortunately, the plan had worked out perfectly, though they were quickly approaching the most important part of the ruse—a moment which could turn the battle from a massive victory to a colossal defeat. He refused to think about the backlash that would cause.

"There," Ren whispered. "Here he comes."

Allyn sank deeper into the weeds, the soft, cold mud of the bank further soaking his compression armor, as a small group of Knights emerged from the back of the manor.

"Wait for it," Allyn whispered. Then two heartbeats later, "Now, Canary. Now."

Canary nodded and closed her eyes, placing two fingers on her right temple. Since she'd embraced her machinist abilities, they had grown at an exponential rate, and where she had previously only been able to receive communication signals, she could now send them, as well. And that was exactly what she was doing now.

When she opened her eyes, Allyn knew that she was done, and he refocused his attention on the rear of the manor. If he hadn't known where to look, he might have missed the two dark figures slipping from the shadows at the rear of the garden. Myanna and Rohn, two of the arch mage's Elemental Guard, had taken on the most dangerous part of the mission.

They stalked forward toward the Knights from opposite angles, Myanna from the front, Rohn from behind. Then just when Allyn thought they couldn't get any closer without being seen, Rohn buried an ice blast in the nearest Knight's back. The man fell to the stone patio with a sharp yell, startling the other Knights, who spun around to find their comrade bleeding at their feet. They switched to combat mode in a fraction of a second, scanning the darkness, guns at the ready.

Then Myanna struck. She too attacked with an ice blast, but inside the magical creation was a torrent of air. Upon impact, the ice shattered and the concussion of air exploded, sending out a dangerous shockwave.

The explosion of air wasn't enough to hurt the Knights beyond the bits of icy shrapnel they hurled, but the sudden movement was enough to ignite the magical creations Myanna and Rohn had hidden on the patio earlier in the night. The inferno mines were a combustive mix of air and fire encased in an icy wrapper. The melting ice had weakened enough that the concussion from Myanna's attack detonated the magi creations.

A sharp *crack* was followed by a flash of orange light as the two inferno mines detonated. Then the bulk of the Knight's force was down.

"Now!" Allyn commanded. "Go! Go! Go!"

Allyn rose from his cover and willed himself forward. Around him, his squad did the same, and within seconds, twelve magi were descending on the Knights.

Gunfire erupted as a small number of Knights clustered into a pair of groups, three men apiece, and fired at the incoming magi. Allyn's squad split, dodging the gunfire, and came to a stop on either side of the patio, where they were protected by a brick retaining wall. Using the wall for cover, they sent their own fireballs and ice blasts in return.

Through the chaos, Allyn only had eyes for one man— Sedric. The Knight Commander organized the counterattack and ordered his remaining men back inside the manor, where they could use the home's architecture to their advantage. But the magi had foreseen that possibility and had strategically placed the inferno mines near the doors so that their detonations would cause enough damage to block re-entry.

Magi attacks cut down the first two Knights who tried to force their way back inside, and as the third moved to try again, Sedric issued new orders. The two enemy clusters merged, reforming their original squad's larger contingent, and backed their way off the patio toward one end of the manor.

"Canary, how many Knights entered the manor?"

"At least twenty," she said.

"Then that wasn't all of them." Allyn turned to Ren. "There's still a squad and a half inside. Can you handle that?"

"Of course."

"They'll have you outnumbered."

She waved away the words as if they were nothing more than an annoying fly. "We have superior firepower."

Allyn wasn't sure he agreed, but he did have full confidence in Ren's abilities—both as a leader and a fighter. If she thought she could handle the remaining Knights, then he wasn't going to argue with her.

"Make it happen then," Allyn said. "The rest of you, with me."

Allyn left Ren and her sub squad behind, moving in the direction Sedric had fled. Behind him on the patio, he heard the muffled sounds of ice blasts finishing the wounded. They would take no prisoners. Today, the magi were making a statement.

As Allyn cautiously rounded the corner of the manor, he heard the first BearCat fire up. He froze, his gaze going to Myanna.

"They're retreating," she said.

"Come on!"

Allyn broke into a run, pushing for the corner of the manor. When they arrived, Allyn slowed and, using the edge of the manor as cover, peered around its edge. A burst of gunfire erupted immediately, and Allyn pulled back behind the corner as bullets tore into the home's exterior. Chips of brick and splinters of wood flew into the air, peppering Allyn's face.

"Nolan," Allyn said. He motioned toward the direction of the Knights then backed away from the edge of the manor to give his fellow machinist space to operate.

Nolan took Allyn's spot and wielded an energy blast. He shot a glance around the corner once, twice, then after two sharp breaths, he hurled the blast toward the BearCat. Myanna stepped out from behind him a fraction of a second later and propelled the blast forward with a concussion of air.

As soon as the blast detonated, Allyn sped forward, already wielding. He kept his head as low as possible, expecting bullets to hiss past his ears at any moment. But the Knights were already in the BearCats.

"Myanna, Nolan!" Allyn shouted. "Again!"

Nolan launched another energy blast, and Myanna sent a fireball directly behind it. The first energy blast struck the side of the BearCat, rocking it onto two wheels and allowing the fireball to strike its undercarriage. When the BearCat didn't ignite as the one at the Freidl Manor had, they tried a second time but without any more success. Instead, the remaining BearCats rumbled to life and screamed away from the manor.

The driveway was blocked, however, by a pair of full-size black SUVs. Fireballs and ice blasts shot from magi inside the SUVs exploded against the front of the BearCats, but Allyn watched in horror as the larger tactical vehicles raced toward the SUVs without sign of slowing.

Magi dove out, rolling to safety only split seconds before the BearCats tore through the SUVs like football players through a banner at a homecoming game. As the magi vehicles tumbled out of the way, the BearCats disappeared down the driveway.

That's when Allyn heard the shouts and curses behind him. He turned, spotting a squad of Knights remaining upstairs. Sedric had left them behind. Allyn readied an attack, half expecting gunfire to rain down from their tactically advantageous position. Before they could, though, a second force entered the room behind them.

Ren. Allyn watched as the magi quickly cut down the

Knights. The threat neutralized, Allyn turned back to the driveway, not yet ready to accept only a partial victory.

"Stay with me!" Allyn broke into a sprint, racing down the driveway after the BearCats. "Canary! Have an SUV waiting for us at the end of the driveway!"

"On it!" Canary shouted back.

The run took longer than Allyn expected, and by the time he and the squad made it to the end of the driveway, he was out of breath. Fortunately, Canary's message had found its recipient, and another black SUV was waiting for them.

"Inside!" Allyn shouted, jumping in behind the wheel. His squad piled inside the vehicle. "Which way?"

Canary closed her eyes again as she focused on the various radio waves. If Sedric or any of the Knights were attempting to communicate with someone, Canary would be able to pick it up and triangulate their position.

"That way!" Canary pointed in the direction the SUV was already facing.

Allyn punched the gas, and the one-ton SUV roared forward. "Stay on them. If they deviate from their course, I need to know."

Canary closed her eyes again, though Allyn doubted Sedric would change course. The narrow, two-lane road wound through the Austrian countryside with little interruption. Allyn continued on his original course, moving at an uncomfortable one hundred twenty kilometers an hour.

They drove for several minutes before the BearCats came into view. Driving in a diamond formation, the Knights' vehicles took up the entire road, kicking up dust from both shoulders.

"Nolan," Allyn commanded, flooring the SUV. "Go for the tires."

"On it!" Nolan rolled down the right-rear window, and a

roar of wind drowned out all other sound. He leaned out the window, wielding a small energy blast as Allyn pulled the SUV up beside the BearCat at the rear of the formation. Nolan hurled the energy at the BearCat's left-rear tire. The energy blast struck the tire, and with a loud *pop*, the oversized off-road tire exploded.

The BearCat swerved. The driver counter-steered into the blast but overcompensated and lost control. Suddenly, the BearCat was skidding and tumbling down the country lane with a shriek of metal on asphalt.

Allyn yanked the steering wheel left, narrowly avoiding the tumbling vehicle, and nearly lost control himself. By the time he regained control, the smoking wreckage of the tactical vehicle was far behind.

Ahead, the remaining BearCats adjusted formation. The two making up the left and right points of the diamond formation sped up, blocking the entire road.

"Nolan!" Allyn shouted. "See what you can do!"

But before the machinist could wield, the middle BearCat's rear hatch fell open. The steel ramp landed on the asphalt with a bang, shooting sparks into the night as it skidded across the blacktop. A handful of armed Knights waited inside, and at their center was Sedric, holding a full-size assault rifle trained in their direction.

Allyn cursed, slamming on the brakes as the Knight Commander opened fire. Tires squealed, and Allyn watched as a single projectile was launched from a second barrel mounted under the first on Sedric's weapon. The projectile hit the road under the front of the SUV, and the next thing Allyn knew, the front of their SUV was thrown high into the air, accompanied by a momentary, nauseous feeling of weightlessness.

The front of the SUV landed with a jaw-rattling *thud*, and

the vehicle was pitched sideways into a roll. Down became up, and up became down as the world spun.

Metal shrieked. Glass shattered. Wind roared. People screamed. And then it was over.

Allyn blinked, struggling to reorient himself. He was upside down, somehow still facing the Knights' BearCats. Blood rushed to his head, filling his ears with pressure, and more dripped onto the top—now the bottom—of the cab. Behind him, he heard others moaning, stirring.

"Everyone all right?" he asked, his pained voice barely audible over the ringing in his ears.

"I'm good," Nolan said.

"Me too," Myanna said.

One by one they checked in, and in the end, three of his squad were injured or unconscious—a remarkably small number, given their speed when they had crashed.

"Oh shit," Nolan said, suddenly alarmed. "Allyn!"

The BearCats had stopped, and the Knights streamed out of the central vehicle, guns already raised.

"Everyone out!" Allyn undid his seatbelt and fell to the roof of the cab. He tried opening his door, found it jammed, and had to kick it open with both feet. Crawling out, he used the door for cover. Behind him, his squad emerged. Seven in all, bloodied from the crash and wielding, they must have looked like a frightful sight, though Sedric appeared unfazed.

The Knights stopped halfway between their BearCat and the wrecked SUV, their guns trained on the magi. Sedric separated himself from the rest by a couple steps and watched Allyn with a wry smile.

"Allyn, Allyn, Allyn," he said in his mocking Southern drawl. "You just don't know when to quit, do you? You won today, and now you risk everything because you just can't help yourself. 'The greedy bring ruin to their households,' Allyn. And you are very, very greedy."

Allyn watched the Knight Commander, unsure how to respond. From the perpetual scowl to the sarcastic humor, Sedric had the look and feel of someone who had been career military. His salt-and-pepper hair was cut short, and his weathered face was sharp and angular, as if his features alone could hurt someone.

"What gave us away?" Sedric asked. "How did you know where we would be?"

Allyn locked his jaw. He wasn't about to give the other man information that he could use against them.

"Come on, Allyn, we did this last time. And I grow tired of talking to myself."

"What do you want to hear?" Allyn finally asked. "That we have a mole in your outfit? That you made a mistake? That you left behind vital information when you retreated from the catacombs? There's no one answer, Sedric. There are many."

Sedric laughed—he actually *laughed.* "Truthful lips endure forever, Allyn, but a lying tongue is but for a moment."

"What's that supposed to mean?"

"It means I know you're lying, Allyn. And the Lord hates a lying tongue."

"What does he say about the hands that shed innocent blood?"

Sedric raised an eyebrow. "Very good, Allyn. Proverbs. I'm impressed. Of course, we've already covered this—you and your kind are not innocent, nor are they righteous, so let's not dwell on your sudden and suspicious Christian awakening and get right down to the heart of it. Tell your men to stop wielding, and I'll let you live."

It was Allyn's turn to laugh. Not that he felt like it—he just needed to stall Sedric while he put together a plan.

"Let us live?" Allyn repeated. "There are ten of us here and only eight of you. Why would we surrender when we have you outnumbered?"

"There are seven of you," Sedric corrected. "And even then, we have the greater firepower."

"You sure about that?"

Sedric held up his gun for all to see. "Do you see this? This is an M4A1 Carbine. It's capable of shooting up to nine hundred rounds per minute, and *all* of my men are equipped with one. Eight people at nine hundred rounds per minute— that's seventy-two hundred rounds fired in your direction in the next sixty seconds. So, tell me again, Allyn, how exactly do you have us outnumbered? How do you have the greater firepower?"

Allyn's mouth went dry.

"That's what I thought," Sedric said. "Don't get greedy for a second time, Allyn. Tell your squad to stop wielding, or I'll have my men open fire and we'll end this right here and now."

Allyn turned, spotting Myanna. She shook her head and showed him the volatile inferno mine glowing in her hand. *She won't let herself be taken hostage.*

Allyn found Nolan next, and he too shook his head, his own magi creation shimmering in his hands. Then Nyla and Canary did the same. They were unanimous in their decision. Allyn nodded and was about to turn back to Sedric when something caught his eye—three pairs of headlights were quickly growing on the horizon.

SUVs, Allyn realized. *Reinforcements.*

He turned back to Sedric, his confidence and swagger returning. Sedric had spotted the incoming vehicles too, and his face twisted with surprise and irritation.

"Like I said, we have you outnumbered," Allyn said. "Myanna, now!"

Myanna hurled her magical creation at the Knights while Allyn and the rest ducked behind the protection of the SUV. The volatile concoction of fire and air encased in ice cracked open, and living flame lashed out angrily, blowing the Knights back. They crashed against the BearCats while others dove for cover and were buffeted by the incredible heat.

For a brief moment, nothing else happened, and Allyn thought Myanna had killed the entire Knight force, but the barrage of gunfire told him how very wrong he had been.

Bullets slammed into the reinforced steel of the SUV, bouncing off the bulletproof shell with a series of thuds and sparks. Allyn wielded, preparing to lead the counterattack, but realized Sedric wasn't attacking—he was *retreating.*

The Knights who could walk staggered backward with him, some making half-hearted attempts to save the injured, and leaving those who were obviously dead behind.

Myanna launched another volley of fireballs. The rest of the magi followed her lead, but the Knights had retreated to the safety of the BearCat. Fireballs and ice blasts crashed against the hatch as it closed.

Allyn slid away from the protection of the SUV and watched as the BearCats rumbled away. Behind him, the other magi SUVs skidded to a stop. Magi streamed from them, ready for battle. Jaxon was among them, and he quickly found Allyn.

"Was that him?" Jaxon asked.

Allyn nodded. "We almost had him, Jaxon. We almost ended the war."

He and Jaxon watched as the BearCats disappeared on the horizon.

CHAPTER 11

THE MAGI DIDN'T RETURN TO the Klausner Manor until the Schuster Manor had been cleared of the fallen, the fires put out, and entrances and windows boarded up. Even in victory, there was defeat. The McCollum forces had repelled the Knights' attack but had lost six of their number in doing so, and the damage to the manor would take months to repair.

Allyn found strange solace in the fact that, as they had so many times before, the dead came from outside the McCollum Family. The comfort wasn't without guilt, but knowing his friends were safe was the only thing keeping him from completely breaking down.

The long drive back to the Klausner Manor provided Allyn with an opportunity to sit in silence. For the first time in nearly a full day, he didn't have to lead. Didn't have to analyze, command, or make life-and-death decisions. He should have been ecstatic that the battle had gone so well, but as it had after many of the previous battles, his mood took a dark turn.

Upon returning to the manor, he ordered the injured inside and quickly retreated to the quiet comfort of his room.

His mood hadn't improved by the next afternoon, either, when he and the rest of the War Council deconstructed the battle. They didn't expect the Knights to continue with their same strategy, not after the magi had routed their forces, but the council could still glean details that might help in future conflicts. Besides, improvement was the result of honest reflection. The council could determine where they had made mistakes, not only where the Knights had erred.

The task left Allyn with a sour taste in his mouth, which was made worse by the council's buzz of excitement. He wanted to scream. Six more magi were dead, and the magi leaders were smiling and quick to laugh. It all felt so wrong.

When the session ended, Allyn returned to his room and collapsed onto his bed. He was emotionally and physically exhausted, but the hard, dreamless sleep was cut short when he woke to the manor alive with activity. Music echoed through the walls, dancing footsteps bounced through the floors, and laughter lit even the darkest corners of the manor.

They're celebrating!

He couldn't believe what he was hearing. Not trusting his ears, Allyn left his room and followed the sounds of revelry. He froze on the first-floor landing. He'd never seen anything like the scene before him.

The magi had turned in their compression armor for traditional cuts of whites, reds, yellows, and blues that flowed when they danced. They lounged in chairs or huddled in corners out of the way, always watching, smiling, laughing, and engaged in their own lively conversations. It felt like a dream. It *had* to be a dream. In the months he'd lived among the magi, they had always been reserved. Never this. Never free-spirited or able to let loose.

Various magi spotted him and immediately looked away, their smiles and laughter dying on their lips. Some even went so far as to leave the room entirely. He looked down, realizing he still wore his compression armor.

It's bringing them down, he realized. *Reminding them of their loss.*

Suddenly self-conscious, Allyn was about to return to his room when he spotted Kendyl approaching. She wore a gentle smile, her cheeks flushed with intoxication, and carried two wine glasses—one full, the other half empty.

"You decided to join us," she said over the commotion. Her words were warm and slightly slurred.

"I must have missed the invite," Allyn said sarcastically.

"Sad. Here, accept this as our apology." Kendyl held the glass of wine in front of him.

"No thanks."

"Take it," Kendyl said. "I don't need a second glass. Or a fourth, whatever this is."

"I was just getting ready to head back up to my room."

"What? Why? I hope it's to change, because your outfit is kind of a downer."

"I just don't feel like celebrating."

"Which is exactly *why* you should be celebrating."

"That doesn't make any sense."

"Sure it does," Kendyl said. "You're just spending too much time up here." She tapped her forehead with her wine glass, spilling red wine on the hardwood floor. "You need to get out of your own mind."

"Goodnight, Kendyl."

"You're really not going to join us?"

Allyn looked around the room, feeling utterly alone in the crowded space. "No. Have a good time, though."

He returned to his room, where he might not be able to find the silence he desired, but at least he could have privacy. Once he was back in his room, though, he felt oddly disconnected, almost like a child who had been told to go to bed while his parents were downstairs, laughing and having a good time. Part of him wondered what he was missing, but no matter how much he tried, he just didn't feel like celebrating. It left him in an uncomfortable limbo—unable to enjoy the company of others, and unable to enjoy the solace of privacy.

So when the knock came, he was simultaneously thrilled and annoyed. He crossed the room and opened the door to find Nyla in the hall. Her silver hair was in a loose braid that was thrown over her shoulder, and she had changed into a well-cut dress similar to the others he'd seen downstairs. Allyn blinked. Nyla was absolutely *gorgeous.*

"So it's true," she said, her tone disappointed as her eyes took him in. "You aren't participating in the festivities."

Allyn shook his head. "I'm surprised you are."

Nyla sighed. "Can I come in? I brought presents." She held up a wine bottle and two empty glasses, flashing another smile that was nearly enough to give Allyn pause. A beautiful woman wielding a smile and alcohol was asking to come into his room? Any other time, he would have a pretty good idea where that would lead, but with the magi, and more specifically, with Nyla, it just left him confused.

"Of course." Allyn opened the door wider and stepped aside, giving her space to enter.

Nyla made for a pair of armchairs beside the window. Allyn closed the door, watching her, hoping for some kind of signal. When he didn't get any, he moved to join her.

Handing him a glass of wine, she held hers high and said, "Cheers."

"What are we cheersing to?"

She shrugged. "A night of distraction."

Allyn took a deep breath and sat down on the arm of

the nearby chair, leaving Nyla and her glass hanging. "Nyla, what is this?"

"What do you mean?"

"You know what I mean. You show up at my room with wine and talk about a night of distractions. To most people outside the Order, that usually means only one thing."

"And what's that?"

"Fuck, Nyla," Allyn said, exasperated. Then realizing the potential double meaning, he felt his face burn with embarrassment. "I mean..."

"Relax, Allyn," Nyla said, laughing softly. "I know you think we're backward sometimes, but we're not naïve. We discovered sex a long time ago too."

"So this is..."

"Nothing more than a concerned friend checking on someone she cares about."

Something similar to relief flooded through Allyn—the relief of not having embarrassed himself further.

"Unless of course my friend needs some kind of *special* attention."

And just like that, Allyn was blushing again. Nyla must have seen it, because she burst out laughing.

"You're messing with me," Allyn said.

"Of course I am," Nyla said. "You're making it too easy." She mirrored him, sitting down on the arm of the chair across from his, and when his expression betrayed his lack of amusement, she added, "The truth is, Allyn, I'm worried about you. Your sister is worried about you. A lot of us are. And I wanted to cheer you up. Make you laugh. See something on your face other than the angry, dour expression I've seen for the last few weeks."

"I'm fine."

"Says the man who only a few days ago told me he didn't

know how much more of this he could take." Nyla leveled her gaze on him. "You're not fine."

"No, I'm not," Allyn admitted. "None of this is, Nyla. Six of our people died yesterday, and everyone is downstairs celebrating. *Celebrating*, Nyla. Doesn't anyone see what's fucked up about that?"

"Of course they do."

"Then why are they doing it?"

"Because a lot more than six magi could have died yesterday. Because this is the first victory we've had against the Knights in a while. And because everyone downstairs needs to be reminded of why they fight. What they live for. Tonight is about hope, Allyn. Maybe not for you and me— though I dare say you need some, but it's about them. *They* need it."

"A night of distraction," Allyn said softly.

"Exactly."

"Then let them have it. I just won't be joining them."

"That's going to be a problem."

"Why?" Allyn groaned.

"Because you were the hero of the day. The change in battle plans was your idea, as were the tactics that secured the victory. Like it or not, Allyn, you're now the face of their hope. And unless you want to destroy that too, you need to be down there."

"I can't. I..." Allyn rose and leaned his head against the cool glass of the window. "If I'm the face of their hope, am I not also the face of the person who killed those six magi?"

"You know the answer to that already."

"Then why do I feel it?"

Nyla stood and drew closer to Allyn, placing a hand against his cheek. He looked at her, meeting her blue eyes. "Because you're a good man, Allyn. And because you care for those affected by your decisions. It isn't a bad thing—except for when it gets in the way of doing everything else that needs to be done."

Allyn turned away and closed his eyes. Part of him thought that if he could just shut it all away and ignore it, that the feelings of regret and loss would disappear too. But even as he thought it, he knew things didn't work that way. He couldn't hide, because there was nothing to hide from except his own feelings. There was only one way to escape, and that was to surround himself with others and distract himself through their differing emotions.

"What are you asking of me?" Allyn finally asked.

"Mingle. Smile. Answer questions, and most of all, be positive. Give them the hope they're all looking for."

Allyn opened his mouth to speak, but Nyla cut him off.

"I know it's not easy, Allyn, and I know it's asking a lot, but I promise it'll help. And who knows? Maybe acting the part will get you out of the funk you've been in."

"You'll be with me?"

"Every step of the way."

"All right," Allyn said. "But let's open that bottle first. A little liquid courage couldn't hurt."

———————

Nearly thirty minutes later and a full bottle of wine down, Allyn and Nyla made their way to the celebration downstairs. More than an hour after Allyn had been downstairs before, the celebrating magi were farther into the bag, more jovial and raucous, and showing no signs of slowing down.

Upon seeing him in his more appropriate attire, the same magi who had given him blank stares or scoffed at his compression armor smiled and slapped him on the back, excited to have the hero of the Battle of the Schuster Manor joining them. And true to her word, Nyla remained with Allyn through it all, often taking the lead and moving him from group to group, avoiding getting stuck with any overly intoxicated magi men who wanted to talk his ear off or magi women who wanted his hand for a dance. She effortlessly steered conversations, allowing him to nod, smile, and add color commentary when appropriate. They spoke to every member of the Forum then the arch mage himself, always just long enough to pay their respects and receive the praise the Forum members wanted to lay at his feet.

Allyn struggled with the responsibility laid before him, but forcing his best smile, he repeated to each thankful Forum member that he was content to score a victory against the Knights. Each time, he insisted that the magi needed to remain vigilant. In most cases, the magi would nod in agreement, tap glasses with him, finish with a drink, and allow Allyn to move on.

"Was that the last of them?" Allyn asked when Nyla finally directed him away from the magi leaders and to a table with wine-filled glasses.

"It was."

"Thank God."

Nyla set their empty glasses out of the way and grabbed two more, handing one to Allyn. "You did great."

Allyn barked a laugh. "I barely did anything. You, on the other hand, were amazing. I couldn't have done that without you."

"You don't have to say that."

"No," Allyn said. "I mean it. There's no way I would have remembered all of their names."

Nyla smiled, no doubt understanding what Allyn truly meant, but she had the grace not to say anything. She raised her glass to his. "To getting through it, then. Together."

"To getting through it." Allyn tapped his glass to hers and took a drink. He felt her eyes on him as he surveyed the room. Magi circled the foyer, leaning against walls, talking, joking, and watching other magi dance in the center of the room. Seeing the unburdened magi, Allyn thought he was beginning to understand what the night meant to them.

"Is this what it was like?"

"Hmm?" Nyla asked.

"Before the war," Allyn said. "Before Lukas and Darian. Before the splinter."

Nyla's smile widened, and she seemed to glow from within at the fond memories. "I suppose. Though, parties and festivities were still rare, often saved for special events or holidays. The carelessness is new. Magi have never been careless—you know that—but there was an unburdened-ness, if there is such a thing."

"It's beautiful," Allyn said softly. "I've never seen... I didn't know..." He winced, struggling to find the words.

Nyla laid a hand on his arm. "You joined our Family at a strange time."

Allyn nodded. "I wish I could have seen it before. Wish I could have met you before."

"We'll get there again," Nyla said then turned her attention to the dancing magi.

The fast, upbeat music had changed to something slower, and the lively, spirited magi dance had changed with it. Where the magi dance before was lively and spirited, something akin to a Native American dance, it now resembled something closer to a traditional slow dance—something Allyn felt much more comfortable with.

His eyes lingered on Nyla, watching the way she followed the flowing bodies. She seemed to long to join them. "When was the last time you danced?"

"Me?" Nyla said. "Not since... It's been a while."

Not since Baylis, Allyn knew, and he nearly lost his nerve.

Baylis had been her lover, and while they had not been married in the traditional sense, they had developed an echo and become as close as any two people ever could be. Because Nyla had used her cleric's abilities and healed Baylis so many times, she had quite literally given him parts of herself and taken on parts of him in return. They had become something else entirely—not just Nyla and not just Baylis, but a combination of the two.

Their relationship had run deeper than that too—the heightened connection was just something of a bonus. But when Baylis died, those pieces of him that were inside Nyla died with him, leaving behind deep psychological and emotional wounds that were more profound than anything Allyn could understand. When he had first met her, Nyla was angry, confused, and struggling to find herself. She'd healed since then, as much as anyone could in that kind of situation, but he knew she would never truly get over it. Never truly return to the person she had been before.

So as it was, five or six—or maybe seven—glasses of liquid courage down, he took her hand and pulled her toward the center of the room. "Let's dance then."

"Allyn," Nyla said, surprised. "I—"

"Come on."

She followed him into the circle of dancing bodies, and once in position, he felt a sudden wave of nervousness that made him weak in the knees. He ignored her eyes on him, flushing slightly at the extra attention, and snuck a peek over her shoulder to see how the other magi held each other.

"What's wrong?" she asked quietly.

"I don't know what I'm doing." He allowed himself to laugh, letting her know he wasn't having second thoughts.

Nyla's face warmed, and as she had earlier in the night, she took control. Taking his hand in hers, she guided his other hand to her hip and moved him in position. "Just follow me," she whispered in his ear, her breath sending shivers through his body.

And then they were off, dancing slowly and moving in unison with the other couples. Allyn was clumsy at first, struggling to follow Nyla's lead. He even stepped on a couple toes like a middle-schooler slow dancing for the first time, but Nyla just smiled and kept going.

As the dance wore on and Allyn got a better feel for the steps, he grew more confident. Before long, he was moving without thought at all. He watched Nyla, swam in the softness of her gaze, felt her body close to his, trembled at the feel of her gentle breath brushing against his ear. There on the makeshift dance floor, dancing a dance he had never danced before, Allyn's worry, sadness, and guilt disappeared. For those few minutes, he was truly in a different place, and for the first time in a long time, he was happy.

Moving on nothing but instinct, Allyn slid his hand from Nyla's hip, cupped her face, and brought his lips to hers. Her body shivered as his lips found hers, and all other sound and sensation disappeared. She was timid at first, and so was he, but neither pulled away. The next kiss was... not better—the first wasn't bad—but it was *more*. It tore through him like the first rays of sun in spring, awakening a desire inside of him that had lain dormant for longer than he had known. Her fingers dug into his back. She felt it too.

As their lips parted and their eyes opened, they each bathed in the loving look of the other. There was nothing else in the world but that one moment. One person. One breath. There was no war. No death. No loss. There was only them.

CHAPTER 12

ALLYN WOKE TO THREE THINGS: a knock at his door, a splitting headache, and Nyla's silver hair draped across his chest. Unfortunately, the first aggravated the second, and both distracted him from the third.

Nyla groaned and stirred awake. She cast an annoyed look toward the door then looked up from his chest and smiled. "Good morning."

"Good morning." Allyn's voice was coarse, sounding almost as if he were coming down with a cold. Like the headache, it was another symptom of his heavy drinking.

The knock came again, more insistent.

"You should probably answer that," Nyla said.

"Yeah."

But neither made any effort to move.

"Maybe they'll go away."

The knock became an insistent pounding. The handle jiggled. Locked.

Thank goodness for that.

"Guess not." Nyla slid off his chest.

Allyn threw his legs over the side of the bed, his bare feet touching the cold hardwood floor as a sudden wave of nausea hit him. The cool sensation was all that kept him from losing his stomach.

"Are you okay?" Nyla rubbed his back.

"No," Allyn admitted. "I haven't drank that much since college. Hell, maybe high school. I don't suppose you clerics have a hangover cure, do you?"

"Ha! Remember, we use our bodies to heal. That means I'd have to suffer instead, and that's not going to happen."

"You seem fine."

"We heal faster than you do."

"So why can't you help again?"

"Because suffering is good for the soul," Nyla said. "Drink a glass of water, eat some breakfast, and tough it out. You'll be fine."

"You're as bad as my sister."

"I'll take that as a compliment."

The knocking continued.

"Yeah, yeah," Allyn said, his own voice thundering in his ears. "I'm coming."

He stood, suddenly aware and very self-conscious of his nudity. Scanning the floor for his clothes, he attempted to shield himself in a way that made it look like he wasn't doing it intentionally. It probably looked ridiculous, and he wasn't sure what made him more embarrassed, his nakedness or his feelings toward it. After all, Nyla didn't seem to care.

Why am I making this more awkward than it needs to be?

He found his previous night's clothes on the floor and hurriedly pulled them on. Finally dressed, he opened the door just enough so he could see into the hall. Liam waited there, bouncing from foot to foot impatiently.

"What's up?" Allyn asked.

"Hey," Liam said, excitedly. "Good morning. I need to... are those the same clothes you wore last night?"

"You woke me up. I didn't have anything else to put on."

"Oh," Liam said. "Right. I heard voices, though. Who's in there with you?" He tried to peer into the room, but Allyn blocked his view.

"What's going on, Liam?"

"Huh? Oh, I... I need to talk to you about something. Can I come in?"

Allyn glanced uneasily back at the bed where Nyla waited. "I tell you what. I'm starving, and I could really use a couple glasses of water. What do you say you meet me in the kitchen in fifteen minutes?"

Liam made a face that suggested he didn't want to wait any longer than he had to.

"Surely you can wait that long," Allyn continued.

"Of course."

"Okay," Allyn said. "I'll see you downstairs then."

Liam hadn't moved by the time the door closed, so wanting to ensure Liam wasn't trying to eavesdrop on him, Allyn remained just inside the doorway until he heard Liam's soft footsteps retreating. Once they'd disappeared out of earshot, he turned back to Nyla and made his way across the room.

"I love that kid to death," Allyn said, "but, damn, he can be nosey."

Nyla sat up, resting her back against the headboard. "He doesn't like secrets."

Allyn barked a sarcastic laugh. *If Liam only knew half of the secrets and plans being kept from him.* He sat on the edge of the bed and looked at Nyla. "Do we need to talk?"

"About?" Nyla asked.

"About last night. About this."

"Talking is never a bad thing, but if you're asking if I regret anything about last night, I don't."

"That's good," Allyn said. "Me, neither."

That brought a smile to Nyla's face. "That's good. Are you going to go down there dressed like that?"

"I don't know. Probably not. Why?"

She gave him a suggestive grin. "Because if you have to get undressed anyway, we might as well do something else we won't regret."

Allyn laughed... and promptly removed his clothes.

Liam was nearly done with breakfast by the time Allyn entered the kitchen. Half-empty wine glasses, half-eaten, drunkenly prepared meals, and various plates, cups, and silverware littered the granite countertops. The hardwood floor was sticky and had more than one wine stain, but it was the smells of coffee, bacon, and alcohol that sent Allyn into another cold sweat.

Liam was sitting at a table at the back of the room, his back to the large bay windows. He scowled at Allyn as he entered. "I thought you said fifteen minutes."

"I'm sorry," Allyn said. "I got hung up."

"With what?"

"I drank all night, Liam. Use your imagination." It wasn't a lie, not exactly, so Allyn didn't feel guilty for it.

Liam made a sour face and pushed his plate away.

Allyn pulled a mug from the cupboards, filled it with hot water from the coffee pot, and began brewing a single serving of tea. His favorite hangover cure from college had been a Gatorade and Cup of Noodles, followed by a Coke and greasy bacon or sausage an hour or so later, but Allyn had long since realized that the luxuries of outside life didn't extend to the magi community. His options were tea and coffee, and he was forced to take the lesser of the two evils.

After adding a couple cubes of sugar, he took a seat across from Liam. "So what has you up so early?"

"It's after nine a.m."

"You've never drank heavily, have you?" Allyn asked. Then when it appeared he'd made Liam uncomfortable, he quickly added, "Never mind. Let's just say nine is early when you went to bed at four and drank more than your body weight."

"Why do you do it then?"

Allyn took a sip of tea. "Hmm?"

"Why drink the way you did last night?"

"Now probably isn't the best time to ask me that," Allyn said with a laugh. "But if you'd asked me last night, I would have told you it's fun and that sometimes you need to go a little crazy to get away from all the other crap in your life."

"But it just makes the next day even worse."

"Everything has a cost, right?"

"I guess." Liam took on a contemplative expression, obviously trying to make sense of the exchange. Allyn had to hold in a laugh and struggled to keep his amusement off his face. Liam was brilliant and developing more and more into a leader every day, and because of that, Allyn sometimes forgot how naïve he could be.

And he's expected to lead the McCollum Family now that Jaxon is gone.

"I'm sorry for waking you then," Liam said. "If you need to rest, we can talk about this later."

Allyn dunked the teabag into the water a couple more times and shook his head. "I'm already up, Liam. What's on your mind?"

"I need your help getting access to the arch mage's private library."

Allyn coughed. Liam's face flushed with embarrassment, and Allyn attempted to mask his reaction by pointing at the tea. "Sorry, that's just really hot." Again, it wasn't technically a lie... "The arch mage's private library?"

"Yeah," Liam said.

"The one full of magi secrets?"

"That's the one."

"Why?"

"Because it's full of magi secrets," Liam said sarcastically. "For research, Allyn."

"Obviously," Allyn said. "What kind of research?"

"You know the paintings in the Klausner study? The ones showing the different eras of magi?"

"Yeah."

"Well, Arch Mage Westarra said that if you trace magi and human lines back far enough, they converge. That at some time in our ancient past, there were no humans or magi, there were just... people."

"You're wondering who made the split," Allyn said.

"Sort of," Liam said. "That's a piece of it, anyway. Was it the magi who broke the line and manifested their magical abilities, or was it humans who somehow lost magi abilities and resorted to tools?"

"Your father described the magi evolution as being needs-based. They needed fire, so they learned to create it using their bodies, but humans found other means. That makes it sound like it was the magi who diverted."

"Maybe," Liam said. "But that's not the whole story, and my father wasn't a historian. Plus, as you said, the arch mage's library will have information that's not common knowledge to the rest of the Order."

"I suppose." Allyn pointed at Liam's plate. "Are you done with that?"

"What? Oh, yeah. Go for it."

"Thanks," Allyn said, reaching for a leftover piece of bacon. "So why now? Why's this so important?"

"The Blood Wand."

"Sorry," Allyn said. "I'm not following. Hungover, remember?"

"I'm trying to figure out why Sedric has magi abilities. Or more specifically, I'm trying to understand why the Blood Wand, which was imbued with the magical abilities of ancient magi, worked on someone with no other magical lineage."

"In other words," Allyn said. "Why does the Blood Wand work on humans?"

"Exactly."

Allyn finished the bacon strip and wiped his greasy fingers on his pant leg. "Maybe there's an unknown magi connection. Maybe Sedric has magi blood in his veins that none of us are aware of."

"I thought that too," Liam said. "So I looked into it using the same program I built to look into your history. It's not complete, which is partly why I want access to the arch mage's records, but it didn't come up with any matches."

Allyn shrugged. "Maybe the Blood Wand just works on humans too."

"But *why?*" Liam asked. "There's more going on here. Remember, we never discovered where your abilities came from, either."

"Wait." Allyn held up a hand. "What are you getting at?"

"I don't know yet," Liam said. "I can barely make out the outlines of the question, but I know it all starts with the divergence."

Allyn was suddenly uncomfortable, and it wasn't because of his rumbling stomach. Liam had touched on a question that had never been answered, one that Allyn had forced deep into his subconscious. He hadn't given much thought into why he had magi abilities—after all, it didn't matter now that he *did* have them. And even then, the long-standing hypothesis was that he and Kendyl descended from a forgotten magi line—something not implausible due to the fallout from the Fracture.

Lukas had targeted them because of a very specific set of different criteria. Allyn and Kendyl were twins who had experienced a traumatic childhood. But that answer had never been enough for Allyn, and if there was something more to it, then he wanted to know. It was vital to knowing who he was and where he came from.

"How soon do you need to get out there?" Allyn asked.

"As soon as possible."

"I was afraid of that."

"Why?"

Allyn took a deep breath. "There's something you should know, and I'm not the person to tell you."

"What are you talking about?"

"Come on," Allyn said, standing. "Let's see if Jaxon is up."

Jaxon was up, and if looks could be believed, he was in much better shape than Allyn.

I really overdid it last night, Allyn thought as he and Liam entered the gym where Jaxon waited. He was mid-workout, shirtless and glistening with sweat. *That's not a bad idea. Sweat the booze out, like a cold?*

Jaxon finished his reps and grabbed a nearby towel to wipe the sweat from his face. "You're up," he said to Allyn. "I didn't expect you up and about for some time."

"I wouldn't have been if it weren't for *someone.*" Allyn gave an exaggerated nod in Liam's direction.

"Oh?" Jaxon took a long pull from his water bottle.

"Tell him what you told me," Allyn said.

Liam gave him a look that said, "You brought me here so you could tell me something, not the other way around," but he complied and told Jaxon what he had said to Allyn.

"I see," Jaxon said. "And when were you hoping to do this?"

"Why does everyone keep asking me that?" Liam asked. "This is important, very important—tell me you see that."

"We see it, Liam," Allyn said. "He wants to go now, Jaxon. He already asked for my help this morning."

Jaxon let out an exasperated breath, grabbed his shirt, then pulled it over his sweaty form. "I'm sorry, Liam. But I can't let you go."

"Why?" Liam asked. "What is it you're not telling me?"

"I'm sorry to have to tell you like this, Liam, but I've been summoned back to my Family. I am to replace my father as Grand Mage of the Green Family."

"What?" Liam looked to Allyn for confirmation or perhaps some sign of a joke. "When? Why now?"

"Soon," Jaxon said. "I've already begun studying under him and playing a more active role in Family and Order planning. For all intents and purposes, I am the Grand Mage of the Green Family already, even if they aren't aware of it yet."

"But it's not that easy," Liam said. "Your father can't just appoint you grand mage; you have to be ratified by the Family itself."

Jaxon smiled. "I know, Liam."

"Then how can he do this? It's circumventing custom."

"Are you suggesting I'm not qualified to lead the Family I was born into?" Jaxon asked with the smallest of grins.

"You know I'm not saying that—"

"Then maybe the Family won't confirm my claim?"

"Of course they will, but..." Liam stammered, searching

for the words. He must have missed the flicker of amusement on Jaxon's face.

"Nothing my father has done contradicts magi custom," Jaxon said. "He's just leading as he's always done. Being firm and proactive."

Liam didn't look as though he completely agreed, but he didn't press the issue further. "So you don't want me to go because you're leaving."

"Not entirely," Jaxon said slowly. "I can't have you leave because I intend to nominate you as the next Grand Mage of the McCollum Family."

Liam blinked and opened his mouth, but no words came out. He looked from Jaxon to Allyn and back, his eyes narrow and confused.

"Say something, Liam," Jaxon said. "Did I make a mistake?"

"I... uh..." Liam took a steadying breath. "That would make me the youngest grand mage in the Order."

Jaxon nodded.

"No," Liam continued. "Not only that, but the youngest current grand mage is twice my age!"

"There have been younger grand mages," Jaxon said.

"Not in—what? A thousand years? And that was during..."

"During what, Liam?" Jaxon spoke with complete confidence, as if he knew exactly where Liam was headed and intended to meet him there.

"During war."

"Exactly." Jaxon closed the distance between himself and Liam and placed both hands on Liam's shoulders. Liam may have grown since Allyn had first met him, but there, standing in front of Jaxon, he still looked like a child. "War makes many things possible, Liam, but that's not why I want to nominate you. You are the natural heir to this Family. You discovered the machinists. You are the only magi in the Order who can wield both the elements and machinist abilities. You have seen the enemy and defeated them. And regardless of age, you are ready."

Liam looked up into Jaxon's round eyes. His were glassy, and he tightened his lips, fighting back emotion. He spoke softly, almost as if he were voicing his biggest fear and that speaking the words aloud would somehow make the fear come true. "Do you think they'll follow me?"

Jaxon squeezed Liam's shoulders. "To the ends of the earth and back again."

A single tear spilled over the bank of Liam's eyelid and slid down his cheek. Silent, he nodded slightly. Then, as if he remembered Allyn was still in the room with them, he looked at him, the same unspoken question on his lips.

"We'll follow you, Liam," Allyn said. "And we'll help and counsel you when needed. If you'll have *us*, of course."

"Of course." Liam's voice was still soft but more confident than before. "I'd be honored to retain your counsel."

"You don't need to give me an answer now, Liam," Jaxon said. "But you'll need to decide soon. Time isn't on our side."

"No," Liam said. "I'll do it."

"You're sure?" Jaxon seemed a little surprised by Liam's firm answer.

"Yes," Liam said. "It's what I want." And as if the words solidified the confidence he already had inside, he stood straighter, raising his chin strongly. "I will be the next Grand Mage of the McCollum Family."

CHAPTER 13

LIAM STOOD IN FRONT OF the McCollum group, hoping he didn't look as awkward as he felt. It had only been two hours since his conversation with Allyn and Jaxon, but in that time, the former Grand Mage of the McCollum Family had organized every McCollum magi still left at the Klausner Manor and assembled the rest via video conference.

Now that Liam had agreed to take what Jaxon had called "his rightful place as the leader of the Family," Jaxon wanted the transition to happen as quickly as possible. Liam wasn't sure who Jaxon was looking out for more, Liam or himself, but he hadn't argued. Stalling wouldn't help anyone. And besides, he still needed access to the arch mage's private library, and he figured he stood a better shot as a grand mage than he ever would have as a simple magi.

They gathered in a first-level private study. Liam found himself scanning the room, trying not to make eye contact with the others. His eyes found the artistic panels that depicted the five eras of magi that he'd spoken to Allyn about. The irony wasn't lost on him. If he were to break down the major eras in his life, beginning with his birth and ending with his death, this moment would no doubt be near the center of the depiction.

Tearing his eyes off the panels, Liam looked purposefully over at the group in front of him. They sat in armchairs and couches in a loose semicircle with Jaxon and Liam at their head.

I still can't believe this is happening.

For two hours, he had wandered through the Klausner Manor and around its grounds. Deep in thought, he'd paid no heed to where he was or where he was going. He only knew that he needed to move. Maybe it helped him think. Maybe it helped him process. Or maybe he was just too afraid to stop, fearing that stopping meant he'd imagined the whole thing and that his dreams weren't really coming true.

You've stopped now, though, haven't you? Does that mean the dream will come to an end?

"Thank you for joining on such short notice," Jaxon said, beginning the meeting and interrupting Liam's train of thought. "I know it's late for those of you at home at the Hyland Estate, but we've had a new development, and I didn't want to keep you in the dark any longer than necessary."

That's a bit of an understatement.

It was nearly one o'clock in the afternoon local time, which meant it wasn't quite four in the morning at the Hyland Estate. Liam could only imagine what was going through their heads. Jaxon's urgent early morning meeting must have caused a panic. And looking at the image on the television being broadcast from the computer, he could see it in their body language.

The McCollum magi sat on the edges of their seats, elbows on knees, feet tapping against the floor. Parke Hyland, Grand Mage of the Hyland Family, bounced nervously from foot to foot. Others stood with their arms crossed while more paced back and forth behind the bulk of the group. All wore worried expressions or failed to hide them through masks of indifference.

"The McCollum Family is a historic Family," Jaxon continued. "Maybe not an ancient Family by old-world standards, but as old as they come in America, and still one of the oldest in the Order today. A Scottish clan before it was a Family, the McCollum Family was formed under the roots of oppression and the weight of persecution. It was formed by love, strengthened through war, and bound by loyalty. For almost five hundred years, a McCollum has led the McCollum Family, and what a group of leaders they've been."

Jaxon paused, looking over the room. The audience was silent, their eyes glued to the man before them. Even those at the Hyland Estate had stopped shuffling and pacing.

"My father, Wesley Green, sent me to the McCollum Family to study under the tutelage of Graeme McCollum, and I'll forever treasure that experience. Grand Mage McCollum was a great man, a great leader, and someone I'll respect for the rest of my entire life. Following his death, I have done my best to follow in his tradition, to steer the Family in the direction I believe he'd want it to go, and to provide a foundation for future strength."

Jaxon paused, his strength faltering. Liam could hear the tremble in Jaxon's breath and see the sporadic rise and fall of his chest. It was perhaps the most emotion Liam had ever seen Jaxon display publicly.

"But I am not a McCollum," Jaxon finally said. "And as much as I love this Family and the magi within it, it is not mine to lead. So it's after much thought, deliberation, and counsel, that I step down as the Grand Mage of the McCollum Family."

Shock rippled through the McCollum magi then was

quickly replaced by outrage. Magi began talking over one another, shouting, pointing, and cursing. Though Liam had known something like this would happen, he was still surprised by the violent nature of their reaction.

They've been through too much. They aren't ready.

Suddenly, the joy and elation he'd felt in the hours leading up the announcement disappeared, and he realized the monumental task Jaxon had just placed upon him. His job wasn't only to lead the Family, but to heal it, as well. He may be a magi, he might even be a machinist, but he wasn't a cleric. He didn't know the first thing about bringing people together.

Jaxon held up a hand. "Please. Please. Allow me to finish." The clamor died down enough that Jaxon could speak above it. "Please. I'm not done." He waited for it to quiet down further before he continued. "I know this is hard. And I know the timing is less than ideal. But know that I do this now for three reasons.

"First, no time will ever be ideal, and despite the current challenges we face, the Family is ready. The threats of Lukas and Darian are gone. The threat of law enforcement has been dealt with. And the Family is once again recognized by the Forum. The Family has been stable for months. Even now, as war rages, the Family is sheltered by distance. You need someone looking toward the future without their own future clouding the path.

"I was sent to the McCollum Family to learn to lead so that, one day, I could lead my own Family. That day has come, and that is the second reason. My father is abdicating, and I am to take his place. What most of you don't know is my father has pressured me to take his place for months. But because of the precarious position we were in, I didn't do it. The time is right now. Not only because the most dire threats have been taken care of, but because someone worthy has risen to claim the mantle of grand mage. For the first time, I feel comfortable handing control of this prestigious Family over to another. The McCollum Family was led by a McCollum for five hundred years, and it will be again."

Liam felt the weight of almost one hundred eyes turn to him. He stood resolute, refusing to show his unease. His eyes scanned the room, falling on Nyla, Leira, and Allyn. The last gave him a small smile and nod of encouragement. Liam looked directly into the camera, his back straight and chin raised, displaying what he hoped was a portrait of solemn strength.

"The first of the machinists, Liam McCollum, has an eye toward the future because he *is* the future. As the only magi in the Order with both machinist and magi abilities, he has the strength to lead the Family through whatever dark days might come. Having studied magi history for years while curating the McCollum library, he is the foremost expert on where magi have erred in the past. And with McCollum blood, he has the pedigree of history. Liam has proven to me, without the shadow of a doubt, that he is the true leader of this Family."

Liam flushed under the praise. He wished he could deflect and downplay Jaxon's words, but he knew that would be counterproductive. Jaxon could nominate and endorse him, but that opinion alone wouldn't be enough for Liam to take up the mantle. The Family had a say in that. It was a tradition enforced in an attempt to keep Families from splintering under controversial rule.

"By magi tradition," Jaxon said, "you have two days to confirm my endorsement or move to a contest, at which time Liam McCollum will be named as the next grand mage of the McCollum Family, or he will be granted the opportunity to make his argument. Please think on what I have said and reach out to me personally with any questions. Until then, I leave you with the MacCallum Clan's own words—words that have defined this Family and will for years to come.

"*In ardua tendit.* He aims at difficult things."

"How is he doing?" Nyla asked.

"Who?" Allyn asked. "Liam?"

"Of course."

Allyn bit back a sarcastic comment, choosing not to anger the only woman who had given him any attention in months. They walked together through the Klausner Manor grounds. The trees and gardens were alive with vibrant colors of spring, the landscape looking more magical than any postcard he had ever seen.

"He's doing as well as possible, I guess," Allyn said. "It's hard to say, though. I think he's avoiding me."

"He's going to need you."

"He's going to need all of us."

"You know what I mean," Nyla said. "He trusts you. He respects you."

"I'll do what I can."

They walked in silence for a while, weaving in and out of forest trails, traversing the steep rocky ground until they came to a clearing with a view of the town below. Allyn threw an arm around Nyla and pulled her close.

"Look at that," he said. "Have you ever seen anything so beautiful?"

"You're really not very good at talking to women, are you?"

"You know what I meant. But I guess you're not too bad yourself. Not quite as colorful, though."

"Oh?" Nyla pulled away and began searching the ground

until she found some yellow and blue wildflowers. She slid them in her hair behind her ears. "How about now?"

"Better," Allyn said with a laugh. "But hold that pose for a second." He pulled his phone from his pocket and snapped a series of pictures. Nyla went along with it, posing differently for each one. Once they'd taken several, Allyn took a seat on a nearby rock and flipped through them.

"Wow," he said.

"What?" Nyla sat down beside him, attempting to look over his shoulder.

"These actually turned out pretty good."

"Why wouldn't they?"

"My sister's the artist, not me," Allyn said. "I'm not usually very good at this sort of thing."

"Well they are pictures of *me*, so it shouldn't be *that* hard."

"I guess I stepped into that one, didn't I?"

"Pretty much."

"I have to say," Allyn began. "You're... how do I say it?" He made a gesture with his hands as he searched for the correct words. "You're *different* today."

The smile Nyla had been wearing faltered slightly, and she looked away.

"I didn't mean it as a bad thing," Allyn said, instantly knowing he'd said something wrong.

"No," Nyla said. "It's not that..."

"If you don't want to talk about it, that's fine," Allyn said.

"No," Nyla said. "It's fine. It really is. You know about the echo, right? And about how Baylis and I..."

"Yeah."

"Well, when he died, it felt like part of my soul was ripped away. I changed when we developed the echo—we both did— and then I changed again after he was gone. Ever since then, I've been trying to figure out who I am."

Nyla's eyes welled up with tears, and Allyn wasn't quite sure what to do. Was it appropriate to console a woman when she was talking about the dead man who had been the love of her life?

"And it wasn't until last night that I realized I can't understand who I am without discovering who I've become. Does that make sense?" She didn't give him a chance to respond. "Of course it doesn't—it barely makes sense in my own head. The point is, Allyn, I like you. I'm comfortable around you. And I'm starting to figure out who I am, for the first time in a long time."

Okay, now you can pull her close.

Her body melted into his as he pulled her tight. "I like you too," he said, kissing her on the top of the head.

He didn't know how long they sat there. It could have been minutes, or it could have been hours. All he knew was that when the time to leave finally did come, it came too soon.

CHAPTER 14

"WELCOME BACK," ARCH MAGE WESTARRA said, looking over the gathered War Council. It was late in the afternoon, and the council had been assembled in the study Arch Mage Westarra had commandeered as his personal office. "I trust you enjoyed yourselves last night and celebrated our important victory."

The council members shared a series of smiles and stifled laughter, no doubt reliving the highlights of their wild night. Arch Mage Westarra, however, quickly dumped a bucket of cold water on their reverie.

"But it's time to get back to work. One victory does not win a war, and we need to be prepared for the Knights' counterattack."

Laid across the long table in the center of the room was a topographical diagram of the Schuster Manor. Allyn had helped the arch mage put it together after his walk with Nyla, so he found his eyes roaming around the room, surveying the other occupants. The entire War Council was present. Most looked as bad as Allyn had felt earlier in the day. Their eyes were baggy and bloodshot, hair rumpled, stomachs bloated, but it was their attitude that surprised Allyn. The room felt strangely like a high school math class, where everyone questioned why they were there in the first place.

"Allyn," Arch Mage Westarra said. "I understand you've had an opportunity to speak with the other squad leaders and deconstruct the battle. Would you mind walking us through it?"

"Of course, Your Grace." Allyn stood, a gesture that commanded the council's attention, and reached for the red and black markers at the table's center.

"As this council is aware, we didn't know where the attack would actually come. We thought there was a high probability it would come at the Schuster Manor, but we also identified two others, so we evacuated each of the three Families and laid a trap at each. For those of you who were not present at the Schuster Manor, our forces looked like this."

With the black marker, Allyn drew symbols of the magi forces around the map of the manor. "We broke the forces up into three main squads with a sub squad inside the manor itself. The remaining magi forces were located behind the manor—here—and here, in the gardens adjacent to it. The magi inside the manor acted as bait, offering up a small resistance, drawing the Knights in, while the rest of us formed a hidden wall blocking an escape through the rear. The last piece of the attack and the bulk of our force was here, located a quarter mile away. They were to be the hammer that would smash the Knights against our wall."

Allyn surveyed the table, waiting for questions. None came. And more than one had to stifle a yawn. He was telling them something they already knew, but it was important to lay a foundation for what would come next. They had to know where they'd succeeded, or more importantly, where they'd failed, and that was only possible when each of them had a clear understanding of how the cards had been laid on the table.

"The plan worked as well as expected," Allyn continued. "The Knights employed the same tactic they've used for other assaults, using their vehicles to block the entrance to the manor." He drew three red arrows indicating the BearCats' path and put an X where each had parked. "These two squads assaulted the front of the manor, taking the bait of the sub squad inside, while the third, led by the Knight Commander, hung back.

"The inferno mines worked amazingly well, taking out almost a full squad of Knights before the battle ever got underway. Without them, I'm not sure the victory would have been so overwhelming. It not only swayed the numbers in our favor but also made the Knights leery, giving our main force plenty of time to arrive. Once they did, things went as planned. Now, there are a couple important details to keep in mind, but before we move on, does anyone have any questions?"

Again, Allyn was greeted with silence. He took a deep breath. This next part was important.

"Okay, the first thing is the Knight Commander himself was at the scene of the battle, and thinking back to previous battles at the Ferdii Village and the Klausner Manor itself, this seems to be a common trend. The Knight Commander operates much like a field general, commanding from the front.

"Second, and more importantly, after the inferno mines eliminated a third of his squad and the battle went sideways, he took complete command, leading the remaining Knights into the manor himself. He micromanaged the battle, and this poses an obvious opportunity. If we can bait their forces into another trap and inflict heavy losses, we may force the

Knight Commander to take command and step into the open, providing ourselves with an opportunity to end the threat for good."

The council members seemed to perk up at this, their eyes showing a little light, their posture improving. Allyn nodded to the arch mage, telling him he was finished, and sat down.

"Thank you, Allyn," Arch Mage Westarra said. "This is important indeed. I hadn't realized the Knight Commander had been present at every battle."

"I hadn't, either, Your Grace," Allyn said. "But we've only had a handful, and two of those were at the Klausner Manor, when they stole the Blood Wand at the beginning of the war, and in the Knights' temporary base of operations—two places we'd expect the Knight Commander to be. This isn't something I think we could have seen before."

"Nevertheless," Arch Mage Westarra said, "that is no excuse." He cast a disappointed look around the table. "It's our job to see these patterns. The side that discovers the right pattern at the right time may very well win this war." He eyed each one of the members until they nodded or voiced their consent. "Good. So how do we get the Knight Commander to expose himself again?"

"In that, Your Grace," Allyn said, "there is another pattern. When the Knights first attacked the Klausner Manor and stole the Blood Wand, the Knight Commander was at their head."

"So he exposes himself when his forces take heavy losses or if there's an objective too important to trust another with achieving?"

"That was my interpretation too, Your Grace."

Wesley Green was the first member of the council other than Allyn and the arch mage to speak up. Like Jaxon, he appeared to be one of the few who didn't seem to be feeling any ill effects from the night before.

"We can inflict heavy losses from a well-orchestrated assault," Grand Mage Green said, "but what do we have that the Knight Commander would give up anything to get?"

"Me," Allyn said with a wry smile. "You have me. The Knight Commander and I have developed something of a rivalry. We met at the Ferdii Village. He failed to take me hostage during the assault on the Klausner Manor. I bested him during our counterassault, and then we nearly had each other during the last battle. It's grown personal for him. Dangle me, and I promise you he'll come running."

"That's all well and good," Wesley Green said. "But until the battle actually begins, we have no way of 'dangling' you. We're still operating in the dark—not knowing when or where the next battle will take place."

"True enough," Allyn said. "Though we correctly identified which Family would be attacked before, and I'm sure we can again."

"It still leaves too much to chance for my tastes," Wesley Green said.

"I don't disagree with you," Allyn said. "But I don't see a way around that unless we dictate the battle and go on the offensive like I originally suggested."

Grand Mage Green sat back in his chair, tapping his lips with his finger, his face contemplative. "There is logic to what he says."

"You'd have us abandon a winning strategy?" Grand Mage Ricci asked.

"We've won one battle," Grand Mage Green said. "Let's not get carried away by calling it a winning strategy. It was never meant to be permanent."

"Even so," Grand Mage Ricci said, "one doesn't abandon a successful tactic until the enemy shows they can defeat it."

Allyn pressed his lips together tightly, forcing himself into silence. It wasn't as difficult as it normally would have been, since Jaxon's father didn't appear any closer to giving in. Truth be told, it was nice to defer the arguments to someone else for a change.

"In most situations, I'd agree with you, Grand Mage," Wesley Green said. "But this isn't a typical opponent. The Knights have already proven themselves to be a formidable enemy who quickly adapts to new tactics. If we don't stay one step ahead of them, I fear they'll quickly retake control of this war."

Grand Mage Ricci surrendered his argument with Wesley Green, and Allyn got the impression he didn't truly feel as strongly about his opinions as he had let on. Allyn found himself watching the two grand mages intently. There was something between them, something he couldn't place. Were they in this together? Was Grand Mage Ricci building a straw man argument that Grand Mage Green could easily poke holes into, or was he simply challenging the man to make sure they had their asses covered?

Not for the first time, Allyn realized there was more going on than he'd originally seen. Each of the grand mages had his own agendas and wanted his personal stations to rise.

They're no better than bickering politicians.

"What would it take to organize an offensive?" Arch Mage Westarra asked.

Grand Mage Green gestured to Allyn to speak.

"Well," Allyn said. "As I mentioned before, Liam has already hacked the logbook we recovered from the catacombs, and we can use my sister to corroborate its authenticity with the prisoners being held at the magi capital."

"How long are we talking?" Arch Mage Westarra said.

"That depends, Your Grace," Allyn said. "How quickly can we have someone sent to Ukiah?"

Allyn left the council meeting elated, floating through the manor halls as if gravity itself couldn't bring him down. He had done it. Finally done it. The council had agreed to go on the offensive. They'd granted his wish. His only concern was timing.

The chances that Kendyl could be dispatched to Ukiah, interrogate the Rakkaran prisoners on the new information Liam had uncovered, and relay that information back to the council *before* the next battle was slim. No, it was nearly impossible. Still, as long as the next battle wasn't a rout with the magi on the losing side, he didn't see anything that would change the council's decision to move forward. He just had to convince Kendyl to go.

He found her outside the manor on a rocky outcropping with a handful of young magi. The outcropping overlooked a field of emerald-green grass that currently basked under the gold, crimson, and violet hues of the sunset. Had his mind not been entirely elsewhere, he might have taken a moment to admire its beauty, but he stumbled into Kendyl's painting class like a drunken uncle at Thanksgiving.

Kendyl had started the class a couple weeks before as something to do with her spare time, though *started* might have been the wrong word for it. The others had seen her painting in various locations around the manor, always complimenting her work. Then one day, as she began to set up her easel and ready her paints, two others joined her, setting up their own stations. When the newcomers hadn't been asked to leave, two more had joined her the following day, and that was when the questions had started.

"Something's off about mine. Can you take a look?"

"I want to get better—what would you recommend I work on?"

"How did you get so good?"

Kendyl just smiled, gracefully accepting praise and always offering words of encouragement to the struggling young artists. "Art is as much about craft as it is about talent," she would say. "If you want to improve, you need to work at it. Every day."

Since then, the class had only grown, so when Allyn stumbled into the lesson, he was greeted by a stern-faced Kendyl and eight surprised budding artists. She held up a finger, gesturing for him to wait. He nodded and took a seat on a fallen tree as Kendyl wrapped up her class. She spoke kindly, offering words of encouragement as the students gathered their supplies.

Once the last of them had disappeared, Allyn stood and approached his sister. "You're a natural," he said.

"I don't know about that," she said. "It *is* fun, though."

"Maybe you've found your calling."

"Oh God." Kendyl shuddered. "My life's turned into a cliché."

"How so?"

"How many of your art teachers were successful artists?"

"Not many," Allyn admitted.

"Exactly," Kendyl said. "Those who can't, teach."

"Fair point," Allyn said. "Though that's not entirely fair, and I wouldn't say any of *this* is a cliché." He gestured at their surroundings.

"That's true. We're doing things a little different, aren't we?"

"A little bit," Allyn said, laughing at the sheer understatement of the comment.

"So what's on your mind? It's not every day the legendary Allyn McCollum, member of the great magi War Council, visits us lesser folk."

"Someone's got jokes," Allyn said, giving her a sarcastic smile, though the words had come out more bitterly than he'd intended. Kendyl had struggled to find her place among the magi, and Allyn had hoped those feelings had subsided after she'd assisted in rescuing Liam and nearly recovering the Blood Wand. Since the war had begun, though, and Kendyl's role within it was marginalized, she'd become more bitter than she had been before.

"Oh, don't get all sensitive. I was just messing with you."

"Yeah," Allyn said. "I'm here because I need help."

Kendyl's playful expression faltered, her smile melting away. "With what?"

"The council has agreed to go on the offensive, but in order to do so, we need information. They want you to go to the magi capital and learn what you can from the prisoners we took from the church."

"I've already questioned them," Kendyl said. "Before Jaxon and the arch mage ever arrived. What else do you expect to get out of them?"

"That was before Liam cracked the logbook," Allyn said. "We think there's more information out there."

"Who thinks that?"

"Does it matter?"

"It might."

"I came up with the plan," Allyn said. "The council supports me."

"So *you're* asking me to go, not the council."

"I guess. Sure. What's the difference?"

"The difference is you can't even stomach asking me for help."

"That's not true."

"Of course it is," Kendyl said. "Name one time you've come to me and said, 'Kendyl, I need your help.'"

"Kendyl, I need your help."

"Don't be a smart ass."

"I'm not trying to be," Allyn said. "Kendyl, I'm sorry I haven't been there for you or been a better brother. But between Liam and the war... I just... I don't know what I'm doing. I'm making it up as I go along. I can't do this. I need your help. Please."

Kendyl studied him, her face hard, and for a moment Allyn thought she was going to say no.

"Please, Kendyl."

"Okay."

"Okay?"

"I'll do it," Kendyl said. "When do I leave?"

Allyn grinned. "Right now."

CHAPTER 15

UNABLE TO CONCENTRATE, LIAM SNAPPED HIS book shut. If the artifact hadn't been one of a kind, he might have thrown it across the room. He couldn't do that, though. He couldn't bring himself to treat the relic so recklessly. And even then, he reprimanded himself for being so careless with such a fragile tome. Running a gentle finger across its spine, he searched for any damage he might have caused. Satisfied he'd dodged a bullet, Liam rose from the oversized armchair and returned the book to its rightful place on the bookshelf.

He was in one of the various Klausner sitting rooms, this one on the second level of the manor and decorated with bold green wallpaper. Unlike in his old library at the McCollum Manor, or even his temporary one at the Hyland Estate, the Klausner Family preferred to use their ancient magi texts as decoration, as some form of prestige. It was as appalling as it was careless.

The various books, tomes, and framed pieces of parchment were already showing signs of damage from the sun, humidity, or simple mishandling. With so little of their history remaining, he would never understand how someone could have such complete disregard of the artifacts' true value and not go to greater lengths to preserve them. To do so wouldn't be *that* expensive or even take *that* much work.

He sighed and returned to his seat. Crossing his legs, he ran a finger over his lips. He'd come to the sitting room, hoping to do more research about the magi origin story or find something about the first era of the magi existence.

When was the first living magi recorded? What year? Where did they live? What were their abilities? Why weren't they more celebrated among the magi Families? After all, every culture and religion had their version of Adam and Eve. The fact that Liam couldn't find *anything* about the magi equivalent was more than unusual.

It was frustrating to have so many questions and so few answers, and to make matters worse, he was running out of places to search. As the hours and days crept by, he was becoming more and more certain that the only place he would find answers would be within the arch mage's private library inside the magi capital.

Of course, if he were truly being honest with himself, he would also know that his current questions, while important, were little more than a distraction from what was *really* on his mind.

His fingers moved from his lips, massaging his forehead as he closed his eyes. It had been two days since Jaxon had nominated him as grand mage. Two long, miserable, agonizing days. His stomach was a knot of anxiety, stress, excitement, and a million other conflicting emotions. He was exhausted but couldn't sleep, lonely but seeking isolation, a living, breathing, brooding contradiction.

You need a hobby, he told himself for the thousandth time. The problem was, he didn't know what to do. He'd thought about joining one of Kendyl's painting classes, but art was too personal, too exposing. He couldn't stomach the thought of laying himself bare like that. Even thinking about it made his skin clammy.

He took a deep breath, sucking in air slowly, and let it out in an equal measure. He repeated the process until the small panic attack subsided.

And you want to lead a Family.

"No," he whispered. Then louder, more firmly. "No." He wouldn't allow himself to spoil one of the greatest opportunities of his life. For years, he had succumbed to the expectation that because he couldn't wield he would never get the chance to lead the Family. Never live up to his father's legacy. But that reality had changed, even if his mind hadn't caught up yet.

I'm not the same boy. I've changed too. I'm still changing. I can do this.

And as simple as that, his nerves calmed, the knot in his stomach loosening. The only nerves that remained were the nerves of helplessness, of not knowing, and there was nothing he could do about that. Not until the Family made its decision.

Liam pushed himself out of the armchair, stretching his tired legs. He needed to get away, to get clear of the books, questions, and anxiety. Get some fresh mountain air. But as he stepped across the room, he heard the heavy footsteps of someone approaching. When he opened the sitting room door, he found Jaxon in the hall. The older magi froze midstep, clearly surprised by Liam opening the door.

"Everything all right?" Liam asked, seeing the tightness in Jaxon's face.

"They've made a decision."

They. Decision. There was only one thing that Jaxon could be talking about. The Family had decided whether they would ratify Jaxon's nomination, force Liam to go through a more stringent nomination process, or reject the proposition altogether. Liam swallowed, something made more difficult since all of the moisture in his mouth seemed to have evaporated.

"And?" Liam asked, his voice barely more than a whisper.

"And we need to gather the Family here to hear their response."

"Of course," Liam said. "Where?"

"Downstairs," Jaxon said. "I'll gather the rest and meet you in the sitting room."

"Okay," Liam said and moved down an adjoining hallway away from Jaxon.

"And, Liam?"

Liam stopped and turned to face his former mentor.

"Whatever happens, I want you to know I'm proud of you."

The simple words were too much. Liam's appreciation, coupled with the overwhelming wave of other emotions, settled in his chest, filling his eyes with tears. Unable to speak, Liam nodded and gave Jaxon a half smile that he hoped conveyed a fraction of the gratitude and respect he felt for the other man. Then he turned back down the hall and strode toward his destiny.

Once the rest of the Family was gathered in the Klausner sitting room, Jaxon pulled up the video conferencing screen and projected the image onto the back wall. It was meant to give them a better picture of the scene at the Hyland Estate, but what they gained in size, they lost in clarity. The pixelated image was difficult to make out, and the metallic voices coming through the line obscured anything Liam might have gleaned through tone of voice.

Attempting to remain calm, Liam stood at Jaxon's

shoulder, his hands clasped before him. Every member of the McCollum Family at the Klausner Manor was in the sitting room with him. Only Kendyl, who had left two days earlier for the magi capital, was missing, but like everyone in the room, she had already cast her vote. Part of him wished he could make the trip with her—it would bring him closer to the arch mage's personal library, after all—but like many things, that would have to wait.

Once Jaxon confirmed with the Family back in the Pacific Northwest that they could see and hear each other, the process began.

"Before we begin," Mason said, "let me just say that this is a highly unusual course of events."

The familiarity of Mason's stern demeanor brought a smirk to Liam's lips. The man was short, with an attitude and temper that made up for anything he lacked in height. The cropped image cut off the lower half of his body, hiding the metal prosthetic leg he liked to show off.

He'd lost the leg when members of Darian Hyland's rebellion had infiltrated the Family by posing as refugees seeking asylum. Mason was wounded in the fight and would have died if it hadn't been for Allyn and Nyla. Though they had saved his life, they had been unable to save his leg.

"By tradition," Mason continued, "the Family should be whole during deliberations. It is... *less than ideal* to be unable to consult with certain members without complication. Additionally, the grand mage in waiting should be present to hear the Family's pronouncement. But the Family understands the uniqueness of the situation and has amended its processes accordingly."

"Thank you," Jaxon said.

Liam thought he heard a little humor in Jaxon's voice, as well. He knew as well as Liam that Mason wouldn't let an opportunity to complain go unused. Though, in Mason's defense, he was correct. By magi traditions, the Family should have been gathered in the central hall of the manor, encircling Liam, a lone figure in the center of the circle like an isolated rock in the middle of the ocean. Instead, he stood beside Jaxon, with the rest of the Family behind him. He wasn't complaining, of course—it was far less lonely this way.

"I understand the Family has reached its conclusion?" Jaxon continued.

"We have," Mason said. "The Family has considered the merits of your nomination, weighing Liam McCollum's unique abilities with the changing landscape of the magi Order. The Family has debated concerns about his age, lack of experience, and emotional temperament. The Family has also reflected on the growth displayed over the last year, taking into account recent events as told by those of you fighting on the front. And the Family has concluded that Liam McCollum, son of Graeme McCollum, former Grand Mage of the McCollum Family, is worthy of the position he seeks."

Mason's stern expression broke into a smile, the Family behind him doing the same. A few of them even had to wipe tears from their cheeks. Chills went down Liam's spine, his breathing growing short.

"Liam McCollum."

"Yes." Liam straightened his back and lifted his chin confidently.

"Do you affirm that you are of stable mind and capable of navigating the duties of grand mage of this Family?"

"I do."

"Do you affirm that you will, to the best of your ability, preserve the culture and way of life of this Family and the magi Order?"

"I do."

"Do you affirm that you will protect and defend this Family and the magi Order from all of those who wish to seek its end?"

"I do."

"Do you, Liam McCollum, accept the mantle of Grand Mage of the McCollum Family?"

"I do."

"Then I, Mason McCollum, speaking with the authority of the McCollum Family, name you, Liam McCollum, Grand Mage of the McCollum Family."

The celebration was deafening, though Liam heard little of it. *I did it*, he thought, and in his mind's eye, he pictured his father smiling at him, sharing in the moment with him. Liam smiled back, giving himself permission to appreciate the moment, because he knew deep down that the real work was only beginning.

"Thank you for coming," Liam said, looking over the gathered group. "I know it's late and that you all have pressing matters. I won't keep you long, I promise."

Allyn, Nolan, and Leira joined him in his room. After the celebration, Liam had returned to his room, where he'd laughed, cried, and reflected on how far he'd come.

Just a year ago he had been a teenage magi scorned or ignored because of his inability to wield. Searching for a way to be useful, he had confined himself to the McCollum library, overseeing and preserving the deteriorating texts before their history was ripped away by the cruel hands of time.

A year later, he was a dual-born, able to wield both machinist and traditional magi abilities, and grand mage of the same Family who had all but disowned him. It was almost too much to take in, and he still expected to wake up in his library, having fallen asleep while transcribing an ancient diary or faded piece of parchment. But as long as this was the reality he knew, he would make the most of it.

"Mason was right," Liam continued, "when he said I'm young and that I don't have a lot of experience. I know that—it's not a secret—which is why I want you to be my inner circle. Each of you comes from a different background and will provide me with a unique perspective, so while I may not have all the answers, it's my hope that between all of you, *we* will."

"I can't commit to having all the answers, either," Nolan said. "But I owe you and this Family my life, so for as long as you seek my advice, I'm happy to give it."

Liam nodded and turned to Leira.

"You're all I have left, little brother." She smiled, but Liam saw little warmth in her eyes.

With everything that had happened, he hadn't given much thought to how his rise would affect her. Jaxon was leaving the Family; did that mean he was leaving her, too? Liam would have to talk to her about it later, though the prospect did little to excite him.

He returned her smile and gave her his thanks before turning to Allyn. "And you, Allyn? I owe so much to you already that I hate to ask for more. But what we've done, we've done together, and I don't want that to end."

"It won't," Allyn said. "We're in this together. I'll help in any way I can."

Liam let out a breath he hadn't realized he was holding. He hadn't expected any of them to say no, but it was his first real act as grand mage, and the irrational part of his brain said that the moment would set the precedent for his rule. If that were true, then he'd cleared his first hurdle.

"Thank you," Liam said. "Before I let you go, I feel like I'm in the dark about a few things. Allyn, what can you tell me about your sister's objective and the council's tactics for the next battle?"

"Do you want us to leave first?" Nolan asked.

"Leave?" Liam asked. "No. If you're to give me advice, then you need to know all the facts."

Nolan nodded. Liam turned back to Allyn and motioned for him to begin. Allyn told him of the prisoners and how Kendyl was to use her empath abilities to corroborate his discoveries from the logbook and how she likely wouldn't return in time to put together a more offensive strategy.

"What happens if there's another battle before she returns?"

"Then we'll use a tactic similar to what we used in the last battle," Allyn said.

"Do you think it'll work again?"

"I hope so," Allyn said with a shrug. "We're unfortunately limited in our options."

"I guess we'll just hope Kendyl is able to return before the next battle," Liam said. "Is there anything I can do to help?"

"With Kendyl?"

"With anything," Liam said. "I don't intend for this to be a one-way relationship."

The other three looked at each other then at him, shaking their heads.

"Okay then," Liam said. "Thank you for your time. We'll reconvene tomorrow, but until then, get some rest and let me know if anything comes up."

They offered their thanks and congratulations again before filing out of the room. Allyn brought up the rear, stopping in the doorway. He didn't look at Liam, but at the room itself.

"Something on your mind?" Liam asked.

"Yeah," Allyn said. "We're gonna need to get you a bigger room."

CHAPTER 16

THE NEXT ATTACK CAME TWO days after Liam's ascension and, as Allyn had feared it would, before Kendyl returned from the magi capital. Without the aid of additional information, the council hadn't implemented a new strategy and had instead stationed magi squads with the two Families Allyn had already identified as potential targets.

Allyn and a full squad of magi were hidden in a copse of trees on the edge of the forest of the Heilig Estate when he heard the unmistakable rumble of the Knights' BearCats.

"Contact!" Allyn said, demanding the attention of the fourteen others with him. "Alert the others and prepare to move."

He rushed to the edge of the forest, where he had a clear view of the driveway. The late-afternoon sun was all but hidden by the forest to the west, and nightfall only a short time away. Already, the impending battle had taken a new twist, and that left Allyn feeling more than a little nervous.

The Heilig Estate was half a mile from Allyn's position, hidden from view by the rolling terrain. The Family had been evacuated, but those who had wanted to fight remained and filled out the magi ranks. After the council's decisive victory, it seemed that Families were more willing to fight alongside them.

Allyn shrank back into the darkening forest as the first BearCat rumbled into view. Its headlights stood four feet off the ground, protected behind a menacing steel bumper.

"They're not even attempting to hide their coming," Nyla said at his shoulder.

Allyn turned to look at her. He hadn't heard her approach. "No, they're not."

"What does that mean?"

"I don't know." Allyn turned back to the driveway. Two more BearCats joined the first, creating a V formation. "But I don't like it."

He moved deeper into the forest, where his squad was already assembled.

"They're here," Allyn said. "Let's go."

Trusting his squad would follow without further order, Allyn jogged away, moving in a direction parallel to the driveway but staying under the cover of the trees. Ahead of him, the red and white marker lights of the BearCats crested a small rise and disappeared. The route itself would take him to the Heilig Estate, approaching from the west, and arriving after the battle had begun.

The timing and location were prearranged, of course, aimed at hitting the Knights where it hurt the most—the BearCats. If all went as planned, Allyn's team would not only destroy three valuable vehicles but prevent the Knights from fleeing as well.

They had only made it about halfway to the estate when they were met with the first sights and sounds of battle. Fireballs illuminated the purple skies, sailing toward the Knights who were already storming the estate. They used handheld battering rams, making quick order of the front entrance, then tossed in what looked like a full-sized dummy, no doubt hoping to spring any trap the magi had left for them.

The tactic worked. The inferno mines the magi had left behind detonated, spitting lances of fire and debris out the open door. Smoke billowed out of the doorway and shattered windows as the Knights advanced, guns trained on the estate's dark interior. The moment the line of soldiers was entirely inside, the magi sprang their next trap.

In nearly every other assault, the magi had fought tooth and nail to repel the Knights while suffering as little damage as possible—not just in lives, but also in property. Each of the other manors and estates had held historical and strategic significance. The Heilig Estate, however, had fallen into a state of disrepair. Foundational issues had rendered it nearly unlivable, and the Family, with aid from the Order, was preparing for a new build and a major renovation. Because of this, instead of attempting to draw the Knights away from the manor, they were drawing them in.

Still far from the estate, Allyn could see only quick flashes of light and shadows moving frantically inside as the bullets and fireballs flew. In another few minutes, it would be time for his squad to engage. He picked up their pace, hoping to be in position long enough to survey the scene more closely and allow the squad a chance to catch their breath. When they arrived, Allyn moved toward the edge of the forest, taking cover behind the overgrown ferns.

The BearCats had stopped in a different formation than before. Two were parked with their large hatches opened to the manor itself, noses pointed toward their retreat. A third, likely the one led by the Knight Commander himself, was parked twenty feet behind the others, on a small rise that offered a clear vantage of the battle. With the first two parked as they were, it seemed the Knights were interested in getting into the manor as quickly as possible and had already positioned themselves to make a quick getaway should the battle turn ugly.

The tension building in Allyn's gut and lower back loosened a bit. The Knights had shifted tactics, attacking as night approached and positioning their vehicles in a more optimal formation, but they hadn't abandoned their previous strategy altogether. The two sides were like a pair of fighters in a ring, throwing jabs and feints, more concerned with watching how their opponent responded than with landing a heavy blow. The magi had changed that dance a bit, but neither side, it seemed, was ready to commit in a full-scale attack.

But impressions were often far from the truth, and knowing better, Allyn felt a quiet confidence wash through his veins. The magi, he knew, were cocking back, ready to land the decisive blow.

Allyn turned and found his squad's eyes already trained on him. "You know what to do. Eliminate the BearCats, and we eliminate their escape. Three squads. A and B, you take the BearCats nearest the estate. We'll take the third."

Sedric is mine.

Nyla and Nolan, each in charge of their own squads, nodded and quickly ordered their magi to advance. Ready to move only if the Knight Commander showed himself, Allyn and his squad remained behind the tree line as the others streamed toward the BearCats.

The two squads quickly crossed the green landscape then took up positions alongside the BearCats. Working off a predetermined silent count, the two squads sprang into unified action, racing around the backs of the BearCats and up their lowered ramps.

Half a heartbeat went by. Then two. There was no gunfire. No magi attacks. Then to Allyn's horror, magi dove out of the nearest BearCat, scrambling, screaming, pushing to get away.

"No," he heard himself say. "No. Get out. Get away!"

But they couldn't hear him—and there was nothing he could do.

The first BearCat exploded, sending shrapnel and magi flying through the air. He had just long enough to turn his attention to the second BearCat, seeing Nyla with her back pressed against the vehicle's reinforced exterior.

"Move!" Allyn screamed again, terror and desperation amplifying his voice.

Recognition manifested on Nyla's face, and she looked in Allyn's direction, her shoulders slumping in helpless resignation.

The second BearCat erupted into a second ball of flames, consuming Nyla and the rest of the magi nearby. Metal groaned as the BearCat was lifted off its tires, the fireball sailing high into the air.

Allyn dashed toward the fallen magi, racing toward Nyla. He rushed past the dead and dying, eyes only for the slender body with silver hair lying facedown on the charred earth. He slid to a stop beside her crumpled body, kicking up ash and burnt grass.

"Nyla." He rolled her gently onto her back. Her pale skin was blackened and blistered where the fire had kissed her flesh. "Oh, Nyla. No. No."

He tried to brush her silver hair out of her face, but the strands broke free and fell to the ground as if they were bits of dried wheat. Her eyes looked up blankly at the darkening sky.

"No," he repeated, choking with emotion. "No."

He checked frantically for a pulse, but his fingers felt nothing and came away sticky with blood. He collapsed to the ground, his head falling on Nyla's chest, his sobs making it impossible to breathe. Nyla was gone. Dead. Taken from him.

Someone grabbed him by the shoulder, pulling him back. He shrugged it off and slapped the hand away again when they tried a second time. He couldn't leave her.

"Allyn!" The voice sounded vaguely familiar. "Allyn!"

The hands took him again, shoving him back forcefully. He found himself on his back, staring up at a cloudy sky bathed in the same reds and blacks as Nyla's burned skin. A face appeared in front of it, staring down at him.

"Allyn!" Nolan screamed, blood dripping from his face. "Come on!"

Allyn blinked, and the world rematerialized. A chorus of screams and shouts rose around him, but they weren't the same screams and shouts as before. Mixed in with the pain, there was fear.

Nolan pulled him to his feet, and that's when Allyn heard the unmistakable sounds of battle. They weren't coming from the manor, however. They were coming from beyond the trees where the driveway met with the road and the remainder of the magi force waited. The forces there had two purposes— attempt to wall the Knights in should they attempt to retreat, and prevent a second squad of Knights from taking the magi unaware.

The battle hadn't been raging long enough for the Knights to have attempted a retreat, and he could still hear the battle being waged inside the manor itself. This was something different. Something new.

The pieces clicked into place in Allyn's mind. The BearCats were bait. That meant they'd also known the magi would divide their forces and attempt to flank the Knights as they had before. If that was the case, then the new battle being fought near the road was a new squad of Knights arriving to turn the tide of the battle squarely in their favor.

As quickly as they had begun, the new sounds of battle disappeared, replaced by an ominous quiet. Either the magi had successfully held them back, or the Knights had broken through. Allyn knew which was more likely. A moment later, several more BearCats rumbled in the distance, growing louder with every heartbeat.

"Allyn," Nolan said. "We have to go. We can't stay here!"

Ignoring him, Allyn stepped past Nolan, walking toward the incoming BearCats.

"Allyn!"

Red coils of electricity snapped into existence, twisting menacingly around Allyn's arms. Crackling and hissing, they burned away the sleeves of his compression armor. In front of him, three more BearCats crested the rise. He held his arms out wide, making himself visible by throwing static charges into the air like sparks from a fire.

Shouts rose up behind him, but they were indiscernible over the din. Allyn ignored them. He had eyes for only one thing. Sedric. And he was sure the man was in one of those vehicles.

Allyn continued forward, a solitary figure standing against a tsunami of metal and weapons. The lead BearCat roared louder, pulling ahead of the rest.

Allyn smiled. He'd been seen. Sedric was coming for him.

He fueled the electricity with every ounce of grief and anger boiling inside him, willing the coils to burn hotter and pulse with more energy. It was a dangerous game. Burn it too hot, and he risked interrupting the electrical system of his heart and going into cardiac arrest. It didn't matter, though.

Nyla was dead. He was going to die too. He knew it. Planned on it. Whether the BearCats or his own grief killed him, his life was coming to an end.

Something akin to peace washed over him. No more battles. No more death. No more grief. No more guilt. No more nightmares. It would all be over soon.

Allyn hurled a pair of static charges at the charging BearCat, taunting its driver. They struck its nose, enveloping the vehicle in a tangle of electrical tendrils before disappearing without effect. He threw two more—both as ineffective as the first.

The BearCat bellowed louder. Allyn refused to move, keeping his arms outstretched at his sides, welcoming the sweet relief death would provide.

Suddenly, a fourth BearCat appeared, and before Allyn could understand what was happening, the new BearCat slammed into the lead vehicle, throwing it to the side and out of Allyn's path with an angry shriek of metal. The lead BearCat flipped and rolled, coming to a rest with its tires facing the sky.

The next BearCat in line clipped the new vehicle's rear, sending the new vehicle spinning viciously. It rocked back and forth, finally coming to a rest as the two remaining enemy BearCats continued toward the manor.

Allyn rushed toward the new vehicle, but before he arrived, the driver's door opened and Nolan, more bloodied than Allyn had last seen him, emerged. He jumped to the ground, favoring an arm.

"Nolan," Allyn said. "H-How?"

The other machinist didn't have an opportunity to answer before a hatch opened on the wrecked BearCat and a Knight wearing full tactical armor opened fire.

Bullets sparked off the reinforced exterior of Nolan's

vehicle as he and Allyn dove for cover. Allyn readied a pair of static charges and popped out from behind the BearCat, shooting the electrical discs at the opened hatch. The first missed, but the second took the Knight in the chest. The man stiffened then fell back inside the vehicle.

When no other Knights emerged, Allyn and Nolan advanced. Nolan threw open the driver's door and hurled an energy blast inside. Half a second later, the energy blast detonated, its muffled blast rocking the vehicle sideways. When Nolan opened the door again, he peered inside, ensuring his work was done. He nodded his confirmation.

Allyn wasn't satisfied, though.

"What are you doing?" Nolan asked as Allyn began to climb inside.

"Sedric was in here."

"He was?"

Allyn nodded. He was sure of it. Why else would it have raced ahead of the rest? Why else had it attempted to run him down? It was Allyn's turn to repay the favor.

The coppery smell of blood was thick inside the BearCat as Allyn crawled across the driver's seat. Bodies littered the main compartment behind the driver and passenger seats. None looked like they would even move again. Despite every instinct telling him not to, Allyn moved deeper into the BearCat, taking inventory of the faces of the fallen Knights. Sedric wasn't among them.

Allyn's first thought was that Sedric had somehow escaped, crawled through another hatch. But no, they would have seen him. They would have heard a hatch squeal open. Frustrated and disheartened, Allyn climbed back out of the vehicle.

"He in there?" Nolan asked.

Allyn shook his head and turned his attention back to

the manor. The other two BearCats had already arrived, and two full squads of Knights stormed forward, reinforcing the battle.

"Don't," Nolan said.

Allyn looked at the man, realizing he'd taken a step toward the manor.

"It's over," Nolan said. "We lost."

"We've still got people in there."

"The retreat has already been ordered. It's over, Allyn. We have to go."

"But..."

Allyn turned back to the manor and saw ten or so dark shapes running away from it toward the forest. A few more appeared behind them, but didn't pursue. Muzzle flashes popped, and three of the retreating shapes fell. Then more gunfire. Two more shadows dropped as the rest entered the relative safety of the forest.

Elsewhere more gunfire rattled, but it was like the last weak breath of a dying man. The end of a hard-fought life. A hard-fought battle. And like the dying man, the magi had lost.

"Come on." Nolan grabbed Allyn by the arm and dragged him toward the BearCat. "I've got an idea."

Nolan threw open the hatch and pushed Allyn inside then climbed inside himself, closing the hatch behind him.

"They were booby-trapped," Allyn said, strapping in.

"Yep."

"This one wasn't?"

"It was."

"Then how?"

Nolan looked at Allyn as he fired the vehicle up. "Canary."

"She intercepted the signal?"

"Who knows?" Nolan said, kicking the BearCat into gear. "But whatever she did, it worked."

The BearCat rumbled away from the battle, and soon, they were speeding down the driveway, quickly coming to where it intersected with the road. Smoldering magi vehicles littered the road, but in the wreckage, there was also life.

Allyn jumped out of the vehicle, rushing to the aid of the injured magi. They found three and quickly loaded them into the BearCat before racing back down the road.

"The rendezvous point is up here," Nolan said. But when they got there, there wasn't any magi anywhere.

Allyn peered into the dark forest from the seat of the BearCat, hoping to see some sign of life. "Where are they?"

"Maybe they're all—"

"No," Allyn interrupted, refusing to believe they were dead. He rummaged around his seat.

"What are you looking for?"

"A flashlight."

"Here." White balls of light illuminated in Nolan's palms.

"Perfect," Allyn said. "Come on."

Allyn and Nolan slid out of the BearCat and moved toward the tree line. Full night had fallen by now, and Nolan's energy blasts lit their way. Allyn wielded too, the coils of energy casting an eerie red glow across the scene.

Spotting sudden movement in the trees, Allyn readied a pair of static charges.

"Here!" a voice shouted. Male. Pained. "It's okay! It's Allyn and Nolan!"

A dozen or so figures emerged from the trees, and a flood of relief washed through Allyn. They'd found the surviving magi. He rushed forward, taking an injured magi by the arm, leading him to the BearCat.

"Where's the rest?" Nolan asked.

"This is it," someone responded. "This is everyone."

CHAPTER 17

ALLYN FROZE IN THE DOORWAY of his bedroom as his eyes fell upon his bed, where he and Nyla had slept the previous morning. The sheets and comforter were still rumpled, her pillow still turned lengthwise in the way she preferred, the room still smelling faintly of the lavender soap she used.

Had used.

He didn't know how long he stood there, but the longer he did, the more difficult it became to move. He was exhausted, *beyond* exhausted, and upon returning to the Klausner Manor, he'd been immediately ushered into the arch mage's private quarters with the rest of the War Council.

For an hour, they interrogated him about the battle. *What happened? Why didn't we see this coming? How did so many in your squad survive when the others did not?*

The questions came in hard and heavy, and Allyn answered them numbly, wishing more than anything that they would leave him alone. It was an irrational thought, and he knew it, but couldn't they see he wasn't in any condition to speak? Couldn't they see he was grieving? In shock? Suffering?

At some point, the questions ceased, and the other

members began speaking amongst themselves. They talked tactics, morale, and different paths forward, always coming back to ways to keep the various Families among the Order safe. Allyn paid attention to little of it. There was a vote, the decision was ratified, then messages were crafted and sent. Finally, very late into the night, Allyn had been able to return to his room.

Only now that he was there, he couldn't bring himself to crawl into that bed. He didn't understand it. He and Nyla were fond of each other and had found comfort in each other's arms, and though his feelings had grown in the previous days and weeks, he wasn't in love with her.

Was I?

Tearing his eyes away from the empty bed, he crossed the room and curled up in the armchair. Even then, the bed demanded his attention, forcing him to remember the woman who had slept with him in it. He felt the softness of her breath, the tenderness of her touch.

It was too much. He rose, turned the chair so that it faced the window, and crawled back in. Finally, with the bed out of sight, if not entirely out of mind, he was able to fall into a fitful, restless sleep.

At dawn, the early morning sunshine accosted him like a screwdriver to the temple. He groaned, blinked, and attempted to stretch his stiff body. For the briefest of moments, he forgot all about the day before. About the blood and carnage. About Nyla's death. About the council's decisions. But all too quickly, the memories came flooding back. With them came a surprising feeling. His mix of emotions from the night before had solidified into something much more useful.

Anger.

Still wearing his torn and bloody compression armor, Allyn stalked the Klausner Manor, searching for the arch mage. He found him in the formal dining room, enjoying a private breakfast of fresh fruit and oatmeal. His Elemental Guard flanked him and attempted to push Allyn back out of the room, but when Allyn started to make a scene, the arch mage quickly relented.

"You look terrible," Arch Mage Westarra said.

Allyn grunted his agreement, sitting down at the table across from the arch mage.

"Would you like something to eat?" Westarra asked. "I can have—"

"No." Allyn leaned forward, placing his hands on the table. "I need to talk to you about last night. I was... I wasn't in a good place and am having trouble remembering the details of the council's decision."

"Oh," Arch Mage Westarra said. "I see. Unfortunately, Allyn, I don't think this is a good time."

"I disagree."

Westarra leaned back in his seat, tapping his finger on the top of the table. He glanced at the guards behind him, nodding slightly as if taking comfort by their presence. "The problem is, Allyn, after yesterday's *setback*, the council has decided on a more conservative approach. As such, it's been decided your services are no longer required."

Allyn blinked. Surely he hadn't heard the magi leader correctly. "Are you... are you... *firing* me?"

Westarra gave him a tight smile—Allyn wasn't sure if it was meant to be a comforting gesture, or if the arch mage was attempting to hide his amusement. "I'm not familiar with the term," he said, "but if you're asking if we've relieved you of your council duties, then yes, you are correct."

"But..." Allyn searched for the words. "Why?"

"Why? *Why*?" He looked Allyn up and down, a sense of disgust radiating from him, and Allyn suddenly wished he had taken an extra minute to change. "Surely you don't have to ask that question."

"You're blaming me for yesterday?" Allyn couldn't believe what he was hearing. "That's bullshit, Your Grace. With all due respect, that's complete fucking bullshit."

"Well"—Arch Mage Westarra pushed his plate away—"I—"

"The entire council agreed on that plan," Allyn continued. "*You* agreed to it."

"Yes, but—"

"You're not going to pin this on me. You're not going to make me the scapegoat."

"Allyn," Arch Mage Westarra said calmly, "I am the arch mage. I will do whatever I deem necessary to keep this Order intact. If that includes making accountable those who are responsible, then I will. Please know that what I do is not done out of spite or malice, but for the good of the Order."

Arch Mage Westarra stood, dropping his napkin on his plate. His guards fell into step behind him as he moved toward the exit.

"This is bullshit!"

Westarra stiffened and turned from the doorway. Any semblance of warmth or compassion was completely absent from his face. He stepped toward Allyn, stopping only inches from his face. "You've been through a trying time," he said softly enough that only Allyn could hear. "And I'm willing to look past these lapses in decorum, but like you, my patience is wearing thin. I suggest you embrace the magi qualities you've learned and control your emotions. Failure to do so will result in severe consequences I'd rather avoid. Is that clear?"

Allyn glared at the arch mage defiantly.

"I said," Arch Mage Westarra said, raising his voice, "is that *clear*?"

"Yes." It was all Allyn could do to mutter the word.

Arch Mage Westarra raised an eyebrow, apparently unsatisfied with the response.

"Yes, Your Grace."

"Great." Flashing a smile that didn't extend to his eyes, Westarra turned then disappeared from the room.

Fuming, Allyn watched, and for the first time in he didn't know how long, he felt lost.

"Arch Mage Westarra did *what*?" Liam asked. "He can't do that!"

"He's the arch mage, Liam," Allyn said, as if that explained everything. "And I'm pretty sure the council voted on it after I left. Their decision is bullshit, but it's final."

"Wow." Liam rubbed a hand across his forehead and squeezed his eyes shut.

Allyn felt bad for his friend. After little more than two days on the job, he was already facing unexpected challenges. Allyn took a sip of his tea and watched as Liam paced back and forth in his room. Allyn had sought out the new McCollum Grand Mage after he'd been able to calm down.

"Do you want me to talk to him?" Liam asked.

"I'm not sure what good that would do," Allyn said. "I'm pretty sure I pissed him off, so it's probably best we give him some space for a little while."

Liam stopped and faced him. "What did you say?" There was a sense of dread in his voice.

"I'd rather not get into it."

"Allyn—"

"I know, Liam. I was pissed, okay? I screwed up." His tone bordered on disrespectful, which he instantly regretted. Being insolent on purpose was one thing, but to do it by accident was inexcusable—especially in the infancy of Liam's rule. Whatever happened during these first few weeks would set the precedent for Liam's reign, and Allyn wasn't about to damage the still-wet foundation. "I'm sorry... I've just got a lot on my mind."

Liam barked a sarcastic laugh.

"Getting kicked off the council was frustrating," Allyn continued. "Humiliating. But you know what the worst part of it is? I know what they're doing is wrong. Consolidating forces? Sure. I get it. But abandoning any chance of an offensive? That'll just delay the inevitable. It'll be a war of attrition, Liam, and we're not prepared to fight it."

"Not all hope is lost," Liam said. "Your sister should be back any day. She might have learned something that'll change their mind."

Allyn shook his head. "That'll be the day." But the idea did give him a flicker of hope.

Liam sat on the arm of one of the nearby armchairs, leveling a firm expression on Allyn. "Even if she doesn't," he said slowly, "I need to know... Can I count on you?"

"Count on me to what?"

"To fight. To follow the arch mage and the council's orders, whatever they are."

Allyn's first instinct was to be irritated that Liam would question him after everything he'd done, everything he'd sacrificed. But when the flash of annoyance didn't grow to anything more, Allyn realized he *didn't* feel as committed to the cause as he had. But that was crazy. He had fought countless battles for the Order—why would now be any different?

He chalked it up to the aftereffects of recent events, but even then, something didn't sit right. Something had changed—he just didn't know what.

"I..." Allyn paused. "I think so."

Liam drew his lips together in a line and folded his arms in front of his chest.

"I'm sorry." Allyn looked away, his face suddenly burning. "I wish I had a better answer."

"It's the truth," Liam said. "And it's even more important to tell it when it's difficult to do so."

It was a subtle dismissal, an invitation to cut the conversation short, and Allyn would have taken it if his legs hadn't felt like lead. The very thought of moving was exhausting, and even if he did find the strength to rise, where would he go? What would he do? Nyla was gone, Kendyl hadn't returned, and Jaxon was distracted by his father and the council. Liam was the only person Allyn had left, even if their relationship was changing.

"It's been a long couple days," Allyn said, his voice barely more than a whisper.

"I know," Liam sighed. "I still can't believe Nyla is gone."

Allyn took a sip from his small mug, hoping the warm fluid would wash away the lump in his throat. It didn't. "Do you remember when you asked me who was in my room after the celebration?"

"Yeah."

"It was her. It was Nyla."

"Oh," Liam said. "*Oh.*" His face flushing with color, he looked away, likely embarrassed by his own embarrassment.

"We were dancing, and... I don't know. It just felt *right*. I hadn't felt that close to someone in a long time."

Liam watched Allyn, his apprehension clearly displayed on his young face. Allyn knew he was putting him in an uncomfortable spot, talking about something that Liam had no experience with, but he had no one else. Besides, he wasn't looking for Liam's advice; he just needed to get the words out.

"I obviously didn't know about you two until now," Liam said. "But I had noticed a change in her as well. Whatever you felt, she felt too. It's the first time I'd seen her truly herself since..."

"Baylis."

"Yeah."

"Do you believe in God, Liam?"

He shifted uncomfortably, no doubt at the abruptness of the question.

"I only ask because I've never heard any of you talk about it. Never seen you practice any religious ceremonies or..."

"It's a complicated question," Liam said. "Magi and religion have had a very troubled history. But if you're asking if we believe in a higher power, then I think you'll find our beliefs aren't too much different from yours."

"I don't know what I believe," Allyn said. "My mother did, but I lost my faith after she died. I couldn't understand how the world would be a better place without her. How leaving two children orphaned could be part of God's plan. But there's something comforting about the idea. And maybe that's why I've never been able to turn my back on it completely. I need to believe there's something more. That I haven't seen my loved ones for the last time."

Liam remained quiet, the way he got when he was deep in thought.

"For Nyla's sake, I hope there is a God," Allyn said. "That would be the only good thing about this. She and Baylis would be together again."

Liam met Allyn's eyes. They were red and brimming with tears. Allyn looked at the floor and took another sip of tea. It was getting cold.

"Have you heard when there's going to be a funeral for the fallen?" Allyn asked.

"No," Liam said. "Not yet. It's still early and there's a lot of magi to... recover."

Recover. The magi prided themselves on never leaving their fallen behind, but in the most recent flight, it had been all they could do to save the living.

"When will that happen?"

"I haven't heard," Liam said. "It'll have to be soon, though."

"When you do, please let me know. I want to be there when... I want to help."

"Of course," Liam said then repeated softly. "Of course."

Arch Mage Westarra presided over the funeral the following day. Despite Allyn's desire to be among the recovery party, he'd been singled out and excluded, while nearly every other magi capable of wielding had been conscripted into service. The arch mage had given him a bullshit excuse, of course, something about it being easier if the architect of the strategy that had led to their deaths wasn't present.

He still chaffed at being singled out and had taken out more of his frustration on Liam than he'd intended to. For all his worth, Liam had remained calm and had even gone himself to ensure that their people were treated with the respect they deserved on their final journey back to the Klausner Manor.

If the matter hadn't been so disheartening, it would have been a day to marvel at. The sun was high in the clear, blue afternoon sky, not a cloud in sight, and fields of emerald green stretched for as far as they could see. Butterflies flew and bees buzzed, and the very air smelled of the sweet wildflowers that grew among the rolling grasslands.

Allyn stood near the back of the funeral gathering, beside Kendyl, Liam, and Nolan. Kendyl had returned the previous afternoon, and Allyn had spent the day bringing her up to speed on recent events and grilling her about what she'd discovered at the magi capital. Unfortunately, her trip to Ukiah seemed to have been a wasted effort. The captives there had provided no additional insight into Liam's discoveries.

Part of him had wanted to press Kendyl and understand in tremendous detail what questions she'd asked and how the prisoners had answered. He couldn't believe they had *nothing* new to add. When it came to it, though, he trusted her judgment and didn't have the energy to press any harder.

Instead he took solace in knowing that even if the battle hadn't taken a turn for the worst, they still wouldn't have been able to move forward as he'd originally planned. It seemed each of the winding paths of life led to this same place, and he didn't know why, but something about that made him feel better.

The service itself was short. The arch mage's decision to speak of the fallen as one sped up the process, but it lacked the deep, emotional resonance Allyn yearned for. When it came time to look upon the fallen for the final time, Allyn lingered beside Nyla's body, memorizing her fair features.

Leira had personally seen to preparing Nyla for this final moment, and she'd done a masterful job. Even having seen the aftermath of the explosion firsthand, Allyn could barely make out her injuries. She didn't appear to be sleeping— Allyn had seen too much death to make that mistake—but she did look peaceful. And as far as final memories went, it was better than he had ever expected to have, and more than he deserved.

Tears sliding down his cheeks, he leaned over her, longing

to cup her face and run his hand through her hair one last time. After a whispered goodbye, he left the proceedings, making her a final vow.

I will not let your death be in vain.

CHAPTER 18

SEDRIC'S KNIGHTS LED THE MAGI prisoners into the Patron's chamber like a pair of cattle dogs rounding up a group of stubborn stragglers. They prodded the magi with the barrels of their guns, barking orders, making examples out of those who attempted to resist. The magi's heads were covered with black cotton blindfolds, their hands and feet bound, and they moved with a sluggish gait that hinted at their having been drugged.

Not trusting that the magi wouldn't attempt to hurt the Patron, Sedric had ordered them sedated—nothing that would render them unconscious, just enough to slow their movements and inhibit their abilities to wield. He couldn't risk them lashing out. Not again.

The last time he'd brought his prisoners to the Patron had resulted in an unexpected fireball flying in his direction and a fresh bullet hole in the offender's forehead.

Any goodwill Sedric had gained with his ability to abduct the magi had quickly vanished, and the Patron still hadn't forgiven him. *As well he shouldn't. If one of my men had made such a terrible mistake, he might have found himself dead on the floor, too.*

The Patron wasn't as exacting as Sedric, though. He hadn't even informed Sedric's superiors of the mistake—something Sedric filed away for future use. For all his pretense, the Patron wasn't as ruthless as he liked to pretend, and Sedric wondered how much of the man's persona was an act.

The Patron waited in the center of his chamber, his arms crossed over his chest. It was night outside, and none of the lights inside the room had been turned on, leaving the Patron as little more than a shadow against the cityscape.

Sedric imagined the Patron wearing an expression nearly as sharp as his black suit and tie. The combination created an element of awe and what the Patron no doubt thought was a heightened sense of mystery. A successful businessman with a reputation for always finding a way to "yes," the Patron was ever the showman, even when his audience was a group of frightened men and women.

Sedric's Knights lined up the magi in the center of the room and forced them to their knees then ripped the black blindfolds from their heads, giving the magi their first glimpse of their new prison. They looked around the room, eyes squinting from the city lights pouring through the floor-to-ceiling windows. The room was identical to the one where the Patron's daughter rested, except this one was entirely empty—no medical equipment or machines or decoration of any kind. A deeper silence fell across the room when their eyes found the shadow of the Patron.

"I imagine you're wondering where you are and why you're here," the Patron began, his tone mild and somewhat consoling. "And while I obviously cannot tell you where you are, I can tell you that your purpose is a noble one. After all, I do not share the same... *disdain* for your people as the man standing behind you."

The four magi seated in front of Sedric looked over their shoulders nervously, their eyes widening with fear.

"What I am curious about," the Patron continued, "is what you're capable of. What your abilities are."

The Patron strode deeper into the room, leaving his place of shadow behind. The city lights didn't provide enough illumination to make out his specific features, but to Sedric's eyes, the Patron looked worse than ever. His face was gaunt, almost ghostly in the dim blue light, his eyes hollow.

We really are running out of time.

The thought brought him little comfort. The last group of prisoners hadn't netted a single cleric. For precisely that reason, three of the four prisoners he'd chosen were female.

He didn't have any hard evidence that suggested more women filled out the cleric ranks than men, but it made sense. Women were motherly, nurturing, and by their very nature, more empathetic and compassionate. Men, on the other hand, were selfish, violent creatures. Who would really expect an uncompassionate brute to sacrifice his well-being to treat another? Sedric almost laughed at the thought.

"Fortunately," the Patron said, "I don't have to pry the truth out of you. We have more *efficient* ways."

As if on cue, two men dressed in white lab coats stepped forward, each carrying a needle and syringe. The magi, surprised by their sudden appearance, fought against their binds, their imaginations no doubt scarier than what actually awaited them. Sedric waited patiently, allowing his Knights to restore order, and by the time the technicians made it to the magi, the Knights had wrestled them back under control.

Without waiting for further instruction, the technicians plunged their needles into the upper arms of the two nearest magi, and the syringes immediately began filling with blood. Once they were half full, the technicians removed the needles and pulled the blood-filled syringes free. From their lab coats, they removed separate vials filled with blue liquid, which they poured into the syringe before giving the mixture a quick shake. Sedric waited with bated breath. The Patron mimicked his expression, even leaning in as if to watch more closely.

When the two liquids were properly mixed, the technicians held the vials up for the Patron to see. Even in the dim light of the room, Sedric could see that the blue liquid had turned to a bright green.

"What does it mean?" Sedric asked, his voice little more than a whisper.

"It means," the Patron said, his face breaking into a smile, "we finally have a proper sample. You've done it, Sedric. You've held up your end of our bargain." He cast a weary eye at the two technicians. "It's time my team does the same."

The Patron dismissed the rest of the occupants with a flick of his wrist. The technicians fled, no doubt ready to begin work immediately, while the Knights yanked the magi to their feet and shoved them from the room. Sedric was alone with the Patron.

"What happens now?" Sedric asked.

"Now we see if funding your operation was worth the expense or not."

"What of my cause?"

"You mean what happens to the rest of the magi?" the Patron asked. "Give me forty-eight hours. If I have what I need, you're free to continue."

Sedric bit the insides of his cheeks to keep from smiling. The news was too great, though, and the smile split his face. In forty-eight hours, there would be no more conflicting agendas or contrary orders. In forty-eight hours, the extermination of the magi would begin in earnest.

CHAPTER 19

L IAM CIRCLED THE RAKKARAN BEARCAT that Allyn and Nolan had stolen during their flight from the Heilig Estate. The intimidating vehicle had a thick matte-black reinforced steel exterior and beefy, oversized mud-terrain tires. Mud covered it and the shattered LED lights that stretched across the top of the cab, but save for the twisted steel front bumper, the vehicle showed little signs of having been in a serious accident.

The inside was just as utilitarian in design, though each of the front seats were made of surprisingly thick leather— likely to make up for the rough ride from the stiff suspension and aggressive tires. Behind the front seats was a pair of benches that extended down the rear compartment. Beneath were small cubbies storing extra helmets, flak jackets, knee and elbow guards, and more. At the rearmost portion of the compartment was a pair of wall-mounted racks. They were empty now—the magi war council had removed the additional weapons, ammunition, and explosives.

Liam eyed the rear compartment, attempting to ignore the bloodstains the cleaners had missed or been unable to fully remove, before turning around in the driver's seat. He ran a hand along the steering wheel, imagining what it would be like to drive such a large vehicle, then pulled the key from his pocket and turned the ignition into the on position. Lights filled the cab and passenger compartment, and the dashboard dinged to indicate the door was still open.

Doing a quick check to make sure no one else was outside, Liam pulled the heavy door closed. Nobody had told him he *couldn't* inspect the vehicle, but nobody had said he could, either, and it was best to avoid any uncomfortable questions.

Taking in the interior of the vehicle, it was obvious that the Knights had valued strength over comfort, simplicity over technology—except in one place. Despite there being power to the system, the dash remained dark.

Liam traced his finger across the digital display and pushed the power button in the upper-righthand corner. The screen displayed a short loading message before coming to life. By the looks of it, the vehicle had access to satellite communications and GPS, as well as other hands-free features. Liam selected the GPS function then pulled his laptop from his bag, plugging it into the USB port on the dash. After a few quick commands, the two computers were linked.

On the vehicle's touchscreen, Liam toggled through the Favorite Destinations folder in the vehicle's GPS. Finding it empty, he muttered a quiet curse. The Knights may not have expected the magi to take possession of one of their vehicles, but they hadn't been careless enough to store their locational information in its onboard computer, either. At least not on purpose.

"Here we go," Liam said, punching in a few other commands. Almost immediately, data began flowing into the laptop. It wasn't readable in its current format, so Liam couldn't make sense of it, but as soon as the transfer was complete, he would build the necessary programs to decode it. Several minutes later, when the transfer process was complete, Liam unplugged the USB cable, snapped his laptop closed, and exited the vehicle.

Night had fallen over the manor, but its occupants were on edge. The council had set a wider perimeter guard, positioning magi in three layers that extended down the mountainside. If the Knights tried to attack, they wouldn't be able to do so without the magi having some level of warning. Of course, Liam doubted the Knights would attempt another attack on the manor. Not while they were still in possession of the Blood Wand. And not after they'd just handed the magi their largest defeat.

Liam nodded to the magi stationed outside the main doors and entered the manor, making straight for his room. Once inside, he closed the door behind him and got to work.

Before long, he had a working program that could decipher the GPS data, and not long after that, he found something useful.

He sat back in his seat and smiled. Allyn and Nolan had unwittingly provided the magi with two things of incredible value—hope, and something they could use to trace the Knights' location.

Now it was just a matter of deciding what to do with the information.

"What you're looking at," Liam said, "is the route the Knights' BearCat took to the Heilig Estate. Now, I've gone ahead and traced it back to its original location, which is... here." Liam toggled between windows, pulling up a street view of a nondescript two-story warehouse with a pair of oversized garage doors. If he'd passed it on the street any other day,

Liam wouldn't have thought twice about it, but looking at it now, it appeared to be every bit like a location the Knights would use.

"Wait..." Nolan held up a hand, looking confused. "Back up. What are we looking at again?"

Liam smiled. It was exactly the type of reaction he was hoping for. He'd never been an overly theatrical person—he'd never really had the chance—but something about giving a presentation brought it out of him.

Allyn, Nolan, and Leira had come as soon as he'd called. He had toyed with the idea of taking the information directly to Arch Mage Westarra, but he selfishly wanted to play an active role in deciding how it was used. Taking it to the arch mage was a surefire way to ensure he was left out of that process. Instead, he'd brought it to his inner circle first, thinking they might be able to come up with an alternative idea.

"I hacked into the GPS of the Rakkaran assault vehicle," Liam said, "and pulled a log of every trip it's taken in the last three months. This"—he gestured at the image projected onto the white wall of his room—"has been its most-frequented location."

"You can do that?" Nolan asked in disbelief. He turned to the others. "He can do that? How?"

"I stopped asking that question a long time ago," Allyn said.

"But what we're looking at is real?"

"Yes," Allyn said, not waiting for Liam to speak up. It was nice knowing Allyn had full confidence in him and his abilities, and it had allowed them to develop something of a shorthand in situations like this. Allyn gestured at the image of the warehouse. "What are we looking at? It doesn't look like a normal garage."

"I'm glad you asked," Liam said, "because I did a little digging. The warehouse is leased by an organization by the name of the Infinity Corporation, but when I looked into them, I couldn't find anything. They're a subsidiary of another organization, who I couldn't find anything on, either. The more I dug, the less I found."

"Definitely sounds like the Knights," Nolan said.

"Exactly," Liam said. "It'll take some time to untangle the corporate knot they're hiding behind, but it has to end somewhere. When we figure that out, we might finally be able to discover who's behind the Knights. Or at least who's funding them."

Allyn rose from his seat and stepped toward the image, getting a better view. "Where is it? Zurich?"

"Stuttgart."

"Germany?"

Liam nodded.

"That's where the arch mage believed the Knights were originally founded," Allyn said.

"Yep."

"And if they're storing their vehicles there, their base must be close."

"Now you understand why I wanted to talk to you about it," Liam said.

Allyn stroked his chin, his fingers tracing his lips. "Who else has seen this?"

"Nobody."

Allyn gave him a knowing look. It appeared he was thinking along the same lines Liam was.

"And what are we supposed to do with this information?" Leira asked.

Liam crossed the room and took a seat on the edge of his bed. *It really is cramped in here.*

"That's what I brought all of you together for," Liam said. "The way I see it, the moment we take this to the arch mage, we lose any control over how it's used. And since Allyn's been removed from the council, we won't even know *if* it's used."

"Wait," Leira said, her voice suddenly thick with concern. "Are you suggesting we *don't* take this to the council?"

"That's one possibility, yes."

"Why?" Leira scanned the room, no doubt looking for support. "The council was formed to defeat the Knights and ensure the safety of our people. Withholding information undermines their ability to do so. What good could possibly come from keeping this from them?"

Liam shared another look with Allyn before turning to his sister. "We have concerns with the council's strategy."

"Then take it up with them," Leira said, exasperated. "You're a grand mage now—bring it up with the Forum."

"We have," Liam said. "Maybe not since I rose to this station, but the council is well aware of our desire to shift strategies."

"Have you wondered if maybe they know best?"

"Of course."

"And?"

"And my concerns haven't diminished."

"So—what?" Leira said. "You go rogue?"

Liam prepared himself to respond, but Allyn beat him to it.

"Yes," he said. "If we have to."

The room went quiet, the tension palpable.

"The council has already decided that fighting a war is not in the Order's best interests," Allyn continued, unperturbed. "If we give this to them, they'll do nothing with it, and we'll lose the only legitimate lead we've had since this war began."

"The council has already ruled, though," Leira said. "What

you're talking about is *treason*." She turned to Liam. "Are you honestly thinking about this? Is this how you want to define your legacy?"

"Nobody has decided anything," Liam said. "Like I said before, I brought all of you together so we could decide what to do with it. Together."

"What's there to decide?" Leira asked. "We take it to the arch mage."

"Leira," Allyn said. "Listen—"

"No, you listen," she snapped, spinning on Allyn. "We *just* got this Family readmitted into the Forum. What you're talking about will not only guarantee that we're banished for good but that we'll be executed for our sedition. I will not let my Family be disgraced or my brother hung because of your personal vendetta against the magi leadership."

"Let's all calm down," Liam said. "Please."

"I can't do this." Leira stormed across the room.

"Leira," Liam said, filling his voice with every ounce of strength he could muster. "Sit down. Please."

She stopped and let out a frustrated breath, her eyes darting between Liam and Allyn.

"For me?" Liam added. "Please."

Leira leaned against the wall near the door, her body language still tight, as if she might rush out at any moment.

"Thank you." Liam turned back to Allyn. "She makes a good point. Acting against the council's wishes isn't something we can risk. I don't like it any more than you, but we're going to have to put our faith in the council's decisions."

Allyn opened his mouth to speak, but Liam cut him off.

"This is my information to give," he said. "And while I appreciate your counsel, it's also my decision to make." He stood and took a deep breath. "I'll think on it some more and let you know of my decision tomorrow."

Liam nodded his dismissal, and his counselors made their way out. Leira was first, though she seemed much less agitated now that she thought he wasn't disobeying the council's wishes.

"Allyn," Liam said. "Please hold up a second."

Allyn stopped and eyed Liam from the doorway.

"Close the door."

Allyn complied and stepped back into the room.

"My sister is right. I hope you can see that. She only wants to protect her Family."

"If you say so," Allyn said.

"Blatantly disregarding the council's judgment sets a dangerous precedent, and it's not something I'm willing to do."

"I understand."

"*But*," Liam said, hitting the word hard, "nothing is stopping someone from discovering the information on their own. The data is in the vehicle *you* drove, after all. If someone were to learn of the Rakkarran garage and investigate to decide whether it was worthy of the council's attention, that wouldn't be treason. It would be allowing the council to focus on the matters at hand, not chasing whispers on the wind."

Liam watched Allyn, looking for a hint that his words were understood.

"If someone were to investigate," Allyn said slowly, "they wouldn't be able to do so alone. They'd need a team."

"True," Liam said. "Fortunately, the arch mage has requested that all able Families reinforce the Order numbers with additional magi. Someone could pick up the McCollum contingent and investigate the location before returning to the manor."

"Yeah," Allyn said, nodding. "Someone could do that."

"Before that person made up their mind," Liam said. "I'd want to make myself perfectly clear and ensure that they understood that if something went sideways, I would deny any involvement. This would be an unsanctioned investigation, and the person leading it would bear all responsibility for its results."

"That person wouldn't accept failure, then, would they?"

"I suppose not."

Liam pulled a slip of paper from his pocket and handed it to Allyn. "The McCollum reinforcements will be here tomorrow morning. That is their flight information. And that"—he pointed at the German address written at the top of the itinerary—"I'm not sure what that is."

"I don't, either," Allyn said wryly. "I guess I'll have to look into it."

"I guess so," Liam said. "Good luck, Allyn."

CHAPTER 20

ALLYN STOOD WITH A MASS of valets, chauffeurs, and anxiously waiting family and friends, watching for the McCollum contingent. Midmorning sunlight streamed through a large wall of windows, lighting the interior of the airport in a welcoming hue. Stifling a yawn—he'd had to leave before sunrise—he thought back on his own trip to the same airport only a couple months before. The irony of the similarities was not unnoticed by him.

As before, he was about to embark on a mission that was equal parts dangerous and secretive. Only before, they had accepted the terms outlined by Arch Mage Westarra himself to get the Family reinstated in the Forum; now they were embarking on a mission against the same man's wishes. If they were caught, all of their previous work would be undone in an instant, and the conspirators, including Allyn and Liam, would be banished—or worse.

We cannot fail.

Allyn spotted Mason before he noticed anyone else. The hard-faced magi walked with a slight hitch, no doubt a byproduct of his prosthetic leg. Made of carbon fiber, the prosthetic blade was black in color and of a similar design as those used by athletes in the Paralympics. It wasn't ideal for normal everyday use, but Mason had grown used to its flexibility, and besides, there was nothing normal about their general day-to-day.

Mason saw Allyn, nodded, then waved at the rest of the group behind him, making for their driver.

"Welcome to Zurich," Allyn said as he approached. "How was the flight?"

"Happy to be on the ground," Mason said, scratching at his prosthesis absently.

"I bet," Allyn said. "It's a long flight."

"That it is."

"This everyone?" Allyn asked, looking over the group. Behind Mason were Rory, Topher, Andrew, and Charlotte.

"It is."

"Let's go then."

Allyn led them through the airport and back to the car, where Nolan was waiting.

Mason looked at the former FBI agent, his face disapproving. "I wasn't aware anyone would be joining us."

It took Allyn a moment to realize Mason still distrusted the man. Allyn couldn't blame him, exactly. The last time Mason had seen the man was when he'd still been one of the lead FBI agents investigating the death of several police officers who had died by Lukas's hand. That investigation had brought the police, and Nolan in particular, to the magi's doorstep. Mason hadn't been through what Allyn and Nolan had been through, hadn't seen him in action or fought alongside him.

"There's been a slight change of plans," Allyn said.

"Oh?"

Allyn looked around the parking lot. Various families and loved ones climbed out of vehicles, grabbing luggage and saying tearful goodbyes. "Get in the car," he said, "and we can talk about it."

Once inside, Allyn brought the McCollum magi up to speed, covering recent events, battles, and the council's decision to adopt a more conservative strategy. He also told them of the information Liam had discovered and explained how it offered a unique opportunity they couldn't afford *not* to explore.

"Make no mistake," Allyn said. "If we do this, we do it alone. No other help is coming."

"This is Grand Mage McCollum's wish?" Mason asked.

"It is," Allyn said carefully. "Though if we're caught, he'll deny all knowledge of our actions."

Mason glanced at the magi sitting with him, looking for approval. All four of them nodded.

"We know nothing of Forum politics and know only what you have told us," Mason said. "I trust Liam knows what he's doing, and if he believes this is our best course, then who are we to argue with him? Let's see what he's found."

Stuttgart was two and a half hours north of Zurich, making it early afternoon by the time they arrived. Using the SUV's GPS, Allyn drove to an industrial part of the city, rife with manufacturing plants, warehouses, and storage facilities. He spotted the warehouse before the GPS announced they'd arrived, recognizing it from the Google Street View that Liam had pulled up the night before.

In the light of midday, the warehouse was even more nondescript, offering little indication of what waited inside. The windows were dark, the building silent, the two garage doors and metal man-door closed. Allyn drove slowly past the building, one eye surveying the garage, the other on the road, so they didn't hit any of the semitrucks or forklifts cruising down the manufacturing lanes.

Allyn parked kitty-corner to the warehouse and shut off the car. Workers wearing yellow-and-orange safety vests came and went from other buildings, taking lunch and smoke breaks. More than one gave them a questioning look, no doubt wondering what a black SUV with blacked-out windows was doing in the manufacturing district.

"We should move," Nolan said.

Allyn agreed and moved the vehicle to a street several blocks over with less foot traffic, parking beside a group of service trucks. "Wait here," he said. "I've got an idea."

He stepped from the vehicle, scanning his surroundings, then seeing that the coast was clear, he began inspecting the beds of nearby tucks. He quickly found what he was looking for and returned to the SUV, carrying hard hats and safety vests.

"Put these on," Allyn said.

Once the team had their new equipment on, Allyn ordered them out, and they proceeded toward the warehouse on foot.

"Nolan and Rory, with me," Allyn said once the warehouse came into view. "Mason, you take Topher, Andrew, and Charlotte. We'll take the far alley; you take the nearer one. We'll meet at the back."

"What are we looking for?" Mason asked.

"Anything that stands out," Allyn said. "And a way in. Come on."

Allyn led them in a slow walk across the street, keeping the brim of the hard hat low to shield his face. They needed to avoid being stopped, but he was also concerned about surveillance outside the warehouse. The element of surprise was their greatest advantage. If any of them were seen, the

Knights would likely abandon the garage, leaving the magi grasping at ghosts again.

As they neared the closest alley, Allyn pointed and said something he thought a surveyor might say. Mason and his sub squad moved down the narrow alley, while Allyn led Nolan and Rory to the next.

Bits of paper and cigarette butts littered the pavement, pockmarked with pools of oily water. There were no windows or doors in the building, save for an emergency exit accessible only by the fire escape. Unfortunately, the ladder to the fire escape was out of reach for even Nolan.

"We could lift someone up," Nolan said. "Maybe two. And they open the door for the rest of us."

"Let's talk to Mason first," Allyn said, "and see what he found."

The other squad leader was already at the back of the warehouse by the time they arrived.

"Anything?" Allyn asked.

"Yeah," Mason said. "There's another door on the side of the warehouse."

"Locked?"

"Yes," Mason said. "But that won't be an issue." Allyn gave him a questioning look that Mason seemed to ignore. "I can take care of the lock, but I can't do anything about an alarm."

"That's not going to do us a lot of good then," Nolan said.

"These places are meant to be mobile and easily left behind," Allyn said. "Do you think they would really take the time to install an alarm system?"

"It probably comes with the building," Nolan said. "This is when it would be nice to have Canary."

"I know," Allyn said. "But we had to keep the group small. I had to talk Liam into letting you come as it is."

"Thanks for that," Nolan said sarcastically. "So what do we do?"

"We have to see what's inside," Allyn said. "We're going to have to risk it. Show us the door, Mason."

Mason quickly led them to the door on the other side of the building. "You sure about this?"

Allyn took a deep breath. "Yes. Do it."

Mason nodded and began to wield. The polished aluminum knob turned a milky-white color, encrusted in a thin layer of ice. Into the keyhole itself, Mason delicately projected more thin shards of ice.

"You're picking the lock with ice?" Allyn asked in disbelief.

Mason ignored him, continuing about his work. A few heartbeats later, Mason reinforced the ice and, in one motion, twisted the handle. To Allyn's surprise, the ice shards held, and the door opened.

Allyn's breath caught in his throat as he waited for the sound of the alarm. One heartbeat. He didn't hear anything. Two heartbeats. Still nothing. Allyn turned to Nolan. "We good?"

"I think so," Nolan whispered, as if afraid that speaking too loudly would set off an alarm that opening the door hadn't. He held out a hand before him, gesturing toward the open door. "Be my guest."

The inside of the warehouse was dark. Dust hung in the stale air, glowing in the dim light and giving the environment an eerie quality. Tucked between concrete beams and parked near the center of the space were five BearCats.

This is it. We did it.

Allyn shed his reflective safety vest and hardhat, tossing them beside the door, and ordered the rest to do the same. Once his squad had removed their disguises, he stepped inside, his shuffling footsteps echoing throughout the vast space. Nolan and Mason followed him, the rest trailing closely behind. The door squeaked on a dry hinge as Rory closed it. He looked at Allyn, offering a silent apology. Thankfully, the warehouse seemed to be otherwise empty.

"Spread out," Allyn said. "Take pictures of anything you think is important, but don't disturb anything. The Knights can't know we were here."

Allyn made for the BearCats near the center of the warehouse. Just as the one he and Nolan had stolen from the Heilig Estate, these were matte black and covered in mud— the same vehicles from the assault.

The doors were unlocked, keys still in the ignition. He briefly considered stealing them and taking them back to the Klausner Manor or hiding them somewhere else, but as he'd said before, the Knights couldn't know the magi had found the warehouse. They needed to find the headquarters. Beyond that, Allyn had no idea how many similar facilities the Knights utilized. If the warehouse was one of many, then they would have given up their greatest advantage for nothing.

Each BearCat's cab was empty, save for mud and gravel on the floorboards. The rears, however, were stocked with guns, ammunition magazines, and explosives. Allyn's gut twisted at the sight of the explosives. He wondered if they were the same kind that had killed Nyla.

After finding nothing in three of the BearCats, Allyn gave up his search and sought out Nolan at the back of the compound, where a computer with dual monitors sat on a wood desk. Compared with the rest of the warehouse, it looked strangely out of place.

"What is it?" Allyn asked.

"I don't know," Nolan admitted. "I was thinking about turning it on to find out."

"Do it," Allyn said. "Let me know what you find."

"Will do."

Allyn went to each of the magi to see what they'd discovered. By the time he made it to Mason, he was growing discouraged.

"There has to be *something* here," Allyn said.

"They don't look like that kind of outfit," Mason said. "If this is only a staging post like you think it is, what did you expect to find?"

He didn't have an answer but was too irritated to admit it.

"Allyn," Nolan said from the computer station.

"Gather the squad," Allyn said to Mason. "We're leaving in two minutes."

"What do we do then?"

"I'm working on that," Allyn said. "But I'll sit in the car and stake this place out before we leave with nothing."

Nolan had his arms crossed and a frustrated expression plastered on his face when Allyn returned.

"What's up?" Allyn asked.

"That." Nolan pointed at the first computer monitor. It was asking for a password. "We're really unequipped for this, Allyn. I know you want answers, but maybe we should come back with the proper people. I'm sure Liam could crack this in seconds."

"Yeah..."

"But," Nolan said, obviously hearing the hesitation in Allyn's voice, "you don't want to leave."

Allyn frowned and shook his head.

"Well I'm sorry to break it to you, but—" Nolan's eyes suddenly darted past the computer monitors toward the front of the building.

Allyn saw the human-shaped shadows in the garage door windows before heard the muffled sound of voices. Three in all, they'd stopped outside the warehouse. The doorknob jiggled as one of them inserted the key and unlocked the door.

The Knights had arrived.

CHAPTER 21

"*IDE*!" Allyn whispered sharply.

The magi quickly ducked behind crates, boxes, and anything else that would provide a modicum of cover. Rory, caught in the middle of the warehouse, rushed toward the BearCats and dove into the nearest cab just as the warehouse door opened. The three Knights lingered outside just long enough for Allyn to duck behind the computer station. Nolan did the same, but not before he turned off the computer monitor.

"Good thinking," Allyn whispered.

Nolan nodded, held a finger to his lips, then positioned himself so he could see around the corner of the desk. Allyn mimicked his movement, sliding to the edge of the station so that he could see the door.

The Knights stepped into the warehouse slowly, their eyes alert, scanning the area. Dressed only in black fatigues, they were without their normal tactical gear and helmets, but all were armed with pistols.

Allyn and Nolan glanced at each other, eyes wide.

"They know we're here," Nolan mouthed.

The Knights fanned out, two moving to the opposite

corners of the warehouse, while the third remained in the center.

"Looks empty," one said. He was shaved bald and broader in the chest and stomach than the rest. More jarring, he spoke in unaccented English.

"Shhh!" snapped the middle Knight, clearly their leader. He was taller than the rest, with spiky bleached hair and a square face made more intimidating by a scar that ran diagonally from his left eyebrow to his right cheek.

"Come on, Nikolai," the first Knight said. "There's no one here. The door was locked."

"Silence!" Nikolai snapped. He turned from the other Knight, raising his gun and starting toward the BearCats. He motioned for the others to start a similar search down the edges of the room.

Allyn quickly estimated the probability of their entire force remaining undiscovered. The odds weren't good—especially considering the Knights had shown up *expecting* to find something.

There was a silent alarm, he realized.

He surveyed the room with fresh eyes, looking past the armed men walking in his direction, and took note of the equipment. Of the weapons. Allyn was no firearms expert, but he was willing to bet the assault rifles, grenade launchers, and other explosives hadn't been purchased legally.

The beginnings of an idea began to take hold. But first, they had to get out of the warehouse unseen.

The Knights were a quarter of the way through the warehouse now and had already passed Andrew and Topher, who had hidden inside a stack of shipping crates. When the Knights passed, Topher rose, completely revealing himself. Allyn's breath caught in his throat.

If even one of the Knights turns around...

Topher moved silently across the warehouse, disappearing behind the BearCats just as Nikolai whipped around, his gun trained on the space where Topher had just been. Nikolai paused, his eyes darting from wall to wall, corner to corner, then dropped onto his haunches, peering under the BearCats. He remained still for several moments, waiting, searching. When he finally stood again, he returned to his original course, though he was clearly more on edge, his movements sharp.

Having seen Nikolai's jumpiness, the other two Knights began to search more earnestly, and Allyn watched in horror as they neared Mason's place of hiding. There was no way they would miss him. He'd found cover in a shadowed alcove between what looked like large munitions boxes.

As the Knight approached, Mason seemed to come to the same conclusion, and Allyn made out a lance of ice forming in his hand. Allyn prepared to wield too, flexing and unflexing his hands with nervous anticipation.

Mason shifted his position, preparing to spring his attack, but before he could, movement caught his eye. Topher reappeared from behind the BearCat, slowly making his way toward the front of the warehouse.

What's he doing? Is he running?

Topher fumbled with the doorknob behind his back, his eyes focused on the Knights. His body grew rigid as his hand found it, and after a single sharp breath, he shoved open the door, allowing it to crash against the front of the warehouse.

The Knights whipped around, seeing Topher in the open doorway. Daylight poured in behind the magi, making his features difficult to discern. Nothing to trace them back to who he really was. What he *really* was.

Unless they catch him.

Topher apparently had other plans. With a smile, he launched himself outside, sprinting away from the warehouse.

"Stop him!" Nikolai shouted, not waiting for his fellow Knights to respond before he broke off in pursuit. The remaining Knights followed their commander, disappearing out of the compound a moment later.

With the Knights gone, Allyn stepped out from behind the computer terminal. He couldn't believe their luck. *No, not luck,* he decided. Topher had made it possible. Without him... Allyn didn't want to think about it. He quickly led the magi out the side door back into the alley.

"Make sure you lock it," Nolan said to Mason as the other magi was about to close the door behind them.

"Good thinking," Mason said then locked the door before pulling it closed.

"We need to find Topher," Allyn said.

"He'll be fine," Mason said.

"But—"

"I've known the kid since before he could wield," Mason said. "He'll be fine. And once he loses those bastards, he'll come looking for us in the only place he knows where."

"The car," Allyn said.

"The car," Mason agreed. "Let's go. We need to be there when he arrives; otherwise, he might come looking for *us.*"

They emerged from the alley as calmly as possible, finding the main street quiet, with no sign of Topher or the Knights except for a black BMW parked in front of the warehouse. Allyn broke away from the group, approaching the car.

"What are you doing?" Nolan hissed. "Allyn!"

Ignoring Nolan, Allyn pulled his phone from his pocket to take a picture of the license plate then another of the VIN. Satisfied he'd captured both, he crossed the street, returning to the group who hadn't stopped to wait for him.

"What the hell was that about?" Nolan asked.

"We're grasping at straws, Nolan. Something as simple as a license plate or VIN might be enough to unravel this mystery."

"Or get us all killed," Nolan said sarcastically.

"Or that," Allyn agreed. *But it's worth the risk.*

They made it back to the SUV without incident and without sight of Topher or the Knights.

Back in the driver's seat, Allyn started the arduous process of waiting for Topher to return. He thought about texting Liam and telling him that he'd been right about the warehouse. But that would link Liam to the operation, erasing any plausible deniability. No, Allyn wouldn't write Liam until he had something of note to tell him.

Topher appeared a short time later. His face was flushed and he breathed heavily, but he was uninjured.

"Were you followed?" Mason asked once Topher had climbed into the vehicle.

"No," Topher said between breaths. "I... lost... them."

"Where?" Allyn asked.

"Few blocks over. Hid and made sure they didn't follow me. Last I saw, they were returning to the warehouse."

"Good work," Allyn said. "And thank you. You saved our asses back there."

"Just doing what I could." Topher's beaming expression was at odds with his nonchalant response.

Allyn fired up the SUV and turned back onto the road, keeping his speed down and scanning the road for the Knights.

"Where are you going?" Nolan asked.

"Back to the warehouse."

"Back to the... *what?*"

"The warehouse is compromised, Nolan. Sedric will know.

By this time tomorrow, the warehouse will be empty, and all we'll have is a couple of pictures of a license plate and VIN numbers."

"Which is more than we had before," Nolan said.

"It's not enough."

"So what are you going to do?" Mason asked.

"I'm going to follow them," Allyn said. "They came here expecting to find someone, and that means someone sent them. We're going to find out who."

Allyn heard no further complaints and returned to the same corner they'd parked at when they'd originally arrived. The Knights' BMW was still parked in front of the warehouse, though a pair of shadows now occupied the front seats, and the car was running.

"Is the driver on the phone?" Nolan asked.

"Looks like it," Allyn said.

"We were *definitely* undermanned for this," Nolan said, no doubt thinking about how Canary could have helped them again.

"Quiet," Allyn said, though silently agreeing with his friend.

"They're moving!" Mason said. "Down!"

Allyn and Nolan ducked behind the dash as the BMW moved toward them.

"Let me know when they've passed," Allyn said.

"They're gone," Mason said.

Allyn sat up and watched in the rearview mirror as the black BMW turned down a side street. With it out of view, Allyn pulled a U-turn and sped down the street in pursuit. Turning onto the same side street the BMW and turned down, he spotted the black car a block and a half ahead.

"Slow down," Nolan said. "Keep your distance."

Allyn wanted to snap at him, wanted to say that he knew

what he was doing, but quickly bit his tongue. As a former FBI agent, Nolan had much more experience at this type of thing than Allyn did. So he kept his distance, attempting to keep at least two or three blocks between them as they cruised out of the industrial district.

"They're getting onto the highway," Nolan said. "Once you merge with traffic, keep at least three or four cars between us and stay in the right lane as much as possible. We sit higher than they do, which is good. We should be able to keep eyes on them."

"Okay."

Allyn merged with traffic and did as advised, remaining in the right lane several cars behind the Knights. Several minutes went by—ten, fifteen, then twenty—and the Knights' direction became clearer.

"They're leaving the city," Nolan said.

"For where?" Mason asked.

"We're about to find out," Allyn said.

The highway went from three lanes of directional traffic down to two as Stuttgart disappeared behind them then eventually became one as small towns began to dot the German countryside.

"Something's not right," Nolan said. "They arrived too quickly. There's no way they drove this far."

"Maybe they're not going back to where they were before."

"Or they know we're tailing them," Mason suggested.

"Doubtful," Nolan said.

Allyn hoped the man was right. The same thought had been creeping into the back of his mind, especially since the road had narrowed and the traffic thinned. There weren't as many places to hide as before. Nolan had told him to slow down again, opening up the space between them to a couple hundred feet, but if the Knights were being vigilant and looking for a tail, they would have easily spotted the magi vehicle. Allyn had no intentions or turning back, though. He was committed to seeing his plan through.

Minutes turned into hours, and steeper hills and thick forests replaced the grasslands as the sun began to dip on the horizon.

"I think I know where we're going," Nolan said suddenly.

"You do?" Allyn asked. "How?"

Nolan peered out the windows as if the beech trees held answers. "I've been watching the signs. We're west of Berlin, maybe northwest." He gestured to his phone. "There's an old military training area hidden in the forest out here."

"Old military training ground?" Allyn asked.

"Yeah," Nolan said. "Apparently, it was owned by the Soviet Union until the early nineties. It's huge, Allyn. Damn near a city. And there's nothing nearby. No other towns for at least twenty miles."

"Who owns it now?"

"That's just the thing. The German government sold the land, but I can't figure out to who."

"Why would they sell an old military base?" Allyn asked skeptically.

"It was abandoned," Nolan said. "Look." He turned his phone around, attempting to show Allyn the pictures he'd found. The windy road made it difficult to see, but Allyn was able to make out concrete bunkers, watchtowers, and even what looked like an old basketball court.

"But why would the Knights move into an abandoned military base?" Allyn asked.

"Because the infrastructure is there," Nolan said. "Think about it, Allyn. They need places to store vehicles and equipment. They need space to train, and they need to do it away from watchful eyes. This has their fingerprints all over it."

Allyn didn't disagree. "I guess we're about to find out."

The BMW was slowing down, its brake lights glowing.

"Where's it going?" Allyn asked as it turned off the road. "Should I follow them?"

"No," Nolan said.

"Why not?"

"Just don't."

They quickly caught up to where the BMW had turned off the road, finding an overgrown lane, its concrete cracked and potholed, running perpendicular to the highway.

"This is it," Nolan said. "I'm telling you, this is it."

Allyn drove another quarter mile before turning off onto a small turnoff and killing the SUV's lights.

"What do we do now?" Nolan asked.

"Let me see those pictures," Allyn said.

Nolan handed him the phone, and Allyn quickly cycled through. Most of the buildings looked to be completely rundown, their walls crumbling, roofs caving in, though some seemed to be in surprisingly good shape. Nolan was right. This *did* seem like the type of place the Knights would operate out of.

"This isn't like the church," Allyn said, almost to himself. "Or the warehouse. It isn't a staging ground. Isn't a temporary base." He looked up from the phone. "I think you're right, Nolan. I think we just found the Knights' headquarters."

CHAPTER 22

LIAM STRODE THROUGH THE KLAUSNER Manor, hoping his mask of confidence hid the boiling sense of unease twisting in his chest. Allyn's call had eased his concern, only to replace it with something even more troublesome. Liam had told him to be discreet and all but ordered him not to get caught, and Allyn had come back with *this*? What he asked for—no, what he'd *demanded*—was outrageous. It was also brilliant, but Liam doubted the council, let alone the arch mage, would see it that way.

A pair of Elemental Guards stood outside the council's office, their eyes forward, backs stiff. Liam glanced at them as he walked by, absently wondering when they had stopped donning ceremonial weapons. Even guards in the British Palace still held outdated, ceremonial weapons.

Stay focused. He didn't have time to daydream about the swords and spears the magi guard had once carried. He needed to have his speech ready. Needed to be prepared to answer questions, fend off objections, and twist arms. Allyn and the rest were counting on him, and they didn't have much time. Not only did Allyn want to move quickly, but the council session would be adjourning shortly. Reassembling them wasn't a hoop Liam wanted to jump through, since that would require convincing the arch mage first—the one person most likely to be their strongest challenger. No, as much as he would have liked to have time to write out his argument and brainstorm potential objections, they simply didn't have the time. Allyn hadn't given it to him.

Win or lose, there's going to be hell to pay when this is over.

Liam took three more circuits around the manor, finally drawing a questioning look from one of the Elemental Guards. The look was little more than a flick of the eyes, but that was as much as anyone could expect from an Elemental Guardsman. Completing the final pass, Liam took a final deep breath and made for the door. The Elemental Guards slid into position, blocking his passage.

"The council is in session," one of the guards said. "No spectators."

"I'm not a spectator," Liam said. "I have urgent information regarding the enemy."

"The arch mage said—"

"The arch mage is going to want to hear this," Liam said. "I guarantee it."

The guard took an irritated breath. "Very well. Wait here." He opened the door and entered. The door clicked shut behind him, but Liam still could hear questioning tones and agitated voices inside. When the door opened again, the man gestured for Liam to enter.

Liam strode into the council chamber with his back straight, his chin up, and his hands clasped behind his back. The council members sat around a rectangular table that held a color-coordinated map and figurines that Liam assumed were a representation of deployed forces.

Drawing his lips into a tight line, Liam surveyed the

council members. Only a few wore expressionless masks; most radiated hostility. At first, Liam thought it was because of his intrusion, but he quickly realized the council had been in the middle of a heated debate before his interruption. In either case, it wouldn't make his job any easier.

"I apologize," Liam said. "But I have urgent information about the Knights of Rakkar."

"Please," Arch Mage Westarra said, gesturing for him to speak.

"Allyn and a small group of magi have found the Knights' base of operations." Liam let the words hang there, allowing the council to digest them. More than a few sat back in their chairs, obviously surprised.

Arch Mage Westarra, already standing, cocked his head to the side. "The Knights' base of operations?" he said as if testing the validity of the words. "And how did he come by this information?"

"From the tactical vehicle he and Nolan took from the Heilig Estate, Your Grace." Liam said. "I've just spoken with him, and apparently, imbedded within the vehicle's GPS was the location of a staging post. Allyn visited this location and found another lead, which they followed to the base."

The various council members looked at each other, sharing wide-eyed expressions.

The arch mage didn't appear impressed, though, and shot an angry look at the others before returning his judgmental gaze to Liam.

"And where is Allyn now?"

"He's there, Your Grace," Liam said. "At the Knights' base."

"At the Knights' base?" The arch mage apparently had a habit of repeating the last thing he heard.

Liam wasn't used to the practice, and it felt as though he were being interrogated. "That's correct, Your Grace."

"He should be here to present the information himself."

"That wasn't possible, Your Grace."

"Oh?" Arch Mage Westarra said. "And why is that?"

"Because he's preparing an attack on the Knights, Your Grace... *tonight*."

The words hung between them, almost visible, stoking the anger that had already been burning within the room.

"And," Liam said slowly, "he has asked the council to assemble its forces and mount an attack with him."

"Your friend has overstepped his boundaries," Arch Mage Westarra said, his eyes burning into Liam's. It wasn't a question, so Liam didn't respond. "What happens if I refuse?"

"He'll still attack, Your Grace. But he *insists* you join him. If you don't, he'll be forced to take more drastic measures."

"Which would be what?" Arch Mage Westarra smiled. He actually *smiled*. "I've grown tired of your friend's antics. Sitting back while he kills himself on a suicide mission doesn't strike me as a terrible idea."

"He thought you'd say that, Your Grace," Liam said. "The staging post he discovered housed a number of tactical vehicles and weapons—equipment that could be very helpful to our cause. But if the council doesn't provide him with assistance, then he'll use the equipment in another way."

"Which is?"

"He'll call the police," Liam said simply. "The weapons and explosives violate German law and will be confiscated when found. We wouldn't be able to use the equipment ourselves, but neither would our enemy."

Arch Mage Westarra's jaw tightened, and Liam thought he heard the elder magi grind his teeth.

"If I may, Your Grace," Liam continued. "As you said, Allyn

is my friend, and I can tell you he doesn't do this out of spite. He only wants what is best for our Family and this Order. Even you must admit what he's been able to accomplish in such little time is impressive. I am not a member of this council, and since Allyn's exclusion, my Family no longer has a voice among it, but for what it's worth, I agree with him. We have a unique opportunity here, and we need... we *should* take advantage of it."

A little of the heat in the arch mage's expression dissipated, and he surveyed the council as if asking for their thoughts.

Jaxon's chair creaked as he leaned forward. He tapped a finger gently on the tabletop, his expression somewhere between contemplative and pained. He looked around the table as if waiting for someone else to speak first. When nobody did, he opened his mouth.

"I also know Allyn," Jaxon said. "And while I don't always agree with his methods, I usually do agree with his reasoning. If the council will take a moment and remove their feelings for him from the situation, I believe they will see the enormous opportunity that lies before it. We've been attempting to manufacture an advantage, and so far, we've failed. But Allyn has succeeded. As Grand Mage McCollum suggests, this opportunity might never come again."

Jaxon leaned back in his seat, his eyes wide with hope.

Arch Mage Westarra looked about the room. "Does anyone actually *on* the council have anything to add?"

Wesley Green cleared his throat. "If I may, Your Grace. I don't know Allyn of McCollum well, but nothing I've seen or heard has given me any reason to doubt his intentions. If he says he has found the whereabouts of the enemy and that the Knights are ripe for an attack, then who are we to question him?"

"It's not his intentions that I question, Wesley," Arch Mage

Westarra said. "It's his ability to execute those intentions—which is why we removed him from this council to begin with."

"A matter in which I was officially against, I'll remind you, Your Grace," Grand Mage Green said.

Arch Mage Westarra glanced uneasily at Liam. The War Council, like the Forum, worked diligently to provide a unified front, and it wasn't often that anyone saw the inner politics manifest outside private sessions.

"I'm well aware of your objections, Grand Mage," Arch Mage Westarra said.

"Your Grace," Wesley Green said, "if it were any of us coming to you with this information, with this request, would you grant it?"

"I... that's irrelevant," Arch Mage Westarra stammered.

"With all due respect, Your Grace, no it's not," Wesley Green said. "Because Allyn was operating under my orders."

Murmurs, muted questions, and surprised gasps filled the room as Arch Mage Westarra took an involuntary step backward. He looked as if he had been shot, his face showing every bit of the pained surprise he felt. Liam kept his face expressionless—or, at least, what he hoped appeared as expressionless.

Wesley Green had just lied to the arch mage. Blatantly lied. And worse still, he knew that Liam understood. Unless Liam contradicted the elder Grand Mage, Jaxon's father had just turned him into an accomplice.

He's every bit as clever as Jaxon always said he was.

"What did you say?" Arch Mage Westarra whispered.

"I said Allyn was carrying out my orders," Wesley Green said. "I gave him the location of the staging post and asked him to investigate and to follow the trail as he felt necessary."

"You disobeyed the council," Arch Mage Westarra said. "You disobeyed *me*."

"I did nothing of the sort, Your Grace. I was under no order not to lead an investigation of my own."

"But you were aware of this council's lack of confidence in Allyn McCollum," Arch Mage Westarra pressed. "You were aware he had been removed from his position."

"Which only precluded him from conducting official War Council business, Your Grace," Wesley said. "As I said, Allyn was carrying out the orders of my own investigation."

"But he's not of your Family," Arch Mage Westarra said. "Why send a McCollum to conduct a Green investigation? Unless you're saying the McCollum and Green Families have joined together in this."

"We have, Your Grace."

There it was. Any wiggle room Liam had remaining disappeared. Arch Mage Westarra turned to him, no doubt looking for confirmation. Wesley Green did too, his face blank and unreadable.

"The McCollum and Green Families have been close for some time, Your Grace," Liam said. It wasn't a lie, and if push came to shove, he would have some level of deniability of Wesley's ploy. "I have been friends with and served under Grand Mage Green's son for many years. An alliance between our two Families makes sense."

Arch Mage Westarra eyed him intently, looking between Liam and Wesley. *He knows we're lying.*

"Why didn't you bring the information to the council?" Grand Mage Guerrero asked, entering the conversation for the first time.

"Because I wasn't sure there was anything *to* bring to the council," Wesley said.

"And you agree with the McCollum plan?" Grand Mage Guerrero said. "You agree we should attack tonight?"

Wesley Green shot a quick glance in Liam's direction. "If the team on the ground believes that's our best course, then yes."

"But why tonight?" Grand Mage Guerrero asked. "Why not wait until we've had more time to prepare?"

"Because the team tripped an alarm when they entered the staging post," Liam said. "They weren't discovered, but there's a good chance the equipment will be moved to a more secure location after tonight."

"Thank you, Li—Grand Mage McCollum," Wesley said. "There's another reason as well. This council doesn't know when the next attack will happen, and after the last defeat, we don't know where, either. But every second we wait, the closer that attack comes. We need to hit them before they have a chance to hit us again."

"What did you say was in the staging post?" Grand Mage Klausner asked, entering the conversation for the first time. The question gave Liam the strong feeling that he and Grand Mage Green were winning the individual council members over.

"Grand Mage McCollum?" Wesley said, deferring to Liam.

"Huh?" Liam said. "Oh, of course. Allyn found five more of the armored tactical vehicles the Knights have used in previous battles and dozens of guns, grenades, and other explosives."

"The vehicles would be nice," Grand Mage Klausner said, looking away from Liam to the rest of the council.

"And securing their weapons before they have a chance to retrieve them might prove useful," Grand Mage Ricci said. Easily the oldest among the council, he must have been added following Allyn's dismissal.

"Exactly," Grand Mage Klausner said. "It won't win the war on its own, but it'll be a nuisance. One more thing they'll need to be concerned with."

Liam had to bite the insides of his cheeks to keep from smiling. One by one, the council members were making his arguments for him, coming to the conclusions he wanted them to come to. Any sense of amusement quickly vanished when he realized the arch mage wasn't paying the council any attention. Arch Mage Westarra was watching *him*. His feelings were unreadable, but Liam got the distinct impression the arch mage was weighing him. Judging his worthiness.

He underestimated me, he thought. *But it won't happen again.*

Arch Mage Westarra held up a hand, silencing the growing discussion among the council members. "Grand Mage McCollum."

"Yes, Your Grace?" Liam said.

"I trust you're still in communication with Allyn?"

"I am, Your Grace."

"Then tell him the council has preliminarily agreed to his request. Once we have confirmed the location of the Knights' base and our ability to mobilize a sufficient force, we will provide him with an official confirmation. If everything checks out, we will hit them with everything we have. In the meantime, work with Allyn and Grand Mage Green to confirm the key pieces of information vital to our attack. I'll organize the strike force."

"Yes, Your Grace," Liam said. "Thank you, Your Grace."

Arch Mage Westarra straightened his back, rising to the full station of his office. "The rest of you, prepare your forces for battle."

Grand Mage Green's quarters were a small living suite on the second floor of the manor. Complete with a bedroom, private bathroom, small study, and kitchenette, the quarters left little reason to venture into the rest of the manor, which was probably the reason Liam hadn't seen much of Wesley or Talisa Green beyond official settings.

Entering the room, Grand Mage Green motioned for Liam and Jaxon to sit then did so himself. Liam sat and found that the sunlight streaming in through the windows had made the black leather of the couch warm and comforting. Grand Mage Green's face, however, was anything of the sort.

"Tell me everything you know," he said without preamble. "Start from the beginning."

And Liam did. He told him everything, including the orders he had given Allyn about denying his involvement.

"And he's there now?" Wesley asked.

"Yes."

"Good. I'll need to speak with him, of course, but this is a good start. We play a dangerous game here, Liam. I hope you know that."

"I do." The private nature of the meeting made all formal titles unnecessary. "I must say, though, your taking responsibility surprised me."

Jaxon's father waved a hand dismissively. "Westarra wasn't going to act. He needed to be pushed into it."

"I think he knows that it wasn't your idea," Liam said.

"Oh, of course he knows," Wesley said. "He may be a self-promoting coward, but he's not an idiot."

"Then why agree?" Liam asked.

"Because even through his overwhelming disdain for Allyn, he still sees the opportunity. That and we already had the support of the other council members. Make no mistake, though, if this turns sour, he will pin the blame solely on our shoulders, just as he did with Allyn."

"I've got a question about that," Liam said. "Why was Allyn kicked off the council to begin with?"

"Westarra needed someone to blame for our defeat at the Heilig Estate," Wesley said simply.

"I figured that," Liam said. "But *why*?"

The elder grand mage smiled. It wasn't a warming gesture, more like a wolf licking its chops after a doe had accidentally wandered into its territory.

"He's worried about his legacy. Under his watch, the magi have suffered splinters and civil war. Ancient secrets are now common knowledge. And the same enemy that's on the verge of destroying our Order has stolen the Blood Wand, the most sacred relic in our history. How do you think he'll be remembered?"

And my sister was worried about my *legacy.* Nothing he had done came close to Arch Mage Westarra's shortcomings.

"But most of that isn't his fault. It would have happened to anyone."

"Perhaps," Wesley said. "But the lens of history won't be kind, and he knows that."

"All the more reason to win, I suppose."

"Don't do it for Westarra," Wesley said. "Do it for the good of our Order."

Something about Wesley Green's words felt off, but Liam had a hard time placing what. He watched his fellow grand mage and saw the machinations of the man's plans twisting behind his eyes.

He tells me to do it for the Order, but who's he doing this for? Grand Mage Green was planning something. *But what?*

"Call Allyn," Grand Mage Green said. "It's time we understood exactly what we're up against."

CHAPTER 23

I T WAS ALLYN'S ROTATION TO sleep, but despite his exhaustion from the day's events and having been up for nearly twenty-four hours, the sweet void escaped him. The conditions, he decided, weren't exactly working in his favor.

Despite having backtracked to find a secluded mountain road southwest of the Knights' base, the proximity to the large number of enemy soldiers was still more than a little unnerving. Mason had returned with Andrew and Topher from scouting the Knights' base, and that provided Allyn with a modicum of comfort, but compared to the one hundred heavily armed enemy soldiers nearby, the magi numbered too few. And even if Allyn had taken comfort in their relative seclusion and the magi on watch, the interior of the SUV was *freezing*.

He'd wanted to leave the vehicle running and enjoy the warmth of the heater, but Mason had advised against it. There was no telling how far the sound of the running engine could carry. Allyn hadn't needed to be told that, but he had been holding out hope that Mason would talk him out of his paranoia. It turned out the other magi was even more paranoid than he was.

All hope of sleep vanished when the door opened and Nolan climbed inside. "They're getting close." He sat in the passenger seat, blowing his warm breath on his hands and fingers.

Allyn sat up from his makeshift bed in the back of the SUV and rubbed his tired eyes. "How far out?"

"They should be here within the hour."

Allyn peered out the tinted windows of the SUV, looking at the treetops of the forest around them. The sky was still a dark gray, dawn little more than a distant promise.

We still have time.

"That's great," Allyn said. "And Liam was successful?"

"He was," Nolan said. "We got word a little while ago. He won't arrive with the rest, but he shouldn't be long after them."

Allyn let out a long breath that turned into a white mist inside the frigid vehicle. "Good news, Nolan. All good news. I'm not going to lie; I can't believe this came together."

Nolan barked a laugh. "Me, neither."

Liam and Wesley Green had called immediately after the council session to inform him of the council's decision. It hadn't been an outright yes, but it was close enough that Allyn couldn't see them backing out now. Their one request had been for Allyn's squad to better scout the area and have the beginnings of a plan outlined by the time the magi forces arrived.

Almost as surprising as the council's decision had been the unexpected support of Jaxon's father. After their conference call, Liam had called Allyn directly and told him how Grand Mage Green had lied to the arch mage, throwing his full support behind Allyn and Liam.

The sudden support left Allyn a little uneasy and questioning what was in it for the grand mage. If he hadn't been ill and abdicating to his son, Allyn might have thought that the grand mage was angling for the arch mage's position, but with his health problems, Allyn suspected other motivations. In his experience, people didn't often throw their support behind a tarnished person without expecting something in return.

"I hate leather," Nolan said.

"Hmm?" Allyn asked.

"Leather seats," Nolan said. "They're hot and sticky in the summer and cold as shit in the winter. I never understood why they were so popular."

Uncertain what to say, Allyn shook his head.

"Seriously. I feel like I'm sitting bare-assed on a freezer."

"You could always go back outside."

"Then I feel like I'm *inside* the freezer," Nolan said.

"Damned if you do, and damned if you don't."

"No shit," Nolan said. "The rest just need to get here."

Allyn agreed, and the two of them spent the next hour taking comfort in the fact that they were both equally as miserable.

The first magi force to arrive was led by Arch Mage Westarra and Wesley Green. It was little more than a contingent of Elemental Guardsmen and members of the War Council, but it meant Allyn had something to distract him from the cold.

"Arch Mage Westarra," Allyn said, approaching the magi leader. "Thanks for coming."

"Allyn," Arch Mage Westarra said curtly. "Good work."

"Thank you, Your Grace,"

"Good work indeed," Grand Mage Green said. "This is exactly what we needed."

"I hope so."

"You've had an opportunity to scout the area?" Wesley asked as Arch Mage Westarra strode toward the rest of the waiting magi. Rohn Agerland, the Spark of the Elemental Guard, remained at the arch mage's side and quickly ordered his forces to reinforce Mason's perimeter.

"Yes," Allyn said. "Mason returned a little over an hour ago."

"Good," Grand Mage Green said. "Show me what you've got so far."

———————

"This is a sky view of the Knights' base," Mason said, standing over a topographical map he'd built with sticks, stones, and bits of bark scavenged from the forest. "The base likely once held hundreds, if not a couple thousand, but many of the buildings have collapsed or fallen into such disrepair that the Knights' forces seem to only be occupying this section of the abandoned city."

Allyn stood with Nolan, Jaxon, Grand Mage Green, and Rohn as Mason explained the layout of the abandoned military base.

"Help me get my bearings," Wesley said. "Where are we on this map?"

"Here." Mason pointed to an area southwest of the buildings. "So when we approach, we'll come at the city from this angle here." He drew an arrow pointing at the rear of the southernmost building.

"Okay," Wesley said. "What do we have to contend with to get there?"

"There's a fence that circles the base." Mason drew a circle in the dirt around his map. "Chain-link with barbwire and a couple nasty signs that say 'trespassers will be shot,' but we were able to dig under it without issue. The Knights have posted a handful of sentries closer to the base, but we were able to slip past them too. There's no way we'll be able to sneak a larger force past them, though."

"We'll need to neutralize them," Wesley said. "Can't afford to let them sneak up behind us or raise the alarm."

"Exactly. From there"—Mason drew another circle, this one closer to the buildings—"the forest ends, and there's a green space between it and the buildings. Fortunately, there's still debris and the grass has grown wild, so there *is* cover. More concerning are the watchtowers here... and here." He indicated a pair of small twigs that stuck up out of the ground. "They're not in the best shape, and one of them is leaning pretty badly, but they appear to be manned. We'll need to eliminate them as well."

"How close are they to the buildings?" Jaxon asked.

"Pretty close," Mason said. "If they raise the alarm—"

"I mean if they were to fall, what would they hit?"

Mason made a confused face, the line in his forehead growing deeper as he furrowed his brow. "Depends on which way they fell, I guess."

"If they fell toward the buildings?"

"Well," Mason said. "Like I said, this one is already leaning, so if it falls, it's falling this way." He pulled the stick from the ground and laid it down so that it had fallen away from the buildings. "But this one, if it were pushed the right way, it would take out this building here."

"What are you thinking?" Allyn asked.

"Just wanted to know what our options are," Jaxon said then turned back to Mason. "Please continue."

"There's unfortunately not much else," Mason said. "Except that only two of the three buildings seem to be used for housing. These two here." He pointed to the northern and southernmost buildings.

"What's the middle one used for then?" Wesley asked.

"I have no idea," Mason said. "It almost appeared to be vacant."

"Maybe that's where they're keeping their prisoners," Jaxon offered.

Mason shook his head. "No. We searched for our people but couldn't find any sign of them. My guess is they're either being held somewhere else, like the Knight Commander's quarters here"—he pointed at another rock separated from the rest of the buildings—"or not at this location at all."

"You're sure?" Jaxon pressed.

"As sure as I can be," Mason said.

"Okay," Wesley said. "So we approach from the south, burrow under the fence, neutralize the sentries, and eliminate the towers."

"Yep."

"What do you think?" Wesley asked, turning to Jaxon. "Two squads to take out the sentries and another for the towers?"

"Yes," Jaxon said. "One approaching from the south, as you said. The other approaching from the north, here. They'll need to be able to communicate with each other to attack in unison. What I'm fuzzier on is what happens next. How many Knights do you think are housed here?"

"Somewhere around fifty in each," Mason said. "But that's a very rough guess. Could be more. Could be less, though I'm not betting on that. You don't hole up in a place like this if you only have a handful of soldiers at your disposal."

"That's what I was afraid of," Jaxon said. "One hundred Knights, maybe more. We can't overpower them with force of numbers, even if we do take them by surprise. Not on enemy ground."

"We need to break them up," Wesley said. "It has to be a series of individual battles. We can't let them mount an organized counterattack."

"I agree," Jaxon said.

"How do we do that?" Allyn asked, voicing the question already on everyone's lips.

Wesley Green smiled. It was a sinister thing, devoid of all amusement, and if Allyn hadn't been on the same side as the grand mage, he would have been terrified.

"You kick the hornets' nest," he said.

The sky had turned the color of a deep bruise by the time Liam and his squad arrived. Allyn could hear the deep rumble of the BearCats before he saw them. Dark gray in color, they would have blended into the night if it hadn't been for the headlights and the LEDs across the tops of the cabs.

Seeing the enemy vehicles quickly approaching their hidden position, Allyn might have thought their force had been discovered and was about to be waylaid by the enemy, except that one of the magi SUVs was at its lead. The SUV and BearCats came to a stop, killing their lights. Liam jumped out of the passenger side of the SUV, a smile splitting his face.

"You made it," Allyn said.

"Yeah," Liam said, his eyes falling over the gathered magi force behind Allyn. "It looks like just in time, too."

Liam had been the last to arrive, but unless they'd been stopped and the vehicle confiscated, there was no way the attack would have begun without him and his squad. The BearCats were too important to their plan, as were the magi and machinists within Liam's squad.

"You run into any issues?" Allyn asked.

"No," Liam said. "You were right, though; there was a silent alarm. It's a good thing we had Canary with us."

"That's good to hear," Allyn said. "What about the computer? Find anything useful?"

Liam grimaced. "Not so much. I'm not even sure why it was there, to be honest. I couldn't find anything on it."

"Nothing?"

"Nothing," Liam said, shaking his head.

"How often does that happen?"

"That there's nothing on a computer?" Liam said. "Never."

Something about that didn't sit right, but Allyn didn't have any answers for it, so he left it alone. "Grab the rest of the squad. The arch mage is about to speak."

A few minutes later, Allyn and Liam gathered with the rest of the magi force, finding a spot with a clear view of the arch mage. Word had come only minutes before that the operation was about to get underway, but before it did, Arch Mage Westarra wanted to say a couple of words.

The leader of the magi Order stood atop a boulder, flanked below by his Elemental Guard and remaining members of his War Council. Allyn watched them with a sour expression, not really caring how much of his distaste for the magi leader was visible on his face. Deep down, he knew he was being childish, but like all petty children, he didn't care. The council had voted him out, embarrassing him. Even Wesley Green, who had come to their aid, stood to gain all the glory and recognition.

There are worse things than being ignored, he told himself. But he was cold, exhausted, and more than a little cranky. Even his own positivity was getting under his skin.

The murmurs and whispers of the crowd quieted as the arch mage held up a hand, indicating he was about to begin.

"In just a few moments, you will be embarking in the largest magi assault in more than half a millennium. Magi, clerics, and machinists from seven Families, four countries, and two continents have been brought together for one, single purpose: survival."

Allyn surveyed the crowd, studying the faces of the men and women he was about to go into battle with. Magi and clerics from the Klausner, Schuster, and Heilig Families mixed with other European Families and were reinforced by more from the States, including McCollums, Hylands, and Greens. At more than a hundred strong, they were truly a remarkable sight and had come together more quickly than he had ever dared to imagine.

The largest magi force in over half a millennium, the arch mage had said. All brought together by Allyn. That in itself was an incredible achievement, but it would pale in comparison to what they would accomplish next.

"Make no mistake," Arch Mage Westarra continued, "the enemy we fight today is unlike any we have ever fought before. They're better equipped, better funded, and more deadly than ever. The Knights of Rakkar are the largest threat our Order has ever faced. And if left unchecked, they will succeed in their five-hundred-year mission to eliminate the magi existence from this world."

Arch Mage Westarra paused and took on a somber expression. He looked over the crowd, making eye contact with many, offering small nods and tiny smiles of encouragement.

For all the issues I've had with the man, he is a good speaker, Allyn thought, silently chastising himself for his earlier behavior. *Maybe I was too hard on him.*

But no, Allyn decided, he'd done what needed doing and pushed the magi leadership into action. Good leader or not, best intentions in mind or not, the arch mage had needed to be pushed in the right direction.

"I tell you this, not to scare you or lay out the odds. I tell you this to prepare you. To let you know why there can be no other outcome but victory. Failure is not an option because it means the end of everything we hold dear. I tell you this because I know you won't let me down. You won't let the men and women beside you down. You won't let your Families down. Because not only are you the *largest* force marshaled in our lifetime, but you are the *greatest.* Magi and cleric and machinist, you are the most deadly contingent ever assembled, and it is you who will go down in history as the magi who faced our greatest threat and prevailed. Who guaranteed our existence and ushered in a new era."

Westarra's voice was growing louder now, building to a climatic crescendo. "You are the greatest of magi heroes. Yours are the faces who will be etched into eternity! Fight with me, now and forever, and together, we will show this enemy the true might of the magi. Together, we will show them we have and will always fight as one!"

"We are of One!" the magi shouted.

"We are of One!" Westarra shouted back.

"We are of One!" the crowd responded. Allyn, throwing aside all previous concern about noise, joined in this time.

"We are of One!" Westarra screamed, showing no signs of letting up.

"We are of One!"

Arch Mage Westarra looked over the energized battle force, his face like stone, looking every bit the leader of the magi Order. "Go now and secure your position in history."

The crowd erupted into motion and shouts of approval. Allyn saw Jaxon through the throng and made for the former grand mage of the McCollum Family.

"Jaxon," he said over the din. "Jaxon."

Jaxon saw Allyn approaching and turned from his father, stepping up to greet Allyn.

"I heard you're leading the vanguard," Allyn said.

"Yeah." Jaxon's voice lacked any hint of emotion.

"I couldn't think of a better man to do it," Allyn said. "I wanted to say good luck."

"Thank you," Jaxon said. "And good work. This is really something."

"I couldn't have done it without help," Allyn said.

"Such are all things, I suppose."

"I guess," Allyn agreed. "But I appreciate it. Everything you've done for me and our Family."

Jaxon waved a dismissive hand, but Allyn wasn't having it. Nyla had been torn from him before he could express how he felt, and he wouldn't let the same thing happen again.

"I mean it, Jaxon. You've been around lately, but you haven't been close, not like before, and that's taken some getting used to. I just hope when this is all done that we're still friends."

Jaxon sucked in a sharp breath. His cheek twitched, and he glanced away. When he looked back at Allyn, he held a hand in front of him. Allyn took it, grasping Jaxon's wrist in the magi fashion.

"Always," Jaxon said. And then the thick man pulled him tight, slapping him on the back. The gesture took Allyn by surprise. It was the most emotion he'd ever seen out of the man. "Take care of yourself, Allyn."

"You too."

"I'll see you on the other side," Jaxon said.

"That's the plan."

It wasn't until Allyn was walking away from his friend that he realized the potential double meaning of Jaxon's words.

CHAPTER 24

JAXON SLIPPED THROUGH THE TREES, wincing with every snap of branch and rustle of underbrush. The lingering darkness was both a blessing and a curse. It provided necessary cover for him and the other four members of his squad, but it also made their trek that much more treacherous.

Rustling through an alien forest without light, Jaxon's squad made more noise than he would have preferred. He just hoped that this close to the enemy border it wasn't enough to catch the attention of any of the sentries.

Their first landmark was the chain-link fence circling the perimeter. If Mason's directions were correct, Jaxon and his squad were getting close. Their mission was simple: sneak inside the enemy perimeter, neutralize the sentries, then rejoin the main magi contingent to prepare for the full assault.

Mason had said the sentries were inside the perimeter, so as Jaxon neared the fence, part of his mind drifted back to his conversation with Allyn. His friend had taken a great risk by disobeying the arch mage's wishes and an even greater one by strong-arming the War Council into action. As Jaxon had said during the meeting, Allyn could be impulsive and bullheaded and had grown even more so lately, so his rash behavior wasn't terribly surprising. What *was* surprising was Liam's willingness to go along with it.

Leira had warned Jaxon that Allyn and Liam were working on something behind the arch mage's back. She had been worried Allyn was manipulating Liam in the same way he had eventually manipulated the council. Jaxon didn't accept that accusation, though. That wasn't in Allyn's character. He was Liam's friend, and he valued loyalty and trust, two things Jaxon believed he wouldn't abuse. That didn't mean Jaxon hadn't kept an eye on him, or taken precautions to protect Liam, of course.

When the time came to come to Liam's aid and provide his support, he had. Since then, Liam had eyed Jaxon's father warily, no doubt attempting to understand why he had lied to the arch mage and assumed responsibility for Allyn's actions.

The thought brought a smile to Jaxon's lips. Neither Liam nor Allyn had realized that Jaxon, not the great Wesley Green, had manipulated the arch mage. His father was merely the face of the manipulation, working on Jaxon's behalf and from the limited information Jaxon had provided. His father may have done it for him, but Jaxon had done it for Liam.

Maybe I'm not so bad at this politicking stuff after all.

The smile disappeared, replaced by the battle-ready coldness as the chain-link fence came into view. Jaxon stopped and held up a hand, ordering his squad to freeze. This close to the perimeter the sentries would no doubt be within earshot.

Signaling for his squad to remain, Jaxon crept toward the fence as silently as possible. Nearing the fence, he eyed the land beyond, searching for shapes and shadows in the darkness. A gentle breeze rustled leaves and branches, but Jaxon didn't see anything that resembled a guard.

He waved the squad forward, and the next magi in line snuck toward his position. Once they'd arrived, the next in line moved. By the time the final magi was in position, Jaxon and Michael, his second in command, had unfolded the compact shovels they had taken from the SUVs' roadside emergency kits and begun digging.

The ground was soft, and within a couple of minutes, they had made a significant impression in the soil. A few minutes more, and they had dug a hole big enough for even Jaxon to slip through easily.

Michael was the first under the fence, slipping easily into enemy territory. Rayna and Moreland were next, followed closely by Charles. Jaxon brought up the rear. Each member of the squad had been handpicked by Jaxon and endorsed by his father.

Nearly twice Jaxon's age, Michael was one of his father's most trusted advisors. Where Jaxon had trained the young magi in the McCollum Family, Michael Green had trained all the young magi of the Green, including Jaxon. There was no one Jaxon trusted more in his Family than Michael Green.

Although Rayna and Moreland were two of Jaxon's childhood friends and Charles was one of the Greens' most accomplished clerics, Jaxon secretly wished he could have replaced them with Allyn, Ren, or Leira, someone who he had been in battle with before. But the McCollum magi had other roles to play in the coming battle.

Once on the other side of the fence and officially in enemy territory, Jaxon ordered their squad to fan out. He took the middle position with two magi each to his right and left. Dressed in black compression armor, they easily disappeared into the darkness of the forest.

Jaxon smelled the first sentry before he saw him. The smell of cigarette smoke marked his coming, the small orange embers of the burning tobacco indicating his location. He stood a couple paces from the tree line, near a pile of scrap metal. Beyond him were the three large buildings Mason had said were being used as barrack. Nearest to Jaxon, the guard was his responsibility.

Dropping into a low crouch, Jaxon snuck forward and wielded a pair of jagged ice shards. He preferred using concussions of air over pulling water or heat from his body—air was replenishable, after all, and wasn't as dangerous to use over prolonged periods of time—but the blast of air left an audible crack and wasn't a solid alternative when stealth was necessary.

Jaxon made it to the edge of the tree line without issue and used the thick leaves of a large fern for cover. The guard—a man with a pronounced forehead and a wild set of eyebrows—couldn't have been older than twenty-two. He looked into the forest, his eyes glazed over with boredom, more interested in puffing on the cigarette between his lips. Jaxon waited, and finally, his patience was rewarded.

After taking a final drag off his cigarette, the guard threw it on the ground and smashed it with a foot. When he did, Jaxon leaped from the tree line. The sentry looked up just as Jaxon brought the pair of ice blades into his neck, plunging downward at an angle into his chest. The young sentry's eyes widened with fear and pain, and his mouth opened to shout, but his words died on his lips. He went limp in Jaxon's arms, and with a quick look at the nearby watchtower, Jaxon dragged the guard back into the forest.

Back under the cover of the trees, Jaxon held his breath and waited. His eyes went from the barrack to the watchtower and back, searching for motion. He strained his ears, listening for sounds of alarm and movement. The seconds ticked by, and he saw and heard nothing, save for the pounding of his heart. Jaxon felt more confident his attack had gone unnoticed, but while he had avoided immediate detection, the attack started a second clock. Eventually, someone would notice the missing guard and come searching. The magi had to spring their attack before that happened.

With the guard neutralized and no others in sight, Jaxon began to circle the perimeter. His squad had already started doing the same, widening the distance between each other and seeking out additional sentries. When Jaxon came upon Michael, the elder magi had already eliminated a second guard, another who was closer in age to a child than a man. In the opposite direction, Rayna had done the same.

After it became clear there were no other guards in their section of the compound, Jaxon ordered his squad to return to him and alerted the arch mage that they were ready for the next phase of their assault.

It was time to take out the watchtowers.

CHAPTER 25

LIAM COULD HARDLY BELIEVE HIS luck. After years of dreaming, he was finally behind the wheel of a vehicle—and not just any vehicle, but one of the biggest, baddest machines he'd ever laid eyes on. The Knights' BearCats had been things to be feared, vehicles that transported soldiers of death who needed to be destroyed, but powering one from the driver's seat was an altogether different experience. It was *awesome.*

The vehicle rumbled underneath him, roaring across the potholed road leading into the Knights' compound with ease. Low-hanging branches, brambles, and underbrush slapped the sides of the vehicle as the BearCat swayed stiffly, its oversized tires rolling over broken slabs of asphalt.

Liam had kept the lights on, seeing no advantage to shutting them off. Allyn had mentioned the need for stealth, but the moment Liam and the other drivers had fired up the engines, they'd known that there was no stealth with these machines. There was only strength—pure, awesome, unbridled power that made men shiver as if they'd been touched by a beautiful woman.

Liam grinned—he couldn't help it—and stomped on the

gas, spurring the vehicle forward with a roar. He knew the display of emotion was unbecoming of a magi, but he didn't care. Besides, no one else was there to see it. The BearCat behind him, the one driven by Nolan, let out a mechanical scream as it accelerated to keep up. They were the only two vehicles on the road. The remaining three BearCats were still at the original rendezvous point, waiting for the next phase in the assault.

As he tightened his grip on the steering wheel, Liam's grin slowly faded, replaced by focus on the mission at hand. The road opened up in front of them, the forest becoming a debris-ridden field of tall grass. Liam steered the vehicle right as Nolan's headlights veered in the opposite direction, heading toward a separate target. Liam's BearCat shrieked, rocking to the side with a shower of sparks as it scraped against the rusted remains of an old truck. Liam jerked the BearCat away then overcorrected as the vehicle slid on the moist ground.

Focus, you idiot. He wouldn't crash. He wouldn't—at least not crash into something he wasn't supposed to.

His target came into focus ahead of him. Over fifty feet tall, the watchtower easily cleared the tops of the trees that surrounded the enemy base. Cylindrical in design and made of red brick with an exposed steel-grated platform more than three quarters of the way up, the watchtower was something out of another world.

According to Nolan, the base had been built by Nazi Germany during World War II then run by the Soviet Union until its fall in the early 1990s. As such, its unique history echoed that of two fallen empires. Liam doubted more than a handful of such places still existed in the entire world.

In many ways, its imminent destruction was a shame. In several more, it was justified, if not overdue.

He adjusted his grip on the steering wheel and leaned forward, putting pressure on the seatbelt. It resisted, holding him in place. That was good. He wasn't about to be ejected from the vehicle because he forgot to buckle his seatbelt.

That would be an unfortunate way to go.

The tower was getting closer now. He readjusted his hands, which had gone slick with sweat—w*hen did I start sweating?*—and once in position, floored the gas pedal.

The BearCat screamed forward. He was twenty feet away. Fifteen. Ten. He yelled and slammed his eyes shut. The last image he had before the world went black was of the red brick speeding closer.

Metal shrieked against stone in a deafening crash as Liam's BearCat slammed into the watchtower. The momentum hurled Liam forward against the taut seatbelt. Pain exploded in his chest and shoulder, and the world lurched as the BearCat's rear tires came off the ground then spun, its rear crashing into the watchtower again from another angle before coming to a complete stop.

Liam opened his eyes, absently rubbing his shoulder where the seatbelt had bit into him. Dust filled the vehicle's compartment, and it smelled of mud and stone and scorched metal. With a groan, Liam shifted in his seat, gazing out the window. The vehicle was facing an unfamiliar section of forest, but out the passenger-side window, Liam could still see the watchtower. The sight of it still standing was nearly enough to send him into despair.

Destroying the watchtower was his one and only objective, and the fact that it still stood was an impossibility in and of itself. Liam's BearCat had left a gaping hole in the tower's base, and the upper column was swaying gently back and forth. Liam had no doubt that given time and a big enough gust of wind, the tower would collapse, but time was the one thing he didn't have.

Wincing as pain exploded across his chest, Liam found the keys in the ignition and tried to start the vehicle again. The engine made a pained sound but didn't turn over.

"Come on," Liam said, trying again. The engine made a similar sound, this one slightly stronger. "There you go. Come on. You can do it."

And as if at his prompting, the engine sprang to life. It didn't rumble with the same strength as it had before, but as long as the vehicle moved, there was hope.

He threw the BearCat into reverse, steering the vehicle into position for another run. He heard another distant crash and spared himself a brief moment to search for the other watchtower. But where it had stood, a plume of dust was rising into the sky.

He succeeded—Nolan did it.

With something similar to resolve taking shape in his sore chest, Liam prepared himself for what would come next. He knew what he had to do. He also knew he couldn't take another impact like the one before. He popped open his door and undid his seatbelt. Then, before he had time to talk himself out of it, he slammed his foot on the gas.

The BearCat lumbered forward, picking up speed, but not nearly as quickly as it had before. It didn't matter, though. Liam had given himself plenty of runway, and if the still crumbling brick of the watchtower was any indication, it wouldn't take much to topple it over.

Liam steered the vehicle into position, aiming for the hole he'd created, knowing that once he took his hands off the wheel, the ground would cause the BearCat to veer one way or another. As long as he got close enough, it wouldn't matter. He lined the vehicle up, making one final course correction, then jumped out of the door.

He hit the ground with a solid, wet thud. The moist earth was softer than the taut seatbelt, though, and he rolled, coming to a stop just in time to see the BearCat slam into the watchtower mere feet from where he'd hit it before.

There was an ear-splitting *crack*, and then brick was crumbling. The watchtower swayed backward, away from the barrack, then toward it. More brick crumbled under the weight. Then even more. Another crack split the night as the rest of the brick gave way.

Liam reveled in the sight. He'd succeeded. He hurt like hell, but his mission had been a success. The tower began to fall, and his excitement quickly turned to horror. It wasn't just falling. It was going to fall *on* him.

Shouting a curse, Liam ran. He moved out of the path of the falling tower, knowing that it was falling faster than he could run. He was going to be crushed. Smashed like a bug under a boot. With a scream, he found another burst of speed, then as he could feel the tower bearing down on him, he leaped, throwing himself forward.

He hit the ground as the tower crashed only feet behind him. He rolled onto his back, amazed he was unscathed, taking in the new sight.

Dust filled the air like fog, obscuring his view, but the tower had crashed into the barrack, tearing a hole through its center. Inside were human screams of pain and surprise. The sounds chilled Liam's insides, gnawing at him like a parasite. Liam wanted to be sick, but he didn't have time for that. Already, the Knights would be moving, arming themselves and preparing for battle, and Liam would be in another race against time to clear the scene before they found him.

He rolled onto his feet and ran like hell. Along the tree line, shapes, little more than shadows, emerged. The cavalry, he thought the expression went, had arrived.

CHAPTER 26

JAXON WATCHED AS THE SECOND watchtower fell. From his vantage in the trees surrounding the compound, it almost resembled a stack of toy blocks brought down by an overzealous toddler, except when the tower crashed into the barrack, it was accompanied by cries of pain and death. After the collapse, Jaxon searched frantically for a sign of Liam and was relieved when he caught sight of a slender shadow moving toward the trees.

He made it.

His concern for Liam, and for the larger mission, had grown exponentially when the tower hadn't fallen from the original impact. It had spiked in the long moments afterward when there had been no sound or sign of Liam at all. Jaxon had feared the worst, thinking that they'd lost both Liam and their element of surprise. He hated himself for equating the two, but if Liam had failed in his mission, then many more would perish.

"Let's move," Jaxon said then stepped from the tree line and broke into a jog toward the compound. It was time for the next phase of their operation.

He felt his squad form up behind him, expecting that the

seven other members had formed into the predetermined V formation. He kept his eyes trained on the compound where he and three other squads were to engage the enemy. Another four squads were assaulting the other barrack, with the arch mage directing the battle from the reserve force that remained in the trees.

Breaking up their forces into smaller, relatively autonomous squads with only basic objectives allowed them to remain flexible and adjust to the changing battlefield—a necessity, they had learned, when it came to fighting the Rakkaran forces.

A thick cloud of dust hung over the compound, obscuring their view, but Jaxon could hear movement within the building. Shouts and orders echoed through the collapsed ceiling, mixing with the shouts and cries of the wounded.

Jaxon split his squad into two sub squads, handing over command of the other to Michael, and directed them behind two separate piles of broken concrete each higher than he was tall. Once in position, he watched the barrack's entrance.

Seeing the compound up close, Jaxon wondered why the Knights had chosen it for their base of operations. The buildings hadn't just fallen into a state of disrepair; most had already fallen in on themselves, and those that hadn't were covered with moss, leaves, and mold, and looked like they could give way at any moment. The concrete that made up most of the buildings was pocked and crumbling, exposing rusty steel rebar at the corners.

He had no doubt that, at one point, the base had been something to behold, a show of strength and commitment to military power, but like the regimes who had occupied it in years past, it was now little more than a relic, forgotten by many.

There has to be something I'm missing. Something I'm not

seeing. The thought made him uneasy, and he watched the entrance with even more intensity.

"Remember," Jaxon said, without taking his eyes from the double doors, "don't attack at first sight. Wait until they've had a chance to filter out."

The first wave of the attack would set the tone for the rest of the battle. If they were able to draw enough of the Knights out from the cover of the compound before the first strike, then they stood a better chance at reducing their numbers and demoralizing the enemy. If they failed, however, it would give the Knights an opportunity to dig in and prolong the battle. In that event, their superior firepower would shift the advantage from the magi to the Knights.

"Here they come," Nolan hissed.

He, along with the reinforcements from the McCollum Family—Mason, Andrew, and Topher—augmented Jaxon's squad, mixing with Michael, Rayla, and Moreland. The mix left them without a cleric, which wasn't what Jaxon would have chosen if given the opportunity, but his father had said this was a squad of strength that needed all the firepower they could get.

Jaxon wielded ice and ordered his squad to do the same. Nearby, hidden behind the other stack of broken concrete, Michael would be giving the same order, as would the squad leaders of the other magi squads that formed a loose crescent shape around the entrance of the barrack.

The first Knights that emerged stumbled through the doorway and nearly fell down the stairs. The thick dust no doubt made it hard for them to see, but they were also desperate, fleeing in panic.

"Hold," Jaxon whispered. He knew he didn't have to issue the order, but he hadn't fought with many of the magi in his squad before, and he wasn't about to risk one of them getting overexcited and exposing their position.

More Knights continued to tumble out of the barrack. Many wore their tactical armor, but a good number were dressed only in black thermal underclothes, no doubt having been asleep before the tower came down. Those that were in their armor eyed the terrain suspiciously.

They're nervous, Jaxon realized. *They don't know if the watchtower fell on its own, or if it was the first move in a larger attack.*

The time for them to learn the truth was quickly approaching. Roughly twenty or thirty Knights had piled out of the barrack by now, many of them armed. If he waited too much longer, they wouldn't be able to win the opening salvo so decisively. He was walking a knife's edge. He needed to wait long enough that a large number of Knights would be eliminated in the first few moments, but not so long that the Knights would be able to put up an effective counterattack.

Within only the span of a few breaths, Jaxon had the eyes of every squad leader on him. They waited for his mark. He couldn't shout the order without alerting the Knights to their presence, but he could do the next best thing.

Jaxon stepped from his hiding place and hurled a lance of ice at one of the armed guards, propelling it forward with a blast of air. Then in a blink, he shot a second lance toward a different guard. The ice zipped through the darkness, nearly invisible, and as the lances struck their targets, the magi assault began in full force.

The first volley of attacks cut through the Knights with terrifying efficiency. In a single devastating wave, roughly half of the Knights were down. It was tough to say how many of them were wounded or dead since those who remained unhurt dove to the ground, frantically searching the darkness, finding themselves surrounded.

Ice already re-forming in his hands, Jaxon pressed the advantage. He launched another volley, wielded again, spun, and shot a third. The other magi around him did the same. Screams rose from the battlefield, frantic and terrified, but as the battle continued, the cries of the fallen dwindled until there was only the sound of the magi attacks.

In one final act of desperation, the remaining Knights jumped to their feet and ran for the doors of the barrack. Jaxon was already wielding again, though, and hurled a fireball at their backs. It connected with the unfortunate guard bringing up the rear, exploding with a brilliant flash of orange death. The Knights were thrown forward. Two crashed through the doors and were tossed into the barrack headfirst. The others crashed into the brick exterior with a sickening sound.

The battlefield went quiet. The magi objective had been to draw out as many Knights as possible and squash them. In that, they had succeeded, but Jaxon stamped down the feeling of triumph, knowing it was only the opening frame of the battle. In mere moments the battle would begin in earnest.

CHAPTER 27

ALLYN SLIPPED THROUGH A NARROW ALLEY, leaving the sounds of battle behind. He and the rest of his squad—which included, Ren, Leira, and Canary—were headed north toward the building Mason had identified as the Knight Commander's residence. Since the magi prisoners seemed to be held elsewhere, the battle plan had two priorities: destroy the Knights' force and reclaim the Blood Wand.

The building they moved toward was a mustard-colored two-story Victorian-style house with a large porch that wrapped around three sides of the home. Built within the cold precision of the military base, the white pillars that framed the elevated front entrance felt like they were from another world.

The damp ground muffled their footsteps, and even here the magi had to take care to avoid the broken bricks, glass, and rotten timber that littered the ground. Making for the house, they moved down a stone path edged with a waist-high stone wall, benches, and decorative trees.

Avoiding the front entrance, Allyn made for a nondescript door that had likely been used as a separate servants' entrance. The door was a natural dark brown in color and adorned with several small square windows. The entire structure seemed to be in surprisingly good shape—even the windows in the door were intact.

He took hold of the tarnished brass door handle and turned it. To his surprise, the handle moved without resistance. Keeping the door closed, Allyn looked to Leira.

"Is anyone inside?" he asked.

She closed her eyes and held a hand in front of her as if reaching for something. The first time Allyn had seen the gesture, he hadn't understood it, but he had since grown to rely on the magi ability. In addition to being able to heal more quickly than other magi and use their own bodies to treat the wounded, a cleric could also sense life forces around them. Like many things, it was a skill that could be honed and improved, and Leira, by her own admission, wasn't as good at the ability as Nyla had been.

Nyla... I wish you were here with us.

Leira opened her eyes and dropped her hand, shaking her head.

"Nobody?" Allyn asked, his voice a deep whisper.

"I can't be sure," Leira said quietly. "But I don't think so."

Allyn turned to Canary. The girl's yellow-and-black streaked hair was hidden under a hood. "Any transmissions coming in or out?"

Canary shook her head. "Quiet."

"That's good enough for me," Allyn said. "But be on guard. Sedric has a history of cutting bait and fleeing when it looks like they're going to lose. If he does, he might come back to retrieve something he left behind. Stay vigilant."

Taking hold of the handle again, Allyn gave it another turn then carefully pulled open the door. Ren was the first one inside. She held translucent shards of ice that were nearly invisible in the darkness. Leira was next, followed closely by Canary, with Allyn bringing up the rear.

They entered a room that might have once been used as a communal area. A hearth was set into one wall, its inside black with soot but otherwise clean. In fact, Allyn was again taken aback by the condition of the house. The tiled floors showed their age and were covered in dust, and the paint on the interior walls was peeling, but there was no garbage or vandalism like in the other buildings.

Closing the door behind him, Allyn listened for signs of the Knight Commander or anyone else within the home.

Nothing.

Confident they were alone, Allyn led his squad out of the room, moving toward the front entrance where the stairwell led to the second story. If the Blood Wand was in the house, Allyn expected it to be in Sedric's room, and that, he assumed, was upstairs.

The stairwell connected to a wide hallway that extended in either direction.

"Ren," Allyn said, still keeping his voice quiet. "Take Leira and search that wing of the house. I'll take Canary and see what we can find on this side."

Ren nodded, and she and Leira moved deeper into the house. Allyn and Canary moved in the opposite direction, quickly searching a pair of rooms on the left side of the hall and finding nothing. Allyn had eyes on a separate door, though.

The door at the end of the hall was cracked, giving him a partial view into what looked like a much larger space. He made for it, ignoring another door to his right.

The door at the end of the hall opened with a gentle squeal. Light from the moon and stars poured in through a pair of large windows, illuminating the space with a cold white light. Even though the furnishings were meager—a cot for a bed, an overturned milk crate for a table, and a single lamp with a naked bulb—Allyn instantly knew it was the Knight Commander's quarters.

At the other end of the room was a dresser with an ornate mirror, and hanging from a doorless closet was a set of neatly pressed uniforms. Allyn stepped up to the dresser, pulling open drawers and searching through the underclothes for the Blood Wand. Not finding it, he dropped to his hands and knees, peering under the piece of furniture. It wasn't there, either.

"Anything?" he asked as Canary stepped from the closet. She shook her head.

A cold sweat washed over his body. Something didn't feel right. He couldn't put a finger on it, but an uneasy feeling nagged at the back of his brain.

"Any communications?" he asked again.

Canary's face went blank as she turned her attention to the incoming and outgoing transmissions. "No."

"Nothing here in this house, or nothing at all?"

"There's always something."

"I meant anything from the Knights?"

Her eyes went distant again, her previous blank expression returning. Not knowing how long it would take Canary to sift through the various radio waves, Allyn looked out the window, searching the night for movement. He thought he saw something, but when he didn't see it again, he chalked it up to either a trick of the darkness or his imagination playing games with him.

"Nothing," Canary said behind him, breaking the silence.

"Nothing at all?"

She shook her head.

Allyn made a disapproving face. The Knights were under

attack by a powerful, if relatively unknown, force. They didn't know the size of the magi number, what equipment they had at their disposal, or how they were placed strategically. Allyn wasn't a military man and hadn't been trained in the art of tactics, but even he saw the flaw in that. Good communication was as important as anything in battle, so what in the hell were the Knights doing?

"Come on," Allyn said.

He stepped hastily toward the door... and came face to face with Knight Commander Sedric Lang.

"Allyn, Allyn, Allyn," Sedric said, his face splitting into a smile. "I just *knew* I would find you here."

CHAPTER 28

GUNFIRE RAINED DOWN FROM THE barrack windows. The magi force, thirty-two magi in all—or what was left of them—returned fire. Picking targets at random, they focused on the muzzle flashes in the broken windows.

Jaxon had lost track of how long they'd been fighting, but already, the battle was taking a toll on him. He felt it in the fatigue of his limbs. His legs felt heavy, his arms hung like lead weights at his sides, and his voice was hoarse from shouting orders. But more than anything, he felt it in the way his body was responding to his repeated magi attacks.

Magic had a cost, and Jaxon knew he was paying the price by the dull headache, dizziness, and dry skin that was brought on by using too much of his body's water. He knew it by his low energy levels and sudden lack of coordination, all signs of hypothermia caused by drawing out too much of his body heat.

He ducked behind a stack of broken concrete slabs, dropping to a crouch and resting against the rough white blocks. Reaching into the neckline of his compression armor, he pulled out a thin blue tube and removed the cork from its end. He took a long drink. The water was warm and tasted like the polyethylene bag that it was stored in—the same bag that was strapped to his back under his compression armor.

Knowing they were likely entering into a prolonged assault, each of the magi had been equipped with one. Hypothermia brought on by relying too heavily on fireballs couldn't be avoided, but dehydration could.

Jaxon took another long pull, taking the moment to survey his squad and the ones that surrounded them. His magi were weary and showing signs of the same symptoms Jaxon was suffering from. Michael's face was in a perpetual grimace now, the kind he made when he was pushing himself too hard.

They can't last much longer. Not under these conditions. We have to sway the momentum of the battle, now, before it's too late.

He pulled his phone from his pocket and called the arch mage. Westarra was still leading the battle from the safety of the forest. Once he answered, Jaxon quickly gave him his update.

"Well done, Jaxon," Arch Mage Westarra said. "I'm sending in the bulls now. You'll have your extra firepower in two minutes."

"Thank you, Your Grace." Jaxon hung up and took another deep drink. He stood up, stumbled, and had to lean into the pile to keep from falling over. Andrew and Topher saw him, their bloodied faces contorting with concern.

Jaxon stood up straighter, masking the dizziness with a smile, and slapped each of them on the back. "Reinforcements are coming." Then louder so the rest of his squad and the other magi nearby could hear, he said, "The arch mage has ordered in the bulls. Stay vigilant. It's time to use the Knights' own firepower against them!"

In the distance, Jaxon could already hear the rumble of

the BearCats approaching. Codenamed "the bulls," Jaxon and Arch Mage Westarra had devised a strategy built on the brute force of the Knights' vehicles, and it was one of many they'd come up with that could be leveraged within a moment's time.

A cheer went up from inside the barrack as the BearCats thundered into view.

They think the BearCats are their own reinforcements, Jaxon realized. *They're in for a rude awakening.*

"They're gathering at the windows," Michael said.

Michael was right. Jaxon could make out several shadows behind many of the windows.

"Good," Jaxon said. "Our magi are tired and drained. We can't let this extend much longer."

"It's going to get bloodier."

The cheer grew louder as the BearCats approached, only to falter as they didn't make for the assembled magi and, instead, parked parallel to the front of the barracks between the two forces.

Several of the dark shadows near the barracks windows disappeared, no doubt taking a nervous step away from their exposed positions. It was too late, though. The magi inside the BearCats opened fire, launching grenades toward the broken barracks windows. Being the only one who had ever shot the weapons before, Nolan had run the magi through a crash course on how to fire the gun-mounted grenade launchers earlier in the night. Like most guns, they weren't overly complicated to use. Point. Shoot. Repeat. But also, like most guns, there *was* a learning curve.

Only half of the 40mm grenades launched from the open hatches of the BearCats hit their mark. The others bounced off the front of the compound, detonating on the ground dangerously close to the vehicles themselves. Inside the barracks, the Knights moved back into action, their temporary reprieve disappearing.

Gunfire hammered the BearCats, sending sparks shooting into the darkness as the magi reloaded and sent a second volley toward the enemy. Much like the first attack, half of the grenades found their targets, exploding inside the barracks, while more bounced against the ground outside. Only this time the misses were more catastrophic.

Jaxon watched as a grenade canister bounced off the barracks, rebounding with more force than he'd expected, and rolled under one of the BearCats. The muffled explosion threw the vehicle onto its side, wiping out a third of their heavy force in a single instant.

Despite the mistake, the magi attack was having an effect. Smoke from exploded grenades billowed out of several windows, and while there was no way to tell how many of the enemy they had taken out, Jaxon was willing to bet the number was substantial.

Movement to his right caught his attention. One of the other squads was advancing.

No, not advancing. They were making for the damaged BearCat.

The Knights saw them too and opened fire, and before Jaxon could do anything, two of the magi fell.

"Give them cover!" Jaxon sent a fireball flying toward the Knights firing on the advancing squad. Half a second later, the rest of his squad was doing the same.

From their distance, the attacks largely missed their mark but were enough to force the Knights to take cover and give the rescue force a few more precious seconds to reach their destination.

When the Knights reopened fire, they focused on Jaxon's squad, halting the onslaught, forcing the magi to take cover.

When Jaxon mustered up the courage to peek at the rescue, he saw that the magi had opened one of the larger BearCat hatches and were inside the vehicle. A couple short breaths later, the magi exited the vehicle carrying the fallen on their shoulders, the rest providing cover for their retreat.

"Again!" Jaxon shouted before launching a new series of fireballs toward the enemy. He took cover the moment the attacks were on their way, narrowly avoiding the Knights' next counterattack. Rocky shrapnel sliced the exposed skin of his arms and coated his dark skin with white dust.

"If we're going to do this," Michael shouted from his nearby cover, "we need to do it now."

He was right. At some point during the battle, the magi within the BearCats had shifted to firing their guns instead of their grenade launchers, a sign that they were out of grenades.

"Form up!" Jaxon said. "We're going in!"

Without a word, the two sub squads fell into position behind their squad leaders. Jaxon took three sharp breaths and darted toward the barracks, his men right on his heels. The magi within the BearCats continued their attack, using the Knights' own weapons against them and keeping them preoccupied. Their work allowed Jaxon's and Michael's sub squads to make it to the exterior wall of the barracks without incident.

They waited there for a moment, allowing the other squads to get into position. Roughly thirty magi in all, they formed up with their backs to the wall, crouching so that their heads were below the first-story windows.

Jaxon readied himself, preparing to give the order to advance, when something caught his attention.

Gunfire—coming from the forest, where Arch Mage Westarra commanded the battle with the magi reserve force.

Jaxon focused on the distant sounds of battle, his blood turning to ice. He knew what his orders were—they were more important than anything else—but the sounds of battle were unmistakable. Had the enemy somehow slipped behind the magi lines? The consequences of such a development would be catastrophic. He hesitated, running through possible scenarios in his head.

"Something's wrong," Jaxon said, his eyes still on the forest. "Michael, take the squads and carry on. Nolan, you're with me."

"What are you going to do?" Michael asked.

"I don't know yet," Jaxon said honestly. *But I'll do whatever it takes.*

CHAPTER 29

"LET ME GUESS," SEDRIC SAID, holding up a finger. "You're looking for the Blood Wand." He laughed when he saw Allyn's blank expression. "Come now, boy, I know you educated types like to think us military boys are slow, but that's just rude."

Sedric stepped deeper into the room, trailed by four fully armed Knights with their guns trained on Allyn and Canary. Two more Knights appeared in the hall behind them, dragging Ren and Leira with them. Each was bound and wore a pained expression. Blood matted the back of Ren's short hair and streaked down the back of her neck. Leira didn't look much better.

"Where is it?" Allyn growled, his eyes returning to the Knight Commander.

"Safe."

"And my people?"

Sedric paused beside Allyn's shoulder, his face making an expression Allyn couldn't place. "They're safe, too."

"You're lying," Allyn said.

"The Lord detests lying lips, and mine speak true. But enough about me. Tell me, who's this?"

Sedric made for Canary, his eyes going up and down her body like a man leering at a beautiful woman. "You're not as feisty as that one over there." He pointed at Ren, who was still woozy from the blow to her head. "You're not one of them healing types, are you? That would be something. That would *really* be something." He pushed her toward one of the nearby Knights. "Bind them."

"Bind us?" The words were out of Allyn's mouth before he had a chance to reel them back in. *If I get out of this, I really need to work on thinking before I talk.*

"Did you think we were going to kill you?" Sedric smiled playfully. "Believe me, Allyn, nothing would give me more satisfaction. Lucky for you, I have other orders." His smile disappeared, his expression turning dark. "Of course, people fall in battle all the time. It's the nature of war."

Sedric tapped his fingers against his lips as if contemplating the idea while his Knights yanked Allyn's hands behind his back, cuffing him.

"No," Sedric said finally. "Again, lucky for you, I follow my orders. You'll get what's coming to you, though. That, I know for sure."

"What are your orders?" Allyn asked.

"You'll find out soon enough." Sedric turned to the Knights who had bound Allyn and Canary. "Ready?"

"Ready, sir," they said.

"Good," Sedric said. "Let's go." Then as if it were an afterthought, he added, "And be careful. Just because they're bound don't mean they can't wield. They're still dangerous. Remember that."

"Yes, sir."

Apparently satisfied that his men understood the danger, the Knight Commander strode from the room, his Knights and the magi prisoners in tow. He led them to the first level then down another stairwell leading to the basement. There, he pulled open a secret hatch on the floor, exposing a set of concrete stairs.

"Down you go," Sedric said, waving the group on.

Once the group was at the bottom, yellow lights flickered on, lighting a long corridor complete with concrete walls and ceiling. The corridor itself was wide enough that a vehicle could drive through.

Of course, Allyn realized. *This is how they did it.*

It made too much sense, and he kicked himself for not realizing it sooner. Of course an old military base would have tunnels linking the buildings together. In the event of an attack, command would have to be able to move soldiers and equipment without the enemy being aware.

Did they use these against our other forces too?

Fear spread through his veins like ice water, leaving a helpless anger in its wake. He felt like an animal being led to its slaughter. He should be fighting, should be saving the magi around him and the others above, but with Ren's and Leira's injuries, the odds of successfully freeing them were too great. His only choice was to be patient and wait for an opening.

Sedric set off down the corridor, the Knights pushing the magi after him until the tunnel opened into a larger chamber. It looked like some sort of underground garage, and in it was a trio of parked BearCats.

"Inside." Sedric held open the door as his Knights shoved Allyn and Canary into the first vehicle. One of the Knights climbed into the rear hatch with them and shoved Allyn onto the bench before closing the hatch behind them. Two more climbed in the front, and the driver wasted no time before firing up the vehicle.

Sedric shoved Ren and Leira into the second BearCat, and

within moments, they were all moving. The concrete walls amplified the BearCats' engine noise, making them sound almost like a pair of airplanes getting ready to take off. Then they were moving upward, and a moment later, the BearCats' engine volume was cut in half.

We're out of the tunnels.

Allyn tried to look out of the small windows, earning him a blow to the side of the head.

"Eyes forward," the Knight in the back said. He stood between Allyn and Canary, one hand holding onto a bar mounted to the roof of the vehicle.

"Where are you taking us?" Allyn said.

The Knight hit him again, and Allyn tasted copper. He spit at the Knight, and a thick glob of blood stuck to his chest.

"You little fucker," the Knight said. "You think this is a game? I'll show—"

"What the hell is going on back there?" one of the Knights in front bellowed.

"This fucker thinks we're playing. I'm going to—"

"You're going to do nothing. No one touches him. Commander's orders."

"But—"

"No 'buts,' Livingston. Understood?"

The first Knight growled but didn't push the issue. Allyn gave him a bloody smile.

Livingston leaned in close, his breath thick with the smell of alcohol. "I'm going to gut you."

"Your breath stinks," Allyn said.

The Knight puckered his lips together and blew out long and slow as if he were blowing smoke into Allyn's face, then he laughed and pulled back, a humorless sneer on his face.

Allyn had no idea how long they drove or in what direction they were headed, but the sun eventually rose high enough for him to see through the windows behind Canary. The forested landscape gave way to rolling hills and small towns, and once again, his thoughts returned to escape.

However, as the miles ticked by, he wasn't sure escaping was the best move. He couldn't be sure, but he didn't think their forces had found any of the abducted magi at the Knights' base. Did that mean Allyn and the rest of his squad were being taken to where the others were being held? If so, he wasn't sure he could give up that opportunity. But what would happen when they arrived? Allyn would be a prisoner himself. Then again, if he broke free now, the whereabouts of their kin would remain a mystery.

Unless... unless there's a third option.

He smiled as the thought materialized. It had been so obvious he'd almost missed it.

CHAPTER 30

JAXON AND NOLAN MADE IT back to the forest in good time, the sounds of the battle growing closer with every step. Jaxon cut through the tree line, moving through the thick foliage, treasuring speed over silence, and it didn't take them long to arrive. What they found was complete chaos.

The location—a small rise with sparse trees, which had provided the magi quick access to the road and a clear path to the barracks—was no longer working in their favor. The sparseness of the forest offered less cover, especially against a force that stuck to the forest shadows and harassed the magi from a distance.

The magi had formed a ring around the arch mage and several of the more prominent grand mages, including Jaxon's father. The Knights numbered roughly the same as the magi—maybe thirty in all—but were more concentrated and were conducting a focused assault.

"They're going after the arch mage," Nolan said quietly. "What do we do? We can't take them on all at once."

Jaxon was barely listening, his mind working out the beginnings of a plan. "Wait here."

"Wait here?" Nolan said, incredulous. "For how long?"

"You'll know."

"What are you going to do?"

"I'm going to nip at their heels."

"What does that mean?"

But Jaxon was already moving. He left Nolan behind, trusting the other man would enter the fray when the time was right. Part of him thought he'd made a mistake in bringing Nolan, that the man would have been better suited for the battle within the barracks, but there was nothing he could do about that now. And any lingering doubt disappeared as the Knight force came into view—Jaxon would need all the firepower he could get.

The Knights were pressing their advantage, and already, the magi lines showed signs of breaking. If he didn't act fast, the reserve unit would be forced to retreat, putting the lives of the arch mage and much of the magi leadership in even greater danger.

Moving softly and sticking to the shadows, Jaxon encased his fists in air and made for a human-shaped shadow hidden behind a tree. He had fought the Knights enough to understand their vulnerabilities, primarily the weak spot in their tactical armor.

Using the sounds of battle as his cover, Jaxon snuck up behind the Knight and drove an air-aided fist into his side. The blow landed with a miniature explosion of air, striking with several times the force of a normal punch. Jaxon felt ribs crack as the Knight stiffened and collapsed to the ground.

Already wielding again, Jaxon drove a lance of ice between the Knight's breastplate and helmet, into his throat, silencing the cry of alarm before it could make it out of his chest.

Leaving the ice shard in the Knight's throat, Jaxon moved toward his next target. He found the Knight only ten paces away and neutralized him in much the same way before moving on again, carving his way through the edge of the Rakkaran line. It wasn't until he eliminated the fifth Knight that he was spotted.

Jaxon rolled through the underbrush, ducking behind a large tree as the Knight opened fire. Bullets ravaged the landscape, tearing through ferns and splintering the thick tree trunk that Jaxon hid behind. Keeping his breathing calm and steady, Jaxon readied another attack.

The rest of the Knight force was still too preoccupied with the magi reserves to have noticed one of their own engaged in a battle with a rogue magi. Knowing he couldn't afford to draw the ire of the full force, Jaxon sprang into action.

The air *cracked* as he propelled another ice blast forward with a concussion of air. It shattered against the attacking Knight's battle armor and sent him cascading backward. Jaxon rushed toward him, doubting the ice had punctured the armor, and found the Knight splayed on the ground, his helmet gone. The Knight tried to bring up his gun, but Jaxon landed on him, burying his knees into the biceps of each arm, and drove a lance of ice through his eye.

Jaxon tore his eyes away from the dead Knight just in time to see three more breaking away from the main unit, their guns already trained on him. Apparently, his one-on-one battle hadn't gone as unnoticed as he'd first thought.

He cursed, diving away as gunfire tore through the forest. Sailing through the air, he knew the maneuver was useless. He was dead. It was only a matter of time.

Except when he landed, rolled, and readied himself to spring away again, he realized the three Knights were on the ground. Confused, Jaxon spun, his eyes searching the forest until he found Nolan, carrying a gun of his own.

"You were right," Nolan said, approaching. "I knew when the time was right."

"I'll say." Jaxon raised an eyebrow at the sight of the gun.

"It's more subtle than magic," Nolan said with a shrug. "With this crowd, anyway."

"Speaking of which," Jaxon said, "it looks like we've made a dent in their line. Keep it up, and we might give our people a chance."

Nolan pulled the magazine from his assault rifle, checking his remaining rounds, then dropped and grabbed two more from the fallen Knights. "Let's get to it."

"One last thing," Jaxon said.

"Yeah?"

"The time for subtlety is over. Make our two feel like twenty. Let our magi know we're out here."

Nolan smiled. "All right then."

Jaxon moved before either said anything more. The magi force had to know there was a weakness in the Knights' line—and that they weren't alone. And there was only one way to do that.

Wielding balls of fire in each hand, Jaxon strode toward the enemy. The world slowed as he fell into the deep concentration that the Mahari had taught him. He could almost see individual bullets as they were spit out of gun barrels, smell the sweat and fear of the Knights, taste the desperation of his fellow magi.

The first fireball exploded against the side of a Knight's helmet, bathing a small section of the forest in an orange light. The Knight next to him spun, turning to face Jaxon, but Jaxon's second fireball took him in the center of his chest.

Continuing down the line, Jaxon hurled fireball after fireball, maximizing the element of surprise. He carved through the enemy lines like a rock through water, and it didn't take long for the magi to take notice.

Without a word, or at least words that Jaxon could hear,

the magi force swelled toward him. At their head was Rohn Agerland, the Spark of Arch Mage Westarra's Elemental Guard. His long hair tied into a tail behind him, he surged forward, wielding with a ferocity Jaxon could only dream of matching.

Jaxon made for the magi, noticing as he drew closer that their faces contorted with the pained expressions of overexertion. They kept fighting, though, hurling fireballs and ice blasts into the trees where the enemy hid.

"Jaxon!" his father called out. "What are you doing here? You're supposed to be with the main force."

"I heard the battle," Jaxon said. "We came to protect the arch mage."

"We?"

"Nolan is with me," Jaxon said, his words punctuated by a flash of white light as Nolan continued to harrow the enemy lines. "Where did the Knights come from?"

"I don't know," his father said. "And we don't have time to talk about it now. We need to protect the arch mage."

"Agreed," Jaxon said, moving again.

"What are you doing?"

"Protecting him the only way I know how. By killing them before they kill us."

His father obviously didn't agree with the decision but didn't say anything more. Jaxon melded in with the rest of the advancing magi force. When a scream punctuated the battle, he spun, finding a small knot of magi crowding around a white mass. Most had their backs to it, attacking a knot of Knights who had opened fire, while a few others were on their knees attending to the fallen.

"No," Jaxon said, rushing toward the group of magi. He knew what he would find before he got there, but his heart still sank when he arrived.

CAPTURE

Blood pooled under the arch mage's white battle dress, soaking into the forest floor. His face had gone ashen, his eyes cold as the clerics continued their work. But Jaxon already knew the truth, even if the rest refused to see it.

Arch Mage Westarra, the leader of the magi Order, was dead.

CHAPTER 31

ALLYN BIDED HIS TIME. His plan was audacious, damn near suicidal, but given the circumstances, it was the best he could come up with.

"Hey," Allyn whispered when the Knight who had been riding in the rear compartment with them strode toward the cab.

Canary looked at him.

"How are you doing?"

She didn't answer.

"Are they... are they on the radio with each other?"

She looked toward the front of the vehicle then back at Allyn.

"Yeah, them. Are they talking to the people in the other vehicle?"

She shook her head.

"Good," Allyn said. "Can you block any transmissions from going out?"

She nodded.

"Perfect. I need you to do that. You can do that, right?" It was less a question of her abilities, and more a question ensuring she was mentally up for the task. Unlike the others, Canary had never experienced battle, let alone been taken prisoner by the enemy.

She nodded again, this time with a little more vigor.

"Good," Allyn said again. "I'm going to get us out of here."

Her eyes went wide as Allyn climbed to his feet. There were no seatbelts in the back of the BearCat, and the Knight hadn't bothered to secure them to the bench.

Livingston's back was still to him as Allyn snuck forward. The BearCat shifted and swayed under his feet, its stiff suspension making it difficult to keep his balance. Allyn kept his knees bent, weathering the movement, then with a burst of speed, charged forward and drove his shoulder into the center of Livingston's back.

The Knight flew forward. His face, which was no longer protected by his helmet, slammed into the front windshield, leaving behind a bloody streak.

The driver shouted and reached for Allyn but couldn't do anything lest he take his eyes off the road. Allyn ignored him, already engaging the passenger. He wielded, feeling the coils of electricity more than he saw them, and with his hands still bound behind his back, he reached blindly for the second Knight. When his fingers found flesh, he grasped, and the coils leaped from him to the Knight like hungry snakes. The smell of burning flesh filled the cab.

"Knight Commander! Knight Commander, this is Singh. Do you copy?" the driver bellowed into a wireless radio. "Knight Commander, do you copy? We have a situation back here!"

Allyn didn't have time to worry about the message going through. He had to trust that Canary was able to block it. His hands still bound behind his back, Allyn spun and reached for the driver. Seeing what had happened to his comrade, the driver pulled away, yanking on the wheel as he did.

The BearCat lurched, throwing Allyn in the opposite direction. Landing on the dead passenger, Allyn struggled to his feet then wielded again. He launched himself at the driver, who struggled to regain control of the heavy vehicle. Allyn felt the Knight go stiff. His screams filled the inside of the cabin, but Allyn refused to disengage, and the screams slowly died away as the Knight was electrocuted.

The BearCat drifted right, then left, veering in and out of the lane as the burned remains of the driver slumped in his seat. Allyn let the coils dissipate and grabbed hold of the wheel, bringing the vehicle back under control. It was awkward—no, it was damn near impossible to drive with his hands bound behind his back, and standing as he was, there wasn't anything he could do about it slowing down.

"Canary!" Allyn bellowed as their BearCat fell farther and farther behind the lead vehicle. "Canary, I need you up here!"

She appeared a moment later, her eyes wide as she took in the scene.

"Keys," Allyn said. "There!" He nodded at Livingston. "On his belt."

Canary snagged the keys and quickly undid Allyn's cuffs. By the time she did, the lead vehicle was completely out of sight. Wasting little time, Allyn snatched the keys from her, returned the favor, then yanked the driver out of his seat and climbed behind the wheel. Beside him, Canary did the same with the passenger.

"I think you're going to want to buckle up for this," Allyn said.

He saw the questioning look in her eyes but didn't say anything more. There was no time for answers. He clicked his seatbelt into place and stomped on the gas. The BearCat roared forward, barreling down the four-lane road. They were in the middle of a city now, not a huge city full of skyscrapers but large enough to be well populated.

"Singh, come in," a voice on the radio said, sounding more irritated than concerned. "Singh, where are you?"

Allyn looked at Canary, his mind spinning. He'd only heard the other man speak once and couldn't remember his accent, or if he even had one.

"Singh?" the voice said again. "What is going on back there?"

Allyn grabbed the wireless radio. "This is Singh. Got hung up at a red light, that's all."

"A red light?"

"Yeah," Allyn said. "A red light. Catching up now."

"If this is Singh, tell me the name of the man in the passenger seat."

Allyn cursed, turning to Canary. "Does he have an ID?"

She ran a hand over his pockets, searching for a wallet, badge, or some other form of identification. She shook her head.

"No need for that," Allyn said. "I can see you now. We're almost there."

It was true—they were only about one hundred feet behind it and gaining quickly.

"Who is this?"

Allyn dropped the radio and floored the gas pedal, closing the remaining distance between them and the other BearCat in only a matter of seconds.

Allyn screamed, Canary joining him, as their BearCat slammed into the back of the lead vehicle with a thunderous crash. Allyn was thrown forward against his seatbelt as the BearCat lurched. Fighting to keep the vehicle under control, he yanked the steering wheel left then right. When he had control again, he saw that the driver of the other vehicle had done the same. He mashed the gas pedal again, preparing to ram the lead BearCat a second time.

Instead of ramming it directly from behind, Allyn pulled up beside the vehicle so that he was even with its rear tires then yanked the wheel to the side, smashing into the BearCat again. The maneuver kicked the vehicle's rear tires out, spinning the rear of the BearCat around. Speed and momentum kicked in. The lead BearCat lurched, tipped up on two wheels, then tumbled end over end. Landing on its cab, it slid to a halt in a mass of sparks.

Allyn slammed on the brakes, bringing his vehicle to a screeching halt. He was out of the vehicle a moment later, striding toward the wrecked BearCat.

It was time to cut the head from the snake.

CHAPTER 32

J AXON'S WORLD SLOWED TO A standstill. The bursts of light from muzzle flashes seemed to freeze as if caught on camera. The echoes of their gunfire were drawn out so that every metallic sound and concussive noise was a distinct and separate piece of the same battle concerto. He could almost see the ripples in the air left behind by bullets, see the smoke trailing off fireballs hurled in return, see individual droplets of water dripping from ice blasts.

"The arch mage is down!" someone bellowed.

And immediately, the chaos of battle returned. Following the brief moment before, everything seemed to move in double time, as if being fast-forwarded to catch up.

Though Jaxon stood only a few feet from Arch Mage Westarra's body, he might as well have been a world away. The broiling mixture of shock and confusion rendered him useless.

More of the Elemental Guard had fallen in with their brethren, protecting the arch mage from further attacks. Most had their backs to him, while three of their guard assessed the arch mage's wounds. Westarra's eyes were cold and lifeless, his arms flailing without resistance as the magi removed his battle attire and stripped him down to his bare skin. Two bullet wounds, little more than round holes, spewed blood down his back.

So much death caused by something so small.

The guards laid the arch mage facedown on the ground, working in silence. Their speed and efficiency was a product of process, of knowing what needed to be done, by whom, and when.

Jaxon had gained too much experience with guns and bullet wounds recently, and knew that the first step to treating a gunshot was removing the bullet. Fortunately for the arch mage, one of the bullets had traveled clean through his body, and his guards were already working on removing the other. Cringing, Jaxon tore his eyes from the magi and fell into position with the rest of the Elemental Guard.

"We have to get the arch mage to safety," Jaxon said as he hurled a fireball into the trees.

"No," Rohn said. "We can't risk moving him. There's no time. We have to give the clerics time to heal him here."

Clerics?

Jaxon glanced back to the rest of the guards. Dressed in the same magi compression armor, the Elemental Guards' blacks were embroidered with swatches of color around the sleeve cuffs and neckline. Most were red, but those treating the arch mage's were blue.

As far as he had known, every member of the Elemental Guard was a magi, their lives sworn to protecting the magi leader. But protection, he supposed, could take on many different forms, and it made sense that a small number of them would be clerics. But a cleric only had so much power—they couldn't bring someone back from the dead.

They wouldn't be trying to save him if they didn't think he had a chance.

A sharp cry brought Jaxon's attention back to the battle. A fountain of blood sprayed from the shoulder of one of the guards in their line. He dropped to the ground, writhing in pain, before rising again, retaking his position, his arm hanging uselessly at their side.

"We can't stay here," Jaxon said. "We're sitting ducks."

"We have to give them time," Rohn said again. His jaw was set, his face hard, showing no signs of changing his mind.

Jaxon ground his teeth but didn't say anything more. Who was he to question the Spark, the leader of the arch mage's Elemental Guard, the man whose sole responsibility was protecting the magi leader?

Someone fell into step beside Jaxon. Then another, and he realized that the remaining magi reserves were returning. The number of their small protective force swelled, doubling, and then tripling in size, every one of them providing additional levels of protection for their arch mage. Then he heard shouted commands from a voice he would recognize in any crowd.

"To the arch mage!" Liam bellowed. "To the arch mage!"

He stood twenty paces down the hillside, his slender frame little more than a shadow in the forest, waving the magi forward like a police officer directing traffic.

"Move!" Liam continued to shout. "To the arch mage!"

The size of the circle shielding the arch mage continued to swell as additional lines of magi filled their ranks. Jaxon and the Elemental Guard pushed their way to the front as each new wave arrived, allowing the reinforcements to take their place behind them. Liam spotted Jaxon and took up position at his shoulder.

"Good work," Jaxon said.

"You too."

Around them the sounds of gunfire slowly faded until

there was none at all. Jaxon eyed the forest warily, catching brief shadows moving toward a central location. The sun had crested the horizon some time ago, but much of its light hadn't yet found the forest floor, leaving the battlefield in looming darkness.

"What are they doing?" Liam asked.

"Regrouping," Jaxon said. He continued to watch the forest, his apprehension growing, and was the first to see the figure appear from the trees. "Nolan."

The former FBI agent was a bloodied mess, though judging by his quick and seemingly unpained movements, most of it didn't appear to be his.

"You're alive," Nolan said with a smile, joining the magi ranks.

"You too, I see."

"So far," Nolan said. "The Knights are massing for another assault."

"Did you see them?" Rohn asked.

Nolan nodded.

"Tell me what you know," Rohn said. "Everything. We need to mount a resistance."

Nolan began telling the Spark everything he had seen. While he did, Jaxon pushed his way through the magi lines, making for the arch mage. He needed to know how long their resistance would have to hold out.

Arch Mage Westarra still lay on his stomach, the three clerics on their knees surrounding him. His skin had gone pallid, and one of the bullet wounds had been widened, no doubt to allow one of the clerics to remove the bullet. Their expressions were more distressed than Jaxon remembered.

We're running out of time.

As if coming to the same conclusion themselves, the clerics formed a triangular shape around Westarra. Placing a hand on the arch mage's back, they closed their eyes, and a moment later, three points of white light blossomed from their touch.

They're forming a chain.

Ripples of light emanated through the arch mage's body, and within moments the clerics began showing signs of pain. Eyes still closed, the far cleric's lips parted, her face contorting in agony.

Jaxon couldn't see any outward signs of the arch mage's injuries appearing on her body, but that wasn't unexpected. Most of the injury, especially the parts that required the most medical attention, were within the body, not the puncture wound itself.

Sweat began to bead on the cleric's forehead, sticking her red hair to her forehead. For some reason, the other two seemed in better shape. That didn't make any sense. By forming a chain, the clerics were supposed to share the burden equally.

Something's wrong.

As if sensing it too, the other two clerics opened their eyes and looked at their companion, their expressions full of shock and anger.

"Jayme," the male cleric said, his voice gruff and thick with pain. "What are you doing?"

"What I must." Unlike the other two, she kept her eyes closed.

"This isn't the way," the male cleric said.

"He's too far gone, Kieren," Jayme said.

"Jayme," Kieren said. "Please."

"He needs a *life spark.*"

"Jayme..."

She opened her eyes, looking deeply into his. They were

so filled with love and compassion that Jaxon felt guilty for impeding on their final moments.

"I'm sorry, Kieren," she said, tears pouring down her face. "I love you."

A bright flash illuminated from Jayme's touch, and as if recoiling from an electric shock, the other two clerics jerked away from the arch mage. It must have been an involuntary gesture, because Kieren immediately tried to reestablish his connection.

But Jaxon knew it was already too late. As soon as Kieren and the other cleric's hands had been repelled, the ripples emanating from Jayme's hands brightened, growing more intense.

"No!" Kieren shouted. "No! Don't do this! Jayme, stop!"

The ripples gained in speed, rolling from Westarra's head to his toes so quickly that Jaxon couldn't differentiate one ripple from the next. Jayme cried out as the puncture wound appeared on her back. Fresh blood poured from it like milk from a hole in the side of a milk carton.

Kieren desperately attempted to reestablish his connection, but something Jayme was doing prevented him from being able to do it. He watched helplessly as she sacrificed herself for the magi leader.

His own tears flowing, Kieren reached out a hand, cupping Jayme's face. Her eyes opened, and without breaking her connection to the arch mage, she smiled at her love. And then her light faded, and she fell.

Kieren caught her before she hit the earth and draped her body across his. He stroked the side of her face, tears streaming down his, and whispered something to her. A private goodbye.

So much death, Jaxon thought solemnly. *Is there anyone in the Order who's been untouched?*

"We've got a pulse!"

Kieren looked up from Jayme, his eyes red as they fell upon the other cleric. Anger washed over his face.

"She did it, Kieren. She did it."

Kieren didn't move, his eyes returning to his fallen love.

"Come on, Kieren. Before it's too late."

But the distraught cleric wasn't listening. He cupped the side of Jayme's face, stroking her cheek with his thumb.

"Kieren! Don't let her death be for nothing!"

Fresh tears falling from his eyes, Kieren met the other cleric's pleading gaze.

"Come on!"

Kieren nodded slightly and leaned down and kissed Jayme on the forehead. Then taking a deep shuddering breath, he laid Jayme aside and, together with the other cleric, returned to work.

"Jaxon!"

Jaxon snapped his head around then pushed his way back through the mass of magi. Nolan stood next to Rohn, their attention focused on a point directly in front of them. Following their gaze, Jaxon spotted a group of fifteen Knights streaming out in a line that ran parallel to the magi force.

"What are they doing?" Jaxon asked.

"Preparing for a last stand," Rohn said. "How is the arch mage?"

"He lives," Jaxon said.

A shudder went through Rohn's body. "Then we cannot fail." He took a step beyond the group, turning his back on the Knight force. "Listen up!" Rohn shouted. "Everything you have fought for tonight comes down to this. The arch mage lives, but those men out there want to see him, you, and everyone we hold dear dead. I don't intend to let that happen. Who's with me?"

A cheer rang up from the magi group.

"Who's with me?" Rohn shouted again.

Another louder cheer, this one louder.

"Every man and woman still able to fight, line up!"

The arch mage's protective circle disbanded as magi lined up shoulder to shoulder, mirroring the Knights. They stood a hundred paces away from each other, one dressed in tactical armor and wielding guns, the other wearing black compression armor and wielding magic. Like two ancient armies donning swords and chainmail, they stared at each other, waiting for the order to charge.

Rohn turned from the group, returning his gaze to the Knights. He held up a hand, and a moment later, fire sprang to life around it. In one fluid motion, he hurled the fireball at the enemy. Like a meteor blazing across the sky, the fireball flew toward the enemy.

"For the arch mage!" Rohn shouted.

The magi line charged, prepared to die for their Order's survival.

CHAPTER 33

ALLYN STRODE TOWARD THE WRECKED BearCat. His hands were at his side, fingers splayed, not yet wielding but ready to at a moment's notice.

The BearCat was only twenty feet away, lying perpendicular in the four-lane street and blocking oncoming traffic. Steam rose from its engine compartment, and blue smoke billowed from its tires, filling the morning air with the acrid smell of burnt rubber. Green fluid, either coolant or transmission fluid, ran down its black exterior, pooling on the blacktop.

Cars and pedestrians had already begun gathering around the scene, no doubt ready to lend their aid to the victims of the crash.

"Stay back!" Allyn shouted, motioning for the pedestrians to return to their cars. Most listened, though not all. "I said stay back!" he shouted again, channeling every ounce of authority he could muster. The remaining do-gooders stopped, though, to Allyn's frustration, they didn't return to their cars.

He couldn't worry about them, though. He had to keep his attention on the broken BearCat, on Sedric's whereabouts. He was the key to his plan. Nearing the driver's door, Allyn dropped to a crouch and quickly glanced inside. Not seeing anything immediately dangerous, he pulled open the door, letting it fall against the blacktop, and stole another glance inside the driver's compartment.

The driver hung upside down, held in place by his seatbelt. Blood ran down his face, dripping onto the top of the cab. His eyes were open, cold and lifeless, and he didn't move. The seat beside him was empty, the door—

Someone screamed.

Allyn leaped to the side, trusting instinct over reason, and was rewarded when a wave of searing heat shot passed his face. An instant later, something exploded against the inside of the door.

Disoriented, but uninjured, Allyn rolled and leaped again just as a second explosion erupted. He hit the ground hard, pain flaring in his shoulder, then rolled onto his feet and sprinted toward a nearby car. He slid across the hood and landed on the other side, placing two thousand pounds of steel and glass between him and his attacker.

Allyn wasn't the only one hiding behind the car, though. A middle-aged man with thinning blond hair and dressed in a suit and tie stared at him with a terrified, wide-eyed expression.

Tearing his eyes off the man, Allyn risked a peek through the passenger window. Still donning his black tactical armor, Sedric advanced toward the car Allyn was hiding behind. And in his hands burned a pair of fireballs.

Sedric snarled and hurled the fireballs at Allyn, and Allyn had just enough time to duck back under the window before the fireballs struck. The car lurched as glass shattered and fell on Allyn's head and shoulders. It peppered the ground, cracking against the blacktop as the driver hurried away.

Allyn looked around desperately. He needed a weapon. A

gun. A knife. Anything. Why hadn't he thought to grab one of the Knights' guns?

Stupid! You've become too reliant on your abilities.

But he wasn't truly weaponless. He felt the energy raging inside him. Enhanced by his sudden brush with death, it was ready to be unleashed.

He also saw the people around him. Saw the reflection of Sedric's fireballs in their eyes. Most watched with horrified, confused expressions, though a few were recording the battle with their phones. In one terrible moment, Allyn realized that Sedric Lang, Knight Commander of the Knights of Rakkar, the sworn enemy of the magi Order, had just destroyed everything the magi had worked for since the Fracture.

Even worse, he'd done so in a way that endangered the lives of innocent civilians, harmless men and women whose only crime was commuting to work on the wrong street on the wrong day. The world would have no choice but to come to the obvious conclusion: The magi were dangerous. Someone to be feared. The enemy.

In his mind's eye, Allyn could almost see the fallout. Twenty-four, seven news coverage of marches and protests ending in riots. Hate crimes. The government attempting to restore order by forcing magi to self-register. Bringing in the National Guard when they didn't. Bloodshed when rogue Families were found. Segregation. Internment camps. And it wouldn't be relegated to a single state or country—it would be a global phenomenon unlike anything the world had ever seen. And there would be no escape.

Allyn shook with the injustice of it all. There wasn't anything he could do. He was helpless.

Except...

If he were seen fighting such a threat, that would have to count for something, wouldn't it? It would show the world that not all magi were like Sedric. At the very least, it would show that there were different factions among the magi. Maybe it wouldn't counteract all fear and xenophobic feelings toward his people, but it might be a start.

Another fireball struck the car, shattering the remaining windows, and Allyn was reminded that he had more pressing issues than figuring out the best way to introduce the magi to the world. Issues like surviving the next three minutes.

Seeing no other options, Allyn took a final look around, making eye contact and nodding compassionately to the remaining pedestrians, and wielded. Fear turned to terror as the remaining pedestrians scrambled to get away from the new threat.

So much for showing the world I am the good *magi.*

"Allyn, Allyn, Allyn," Sedric's voice cut through the panic, his tone reminiscent of a disappointed parent. "Why don't you come out here and face me like a real man and not the coward you really are?"

Allyn gritted his teeth and stood, finding Sedric only about ten feet away on the other side of the car. A large cut above his eye spilled blood down his face, staining his gray hair and beard red.

"That's better," Sedric said. He sucked his split lips and spat a glob of congealed blood that fell well short of Allyn. "That was a bold move, Allyn, crashing the vehicle your friends rode in. Do you not care about them?"

"I need to know where you've taken my Family."

"It doesn't matter," Sedric said. "Wherever they are, they're serving the Lord's purpose."

"What are you doing to them?" Allyn growled.

"Drawing the devil out."

"Without the pious bullshit."

Sedric laughed. "Come on, Allyn. You know I'm not going to tell you what we've done with them."

"Then you leave me with no other choice." Allyn held his arms out wide, letting Sedric see the full glory of his magi abilities.

Sedric nodded and let out a long breath. "It was always going to end this way, Allyn. You and me. Alone."

Allyn shrugged, feigning nonchalance, then in an instant and with a powerful step forward, he brought his hands together in a mighty clap. The coils of electricity writhing around each arm collided, flashing a brilliant white, and a single red cord of electricity shot toward the Knight Commander.

Sedric didn't attempt to jump out of the way. Instead, he took a strong step forward of his own and brought his hands and forearms together in front of his face. Just before the cord of electricity struck, Allyn saw a thick coating, vaguely blue in color, solidify around the Knight Commander's arms.

Ice.

Allyn's cord of electricity struck, shattering the ice around Sedric's arms and hurling the Knight Commander backward with amazing force. He landed on his back, his tactical armor sliding across the blacktop and protecting him from harm. Before he came to a complete stop, he rolled onto his feet and brought up his right hand.

Allyn barely had time to register the attack before a translucent shard of ice was erasing the distance between them. He danced to the side just in time to watch it bury itself into the side of the car.

Sedric spun, launching a second lance of ice from his other hand. Expecting the attack, Allyn planted a foot, reversing course and darting in the opposite direction. The move succeeded, Sedric's attack going wide.

No longer on his heels, Allyn readied an attack of his own, and in a blink, he had three static charges racing toward the enemy. The first two sailed wide, but the third flew true and was about to take the Knight Commander in the chest when he *punched* it out of the air. Ice shattered, and it took Allyn a moment to realize the Knight Commander had coated his hands with it.

Sedric flexed, his lips curling into a smile. "You're not the only one who's been training." He took a giant breath and ripped his arms out wide, exposing his chest. The air in front of him warped and seemed to collapse upon itself then exploded with an ear-splitting *crack*.

The concussion of air threw Allyn off his feet and sent him tumbling through the air. He came to an abrupt and painful halt, smashing into the side of a nearby car. The remaining air in his lungs vanished, and he felt something inside him crack.

You need to move, he told himself. *Move or die.*

With a groan, Allyn rose to his feet, only to be met with a second concussion of air. He crashed into the car with even more force, blacking out from the pain.

When he came to, he was face down on the blacktop. Blood streaked down his face, smearing across the street. Every inch of him hurt. He coughed, and the sudden expenditure of air splattered more blood onto the street. Allyn blinked, trying to shake the cobwebs loose. Instead, the world warped, and his vision went dark again.

He woke to a heavy boot rolling him onto his back. He stared up into the partly cloudy sky, the sunlight like tiny daggers plunging into his eyes. Sedric looked down at him, the light behind him masking his features.

"You still with me, Allyn?" Sedric asked. "I'd hate to kill you without you knowing it's coming."

Allyn groaned. Words came to his mind but failed to make it to his lips.

"I'll take that as a yes." New light appeared as Sedric wielded fire. "It's the Lord's time to judge you, Allyn. Good luck."

The final vestiges of Allyn's fight-or-flight instincts flared, and before he knew what he was doing, his hand was reaching up toward Sedric. Red light mixed with orange for a single, indefinable moment. The world didn't just slow, but crawled as Allyn watched the static charge collide with Sedric's fireball.

The bonds that held the two together shattered, turning the fireball into a horizontal wave of flame. Something similar happened to the static charge—the individual coils that made up the flattened disk came apart, spinning off at random angles. Just as the wave of flame washed across Allyn's hand, a single tendril of electricity whipped across Sedric's face.

Allyn rolled onto his knees as Sedric staggered backward, clutching his face. Spikes of pain shot up his arm, and he looked down to see the skin of his hand was red and blistered, blood and other fluids already seeping from the wound. Allyn stared at it, shock removing pain, replacing emotion with cold logic.

Sedric pulled his hand from his face, and a six-inch burn stretched up his right cheek, into his eyebrow, where it had left a cleft in its center. Blood seeped from the Knight Commander's right eye socket, the eye itself *deflated.*

Allyn's stomach threatened to empty itself. The only thing preventing that was the look in the Knight Commander's good eye. He didn't say anything—he didn't need to. His expression said everything. Sedric wasn't playing games any longer, wasn't trying to hide his villainous acts behind a righteous mask. He had only one thing on his mind.

Vengeance.

Allyn let his bloody hand fall to his side and watched as the Knight Commander limped toward him. He had no intention of going out without a fight, but injured as he was, he knew the odds were not in his favor. He started to rise to his feet when movement behind Sedric reminded him he had something the Knight Commander would never have.

Family.

Ren had emerged from the wrecked BearCat and was moving in their direction. Clutching her side, she was a mess of blood, sweat, and anger, but she still rushed toward the unsuspecting magi enemy as fast as her injured body would allow. A lance of ice appeared in her hand at the same time Sedric's fists came alive with fire. She must not have trusted her aim at the distance, though, as she didn't hurl it toward the Knight Commander.

Sedric continued forward, oblivious to the advancing magi.

Allyn let himself fall backward and slid away from the Knight Commander. The move gave him a few precious seconds—and more importantly, it gave Ren a clearer shot.

The first lance of ice exploded through Sedric's upper leg, its tip ripping through his quad. Howling in pain, Sedric fell to one knee, the fire around his hands disappearing. The second lance of ice ripped through his shoulder, sending him face-first into the blacktop.

Ren appeared behind him, already wielding again, ready to end Sedric's reign.

"No!" Allyn choked out. "Wait."

Ren hesitated, confusion on her face.

"We need him alive." Allyn winced in pain. Damn, it even hurt to talk. "He knows where our people are."

Ren gave Sedric a final look then nodded, her hands falling to her sides. She grabbed a fistful of the Knight Commander's hair, yanking his head from the ground.

"He's out," Ren said.

"Good. Help me up." Ren stepped over Sedric and took Allyn's good hand. "Slowly," he added at the last second.

With her help, Allyn rose to his feet. His whole body resisted, screaming in agony, and it was all he could do not to collapse. Once on his feet, he leaned heavily on Ren and surveyed the battlefield. The pedestrians were emerging from their hiding places, heads popping up from behind cars, and stepping out of nearby shops. They stared at Allyn and Ren with a mix of fear and awe, not quite sure if the danger had completely passed.

Allyn's heart thundered, his breath quickening. Commotion was building, the pedestrians growing more comfortable by the second. More and more of them were pulling their phones from their pockets, snapping pictures, and taking more video. At any moment, he expected to hear sirens. In fact, now that the battle was behind him, he was surprised a police presence hadn't arrived already.

"We need to go," he muttered.

"Yeah..." But Ren didn't move, and worse, there was something in her voice, a deep, resounding disappointment that twisted at Allyn's insides.

He looked at her—she was fixated on the crowd of onlookers. And in that moment, he knew his previous assessment of the magi future only told part of the story. Exposing the magi existence to the world wasn't as simple as no longer living in secret. It meant the end to their entire lifestyle, their very culture, everything that they had held on to and made them who they were. Like it or not, justified or not, Allyn's and Ren's faces would forever be the symbols of that change, and in her face, in the tears flooding over the banks of her eyelids, he saw the same regret that pulsed through his own veins.

"Come on," Allyn sighed. "We need to go."

Ren nodded, wiped the tears from her eyes, and left, quickly bringing the BearCat around. With Canary's help, they pulled the Knight Commander into the back of the vehicle. Like Allyn and Ren, she looked worse for wear, though it had less to do with any outward injuries. Her eyes were sunken and skin ashen as if she hadn't slept for days, and suddenly, the lack of police presence made sense.

"You stopped their calls from going through," Allyn said.

"Yes." If exhaustion had a sound, Canary's voice was it.

Allyn laid a hand on her shoulder and gave her his most thankful expression. "Good work."

"Thank you," she said, smiling.

With Sedric securely in the vehicle, Ren pulled the BearCat beside the second, and she and Canary repeated the process, bringing the injured Leira into their care. The cleric had struck her head in the crash, and though her injuries didn't appear to be dire, head injuries were difficult to predict. Canary stayed with Leira in the back of the BearCat, keeping an eye on her and the prostrate body of the Knight Commander.

Ren left the crowd of pedestrians behind, and even as the BearCat pulled away, Allyn knew the onlookers were still recording their retreat. In hours, maybe even minutes, video of the entire ordeal would be picked up by local news stations, and after that, the international networks.

Before the magi even returned to the Klausner Manor, their existence would be known to the world.

CHAPTER 34

THE FULL LIGHT OF DAY showed the true cost of the battle. The total number of the dead was still being calculated, but having been in the thick of it, Jaxon knew it was going to be devastatingly high—for both sides.

After Arch Mage Westarra's fall and following resuscitation, Jaxon and Rohn had led the magi forces against the remaining Knights. With their leader's life hanging in the balance, and having already weakened the Knights' line with Nolan, Jaxon and Rohn had been able to successfully repel the enemy force, killing or taking prisoner every member of the enemy force.

The other prisoners taken from the church months before hadn't netted much in the way of information, but like Jaxon, Arch Mage Westarra didn't believe in killing when he didn't have to. Besides, if only one of them knew something worthwhile, the magi could get it out of them. If nothing else, the Knights would be a good bargaining chip if the Rakkaran leadership every became willing to do a prisoner swap. It all added up the same—the Knights were more useful alive and safely disarmed than dead.

With the dead gathered and the injured tended to, the

magi quickly set their sights on the complex of buildings. Leira had been in Allyn's squad, but no one had seen or heard from the squad since they'd gone in. The turn of events was more than enough to unnerve Jaxon, and when it became apparent that the Knight Commander had disappeared as well, he drew the obvious connection.

"He took them," Jaxon said.

Nolan was walking at his shoulder, his eyes distant, skin pale and blood splattered. "We can't be sure of that."

"No," Jaxon said. "I can feel her. She's..." His face contorted as he attempted to concentrate. The connection was weak, strained—the magical equivalent of losing someone to bad reception. Only their connection didn't rely on towers and satellites. It relied on their well-being. "She's hurt."

Nolan looked at him sharply, a silent question on his lips. Like most of the magi in the Order, Nolan didn't know that Jaxon and Leira had developed an echo. He didn't question Jaxon, though, and Jaxon felt a wave of respect for the man.

"We'll find her, Jaxon," Nolan said. "I promise."

The former FBI agent disappeared shortly thereafter, assembling a team to search the Knight Commander's quarters for clues. Those not wounded or tending to the wounded were quickly recruited into salvage teams. They gathered guns, ammunition, explosives, computers, even personal belongings from the base, not knowing what would aid them in the future.

Jaxon watched the work numbly, remaining aloof until the magi gathered their forces and prepared to depart. Nolan found Jaxon as they climbed into their vehicles. He shook his head but told Jaxon to remain positive. They still had time.

Jaxon nodded, burying his pain deep. He still had a duty to perform, had a Family to lead. He couldn't do that emotionally compromised, regardless of how much Leira's disappearance hurt. He had to stay strong. As Nolan said, he had to stay positive, but that was easier said than done. He was so lost in thought that he almost didn't hear it when his phone began ringing in his pocket.

"Who is it?" Nolan asked as Jaxon pulled the phone from his pocket.

Jaxon didn't recognize the number. "I don't know."

"Are you doing to answer it?"

Jaxon stared at the phone. The truth was, he didn't want to answer it. A random number calling after the day's events was enough to fill his insides with dread. He was being irrational, though, and he knew it. The magi numbers weren't known outside the Order, so unless it was someone dialing the wrong number, it had to be one of their own.

"This is Jaxon," he said, answering the call.

"Jaxon, it's Allyn," the voice on the other end said.

"Allyn?" Jaxon sat up in his seat, suddenly feeling the eyes of everyone in the car with him. "Where are you? Are you all right?"

"We're fine," Allyn said. "We're headed back to the Klausner Manor now."

"We?" Jaxon repeated, fighting with everything he had to keep his hope bottled up.

"I'm with Ren, Canary, and Leira," Allyn said. "We're a little banged up, but we'll be fine."

Jaxon let out a long breath, and the tension he'd been holding slid off his shoulders like ice from a melting glacier. His eyes brimmed with tears as he swallowed the rising lump in his throat. "I can't tell you how good it is to hear that."

"Good," Allyn said, his voice suddenly going straight to business. "Listen, did you take any of the BearCats from the Knights' base?"

"Yeah," Jaxon said slowly. "Why?"

"You need to get rid of them."

"What?"

"I said you need to get rid of them," Allyn repeated. "Ditch them. Hide them. I don't care what you do, but you can't drive them. Not right now."

"What's going on?" Jaxon said. "Are you sure you're all right?"

"I'll explain later, but trust me on this. Do whatever you have to do, but get rid of the vehicles."

"Okay," Jaxon said. "I'll give the order."

"Good," Allyn said, and Jaxon could hear the relief in his voice. "I'll see you back at the manor."

"Wait. Did you...?" Jaxon was suddenly wary of talking over an open phone line. "Were you successful?"

Allyn didn't respond, and the pause lasted long enough that Jaxon nearly repeated the question.

"Yes," Allyn finally said, though his tone suggested there was more to the story than he was leading on. "In a way. I don't have the Blood Wand or our people, but, Jaxon, I have something better. I have the Knight Commander."

Jaxon blinked as the words registered. He shook his head in disbelief then looked at each of the other magi in the vehicle with him. Even the driver was watching him from the rearview mirror. Knowing they suffered from the same sense of loss, Jaxon did something he had never thought about doing before. He hit the speakerphone button.

"Allyn, I just put you on speaker," Jaxon said. "There's a car full of magi who would love to hear what you just said. Can you tell them what you just told me?"

"I said I have the Knight Commander."

The vehicle erupted in cheers, and for the first time since Jaxon could remember, he smiled and genuinely meant it.

CHAPTER 35

HE MAGI FORCE RETURNED TO the Klausner Manor as the afternoon gave way to evening. The partly cloudy sky was a vibrant array of reds and pinks and purples as the sun began its final descent, the gentle breeze, warm and inviting, a direct contradiction to the mass of emotions plaguing Allyn's psyche.

He stood in the center of the driveway, watching as magi poured from the magi SUVs. Allyn had instructed Jaxon to ditch their BearCats, and the future grand mage seemed to have complied.

As he stepped out of the vehicle, Jaxon smiled and immediately made for Allyn. He looked terrible—cuts and scrapes covered his body, his hands discolored from dried blood, his eyes swollen and concerned.

"You look awful," Jaxon said, and it was enough to make Allyn laugh.

"So do you."

"What happened?" Jaxon asked, nodding at Allyn's injured hand. He'd had it bandaged as he'd waited for the rest of the magi to return, and it was now covered in thick gauze. The Klausner clerics had offered to heal it for him, but he'd declined, knowing their abilities would be required elsewhere.

"It's a long story," Allyn said. "One we'll get to shortly."

"Where is she?"

"Inside. The clerics are tending to her. She's fine, Jaxon," he added as he saw the wave of concern flash in Jaxon's eyes. "But we need to talk."

Jaxon nodded but moved past Allyn, striding toward the manor. Allyn grabbed the other man by his arm, stopping him.

"Now, Jaxon," Allyn said. "Bring the arch mage. No, better yet, bring the Forum. Everyone will need to know this."

"What's going on?"

"You'll know soon enough."

───────────────

It only took Jaxon a few minutes to assemble the Forum and Arch Mage Westarra in the arch mage's private quarters.

"Thank you for coming on such short notice," Allyn said. "You no doubt have other things to tend to, but this couldn't wait."

The mood in the room was tense as Allyn quickly recounted his part in the battle. He started from the beginning, taking them through the Knight Commander's sudden appearance and how he and his squad had been taken prisoner, pausing when he came to the point where he'd flipped Sedric's BearCat.

"What happened next?" Arch Mage Westarra asked.

"That's why I gathered you here." Allyn let out a deep breath, and instead of saying anything more, he turned to the television mounted to the wall and powered it on. The image on the screen was grainy and chaotic, moving too quickly to easily make sense of, but when it stabilized and focused, a man took center stage.

"Is that Sedric?" Jaxon asked.

"Keep watching," Allyn said. The magi returned their gaze to the television, their eyes moving from Sedric's figure to the orange banner that stretched across the bottom of the screen. *Breaking News*, it read. *Battle Erupts in Germany*.

Allyn sighed, anticipating what came next, and winced as gasps filled the study. He didn't need to look to know the fireballs had appeared in Sedric's hands.

"What is this?" Arch Mage Westarra demanded.

"Please," Allyn said. "Just keep watching."

Sedric hurled one of the fireballs, sending it crashing into a parked car. The nearby onlookers dove for cover, others attempting to hide. All but a single figure took cover behind the car.

"Is that...?" Jaxon's words trailed off as his eyes met Allyn's.

Allyn nodded.

Jaxon's mouth hung open, but he seemed to be at a loss for words. The lack of anger was nearly more painful than the fury Allyn knew would come next.

Sedric hurled another fireball. Then there was talking. "Allyn, Allyn, Allyn..." Sedric said, erasing any doubt who was behind the car.

The recorded version of Allyn stood, the present Allyn knowing what was going to happen but wishing more than anything he could prevent it. He watched as the recorded version of himself wielded, the unmistakable red coils of electricity springing to life around his arms.

The study remained silent, shocked, angered, and entranced by the video. The recording showed the entire battle, and when the camera grew too shaky, or its angle less than optimal, the footage would jump to another recording taken by another bystander. It all happened in the clear light of day, and there was no denying Allyn's involvement. No denying the magi powers.

"Turn it off," Arch Mage Westarra said. He rubbed his hands through his hair, exasperated. "I don't... I don't know what to say."

"There's nothing to say," Allyn said. "I only hope the—"

"Stop!" Arch Mage Westarra commanded. He waved his hand in the air as if he were trying to wave away smoke. "Just stop. For over two thousand years, this Order has remained hidden. Not by choice but out of necessity, and thousands of magi have made enormous sacrifices to make that possible. Our lives depend on it. Our *future* depends on it. And you have just exposed that secret to the world."

"I understand, Your—"

"No!" Arch Mage Westarra's voice burned with rage. "Don't tell me you understand. You don't know the first thing about the sacrifice others have made or the dishonor you have brought." He turned to his Elemental Guardsmen. "Rohn, this *man*"—he nearly spat the word—"is to be confined to his quarters. Station a guard outside his room and see that he doesn't leave. He can't be trusted, understood?"

"Of course, Your Grace," Rohn said. "For how long?"

Arch Mage Westarra gave Allyn a disgusted look. "Until I know what to do with him."

Allyn didn't say anything as the Elemental Guard closed in around him. He looked to the floor in disgrace, refusing to meet the eyes of the Forum or his friend as he was led out of the room.

"What happens now, Your Grace?" he heard someone ask before the door closed.

Arch Mage Westarra took a long, shuddering breath. "Now we prepare. Our world, and everything in it, is about to change."

EPILOGUE

FORMER FBI SPECIAL AGENT RICHARD Maddox stumbled out of the bar and vomited on the sidewalk. A pair of women dressed for a night on the town squealed and jumped back, trying to avoid getting the splatter on their high heels. They must not have been successful, because one of them cursed and gave him a violent shove that sent him sprawling across the rough concrete, scraping his hands and face.

"Sorry," he said, his voice slurred even to his own ears.

"Asshole," one of them shouted back.

Maddox laughed. There wasn't anything left to do—he *was* an asshole. Letting out a deep breath, he pushed himself to his feet, lost his balance, and grabbed hold of a nearby parking meter to keep from toppling over again. He shouldn't have had that last shot of whiskey. Hell, he shouldn't have had the last *three* shots of whiskey, but like his time in the bureau, once he got his teeth into something, he had a hard time letting go.

"Hey, Maddox," the bartender said from the doorway. His name was Brad, and he was both the owner and operator. "I like seeing you, man, and I appreciate the loyalty. But you gotta get your shit together."

"Yeah, yeah."

"You need a taxi or something?"

"No," Maddox said. "I'll walk it off."

"I don't think that's a good idea, man. Let me call you a cab." Brad disappeared back into the bar.

Maddox didn't wait for him to return. He appreciated the gesture, but it wouldn't be the first time he'd stumbled his way home. Besides, he didn't think his stomach could take the motion of a car, and he had no intention of emptying his guts on the floorboard of some poor soul's Crown Victoria.

The first step was the hardest, but once he had momentum behind him, he was fine. Maddox was more than a block away before Brad realized he'd made a run for it.

"Maddox!" Brad yelled after him. "What the fuck, man?"

Maddox responded with a wave and kept on his way, passing a pair of motorcycle cops. If he'd been a little more sober, he might have thought about how his old self would have taken Brad up on his offer, regardless of whether or not he'd been able to maintain his composure. Walking while intoxicated, though technically safer, was still illegal in the eyes of the law. Drunk in Public, they called it, and Maddox was certainly that.

The only saving grace was his condo's proximity to the bar, and before he realized it, he was standing outside the entrance, one-eyeing the security console. He got it on the second try.

Maybe the last shot hadn't been such a bad idea after all.

His apartment was a one-bedroom affair with a living room taken up by an oversized sectional. Grabbing a beer from the fridge, he collapsed onto the couch and turned on the television. He cycled through channels, taking a long pull from his beer, when something caught his eye. He backed up two channels and sat forward in his seat, dropping his beer onto the overpriced carpet.

Breaking News: Terror in Germany, the caption read. The grainy video seemed to have been taken from someone's cellphone camera, but Maddox would have recognized the man on it anywhere. In an instant, he was sober again, watching the battle between Allyn Kaplan and an unnamed assailant play out.

For months, he'd imagined what would happen if he came face to face with Allyn again. The man had been the root of his demise. Allyn Kaplan was more than the one that got away—the man had ended his career, and for the first time since being left in a bloody mess on the highway, Maddox had a lead worth following. He didn't have much of a plan, but he knew whatever his future held, it depended on apprehending his former nemesis.

He picked up his beer and took it to the kitchen, where he dumped what was left into the sink. Then, grabbing a glass of water, he started planning.

The story continues in...

EXPOSURE

The Machinists, Book Five
Coming Soon

To receive *Heritage*, an exclusive prequel novelette
set in the world of The Machinists, sign up
for the Craig Andrew's mailing list at:

http://eepurl.com/IEjlr

For additional bonus content, and to be the
first to hear about giveaways and
promotions, follow Craig Andrews on Facebook at:

https://www.facebook.com/craigandrewsauthor

ACKNOWLEDGMENTS

I MADE A PROMISE WHEN I released *Martyr* that I would never make my readers wait as long for a book as they did for that one, and so far I've made good on that promise. Go me! That wouldn't have been possible without the help of a lot of people, but to name a few...

There's Tiffany, my tough-loving wife and best friend, who has draged me out of bed to write on too many occasions. Whatever curses I mumble under my breath at those ungodly hours, I promise I don't *really* mean them. Or maybe I do, but I say them with love. ☺

Ender and Callan, who grab their computers (relics that don't even turn on anymore) and sit down beside me to do their own "work." It makes those lonely writing sessions not so lonely anymore. I love you to infinity and beyond and back, and can't wait to read the stories your little creative minds come up with!

Mom and Dad, who taught me how to dream, set goals, and work to make those dreams a reality. I could write an entire book thanking you.

Gary and Gala, to whom this book is dedicated, thank you for your never-ending support and enthusiasm. You've seen early cover drafts, heard me ramble on about plot threads and character ideas, and asked good questions that helped me flesh those things out. More than that, you put up with my cantankerous ass, and that's really saying something!

Grandpa Kenny who continues to gift paperbacks to local libraries and businesses, and Grandma Bunny who has read them all and recommended them to family every chance she gets. To the rest of my extended family, who there's too many to name, thank you for your kind words and continued excitement. It's always fun to talk about this journey with you.

Lynn and Stefanie from Red Adept Editing, who take these books and make them into something coherent and readable. We're four books into this beast now (and a novellete) with many more to go.

And finally, thank you, dear reader. I've said it before, but I go to great lengths to write and produce the best books I can, always with only one goal in mind: to make your reading experience as enjoyable as possible. Without you, this budding career of mine wouldn't be possible, and I'm forever grateful for your support. If you like these books, please consider leaving them an Amazon review and help other readers find them. Every review, every shelf-add and rating on Goodreads, and every time you mention them on Facebook or in an online forum, helps others discover this series and supports this crazy dream of mine. If we ever meet in person, please let me know you're a fan so I can shake your hand or give you a hug (your choice).

To everyone else, of which there are too many to name, here's to ending this series with a bang!

—Craig Andrews

CRAIG ANDREWS GRADUATED FROM PORTLAND State University with a Bachelors of Arts in English. Growing up on a healthy diet of fantasy and sci-  ence fiction, some of his favorite childhood memories include being traumatized by the TV shows *Unsolved Mysteries* and *The X-Files*. He currently lives in a small, rural town outside of Portland, Oregon with his wife and two boys.

Say "hi" at any of the following:
craigandrewsauthor@yahoo.com
http://www.craigandrewsauthor.com
https://www.facebook.com/craigandrewsauthor
http://eepurl.com/IEjIr (mailing list)

www.ingramcontent.com/pod-product-compliance
Lightning Source LLC
Chambersburg PA
CBHW021320250626
47155CB00002B/568